Blood List

By
Patrick & Philip Freivald

JournalStone
San Francisco

JOURNALSTONE
YOUR LINK TO ARTISTIC TALENT

JournalStone books may be ordered through booksellers or by contacting:

JournalStone
www.journalstone.com
www.journal-store.com

The views expressed in this work are solely those of the authors and do not necessarily reflect the views of the publisher, and the publisher hereby disclaims any responsibility for them.

ISBN: 978-1-936564-91-0   (sc)
ISBN: 978-1-936564-96-5   (ebook)

Library of Congress Control Number: 2013947662

Printed in the United States of America
JournalStone rev. date: November 15, 2013

Cover Design and Artwork   Jeff Miller

Edited by: Dr. Michael R. Collings

To The Redhead™. You're why I write.

Patrick Freivald

To the other three Horsemen. Thanks for the camaraderie.

Phil Freivald

Acknowledgements

We'd like to thank our brothers Mark and Jake, for their enormous help on our first trip around the block. *Blood List* wouldn't be the book it is without you. We'd also like to thank all our beta readers, typo-hunters, fact-checkers (dad for guns, Betsy Hutchison for virology, and so many others), and the wonderful staff at JournalStone – Christopher Payne, Joel Kirkpatrick, Norm Rubenstein, our editor Dr. Michael R. Collings and our proofreader Amy Eye. Finally, we'd like to thank Jeff Miller for an awesome cover.

Blood List

Chapter 1

June 22nd, 4:48 PM PST; Café Molto Espresso; Los Angeles, California.

Paul Renner looked across the street at the woman he'd come to Beverly Hills to kill. He blended in with the throng of thirtysomethings crowding up Rodeo Drive: six feet tall, short black hair, a decent tan, and a business suit that cost more than his first car. He pretended to people-watch, his soft brown eyes scanning the crowd sweating in the summer heat, debutantes and nouveau riche Hollywooders spending thousands of dollars on outfits they'd wear once and never think about again.

The blaring TV behind him was difficult to ignore. Some talking-head CNN anchor blathered on about a mass shooting in Des Moines. *Who kills a bunch of people at the mall? What a waste of life.*

He took a sip of his caramel macchiato. Across the street, Jenny Sykes screamed at a shoe-store employee. Paul typed a text message while the beleaguered clerk rang up the purchase and bustled Ms. Sykes out the door. He held his thumb over the "send" button.

Ms. Sykes lugged two full bags of Guccis and Manolo Blahniks to her car. Her body was tight and firm, thanks to Botox and a personal trainer, and she walked like a high school cheerleader. *Her shoe collection probably cost more than my house.* He looked up from the phone and caught her eye. She smiled tightly, averted her gaze, and headed to her car.

Jenny Sykes was too old to be called Jenny and wasn't remotely hip in spite of the hundreds of thousands of dollars she spent to appear to be. *She probably thinks her daughter's ten-thousand-dollar-a-week cocaine habit is her biggest problem.*

Jenny slid behind the wheel of her chrome-silver Mercedes Benz, flashing far too much leg for her age. Paul stood, dropped a ten-dollar bill on the table, and walked away. When she closed the car door, Paul pressed "send" on his pre-paid NetPhone I-590 cellular phone. No annual contract, WiFi digital compatible, and, best of all, paid with cash. Totally anonymous.

Two things happened simultaneously. First, the text message fired off to a familiar number. It read, *Jenny Sykes, Rodeo Drive, Los Angeles, California.* Second, the phone sent another text to an identical phone in the trunk of Jenny Sykes' Mercedes.

The Benz erupted into a fireball, sending Jenny Sykes to whatever heaven or hell shallow socialites go. Shattered glass fell from storefront windows, but most of the shrapnel blew straight up, just as Paul had intended. Like cattle, the herd of shoppers screamed and cried as they stampeded away from the carnage. Paul joined them.

Hurrying along with the crowd, he felt none of the feigned panic he projected for the inevitable YouTube videos. *Some people are too dumb to run.* Several blocks away, he ducked into an alley between a Thai tapas restaurant and a place called Tie World.

He tossed the phone into the restaurant's dumpster. His fingerprints weren't on record, so the G-men who'd been trying to catch him for the past decade would know it was the D Street Killer, but not his identity. Leaving little clues for Special Agent Gene Palomini and his boys was part of what made these operations fun.

* * *

June 22nd, 5:16 PM PST; Jenny Sykes murder scene; Los Angeles, California.

Special Agent in Charge Giancarlo "Gene" Palomini held on as the two black SUVs screamed onto the sidewalk across the street from the smoking mess of what was left of the silver Mercedes Benz. The red-and-blue police lights flickered off the yellow CRIME SCENE: DO NOT CROSS tape that two uniformed locals wrapped around a hundred yards of Rodeo Drive.

Gene looked at the damage as he hopped out of the driver's seat of the front vehicle. Just over six feet tall, in his early forties, with a medium, muscular frame and thinning, military-short blond hair, he exuded confidence and frustration in equal measure as he surveyed the wreckage scattered across the street. His older brother Marty got out behind him.

"Whoa," said his technical specialist as he emerged from the second car. "A car bomb? Are you kidding me, Gene?" Agent Carl Brent was short, black, in his mid-thirties, and looked like a kid playing dress-up. The hair was pure businessman, but his navy suit was a little too big, and Gene was sure he didn't have to shave more than twice a week. Carl was never one to avoid pointing out the obvious.

The last thing Gene's smog-choked sinuses needed was a Carl-induced headache. "Stow it, Carl. Let's make nice with the locals."

Agent Doug Goldman took point, blazing the way with his fierce gray eyes. Barrel-chested and bald, Doug was so tall that his FBI badge was at eye level for Gene. Doug was a wall with a badge and a gun, and Gene used that fact to their advantage. Gene walked at his heels, eclipsed by the large man's presence.

Gene's brother walked next to him. They looked like twins except for Marty's full head of hair and the ridiculous porn-star moustache he grew in the Navy and had refused to shave since. Behind them came Carl Brent, with Jerri Bates to his left. Agent Bates was a small, pretty woman in her early thirties with an angular face, short red hair, green eyes, and curves in places that Marty said made her standard, uptight FBI suit look naughty. Gene had never seen the appeal, no matter what she wore.

A Hispanic LAPD detective saw them coming and avoided eye contact. He whistled to a uniformed officer who was trying to figure out how to attach a pink marker-flag to a square of sidewalk concrete and jerked his head toward their group. "Hey, Jimmy! Bureau's here. Show them around, and don't let them muck up my crime scene."

Jimmy dropped the marker on the sidewalk, pulled off his latex gloves, and trotted over to Gene's group. His smile was too enthusiastic for someone who had just been tagging vaguely-identifiable body parts.

Gene watched as the uniformed officer—J. Anderson by his name tag—walked straight to Doug and stuck out his hand. It never failed. Hidden in the human psyche lurks a primitive instinct that makes people assume the biggest guy is the man-in-charge. It helped the team put people off-balance without seeming to be deliberate.

"Special Agent?" Officer Anderson asked. He looked confident, but his inflection betrayed a touch of apprehension at presenting a part of his body anywhere near the massive, scowling man in the middle.

"That's Agent Goldman," Gene said as he reached out to complete the handshake. "I'm Special Agent in Charge Palomini, call me Gene, and these are my associates, Agents Bates, Brent, and Martin Palomini." The officer's grip was far too strong, carrying on the pointless tradition of local cops trying to prove that they're just as good as the FBI. Demonstrating that it's the cop who makes the badge only tended to make them grumpy, so Gene gave the hand a good squeeze.

"I'm Officer Anderson, Jimmy Anderson. You guys sure got here quick."

"Well, we were in the neighborhood," Gene answered.

Gene held Anderson just long enough for his crew to get past. Jimmy raised his eyebrows. "Um...if you guys want to stick with me, I'll show you what we know so far...." His voice trailed off as the agents ignored him.

Gene noted with pride how his team knew exactly what needed to be done. Jerri Bates approached the witnesses and singled out a crying cashier from the shoe store. She used her disarming looks and personality to pull out details other interrogators might miss. Doug Goldman and Marty Palomini made a beeline for the uniformed PD to make some needed friends, and Carl Brent honed in on the forensics crew to add his expertise to the decades of experience already present. *Meanwhile, I get to play politics. Yippee.*

Gene turned Officer Anderson toward the group of sport-coated detectives next to the wreckage and unveiled his best diplomatic smile. "Why don't you take me to the detective in charge? It's going to be a long night, so let's work together to make it shorter, okay?"

Anderson followed Gene, muttering a barely-heard mantra over and over to himself. "Mustache Martin, the other one's Gene. Mustache Martin, the other one's Gene."

* * *

June 23rd, 1:23 AM PST; FBI Headquarters, Wilshire Boulevard; Los Angeles, California.

The computer screen shuddered rhythmically, no doubt caused by something electronic in the rooms near Gene's makeshift office. His head throbbed in time to the pulses. He closed his eyes and rubbed his temples for the hundredth time. It eased the pain only so long as he kept doing it and felt that much worse when he stopped.

Coffee, he thought. He grabbed his official Department of Justice mug, proudly emblazoned with the red, white, and blue shield with the bald eagle in flight on the front, and pushed his chair back from the desk. *When we find this guy I'm going to beat him to a pulp with that olive branch.* He shuffled down the hall toward the break room.

"You shouldn't drink that piss this late," Marty said from the hallway. He scowled in disapproval. "You won't sleep for shit tonight."

With a dismissive flick of his hand to stave off any more sage advice, Gene stepped around him. Marty seemed to think that once a man's ex-girlfriend could no longer nag him into a pounding headache, it became the sacred duty of the elder brother. Marty spoke behind him. "They found the phone, got prints. We forwarded them to Sam."

Samantha Greene was the invisible sixth member of the team. Two hundred and twenty pounds and five-foot-two, she hadn't passed the FBI's physical for field work in five years. Gene doubted she could walk a mile without dying, much less run three in thirty minutes. She was an expert marksman who practiced at the shooting range three times a week but had never worn a weapon on duty. It didn't matter.

Sam was the best field coordinator in the Bureau. She tracked the team with GPS, listened to and recorded their conversations over the COM, used gadgets and programs with other mysterious acronyms to perform astounding feats of technical magic, and crunched dizzying amounts of data for use in real time. She did all this from in front of a dozen computer monitors, safely ensconced behind a desk in the J. Edgar Hoover Building in Washington, D.C.

Privacy didn't exist in the field anymore. Everything was recorded, flagged for important words by massive supercomputers, and analyzed by the intel weenies back at HQ.

Marty continued, "The prints matched. We know it's him for sure now."

Gene turned around. "We knew for sure a week ago, Marty. We just didn't know who the victim was. Just like Denver. And D.C. And...."

"Yeah," Marty agreed. "Hell of a job we've got here, ain't it? Almost makes me wish I'd dropped out of school."

"Mama would have killed you, Marty."

"True," Marty said. "But then I wouldn't be working for a pencil-neck like you."

Gene grinned and turned back down the hall. "I should be so lucky."

Gene walked into the break room and glared at the half-empty coffee pot. The little red light stared back at him. The stale, bitter smell in the room indicated that this pot was probably brewed during the Rodney King riots, from stale beans.

"Gene, you've got a meeting with the Chief of Police at oh-seven hundred. Get some fucking sleep, boss." Gene nodded as he emptied the pot into the sink, clicked off the machine, and headed back to the couch in his office. He didn't need to see the smirk on Marty's face to know it was there.

He only calls me "boss" when he's telling me what to do. With an exhausted grin of his own, Gene lay down on the lumpy couch to catch as much sleep as his aching head would allow.

* * *

June 23rd, 6:57 AM PST; LAPD Headquarters, Parker Center; Los Angeles, California.

Gene had done his research. By all accounts, Police Chief Logan Stukly was an ambitious and intelligent man. Born and raised in Los Angeles, he was as comfortable in the barrios and ghettos as he was in the mansions of the Hollywood elite. A third-generation police officer and a twenty-two-year veteran of the L.A.P.D., he hadn't just been around the block; he lived there. Add a fierce charisma and a pack of weasels willing to get dirty behind the scenes, and it all added up to a major appointment that had transformed a career cop into a budding politician.

Explosions on Rodeo Drive made the local PD look bad. Given Stukly's mayoral ambitions, Gene could guess his mood. Gene's head throbbed in time with his footsteps as he approached the door.

The man glanced up when Gene walked in. He waved Gene to a chair and kept typing. Twenty seconds later, he clicked his mouse and looked up.

"You Palomini?"

"Yes," Gene said.

Chief Stukly sneered through his teeth and looked across the massive oak table that served as his desk.

"Tell me, how long were you planning on letting a serial killer rampage through my city before you deigned to inform my men of his presence?"

Gene suppressed a groan. He'd hoped for some level of cooperation. "You understand that all of this has to be kept confidential?"

"Yes," Stukly said.

"He's known as the 'D Street Killer' after the location of his first murder. He likes to toy with the FBI, give us clues. We got the city location four days ago, when—" He jumped as Stukly slammed his meaty palms on the table.

"FOUR DAYS?" Stukly roared, spittle flying everywhere. Gene held up his hands and winced at the volume. The chief's face was flushed with rage, but his voice calmed. "I'm sorry, Agent, please go on."

Temper versus ambition, Gene thought. *This man is dangerous, but mostly to himself.*

He licked his lips and continued. "Yeah, well, this guy likes to taunt us. He gives us a state six days before a kill, always by pre-paid cellular, voice-over-IP, or text message. We get a city two days after that. Neighborhood the morning of the kill, almost always with the first and last initials of the victim. Within seconds of the kill, we get a victim ID and a street." He snarled. "Never enough time to catch the perp, though."

Stukly's frown deepened. "And you couldn't tell LAPD that he was in Los Angeles because?"

"Because we already had. Two of your sections were notified and had classified it as low priority, partly because the Bureau was already on it and partly because your homicide guys are already swamped. Until we found out the neighborhood, of course."

Stukly raised his eyebrows. "What about the neighborhood?"

"Rodeo Drive is not South Central," Gene said.

The chief raised his bushy eyebrows and shuffled the papers in front of him. Instead of answering the charge, he changed the subject. "Why this vic? Why Jenny Sykes? Why Rodeo Drive?"

"I wish we could tell you, sir," Gene said. "This guy's one of the slipperiest the Bureau's ever encountered." He told the man what precious little they knew and was asked the same old questions. M.O.? Usually a gun, but no consistent model or caliber. Knives on a couple of vics, but different kinds, usually taken from the area of the kill and always left behind, just like the guns. On top of that, they had a baseball bat, a lamp, a steel-toed boot, a television in a bathtub, and a ten-story drop to pavement. And now a car bomb.

It took Gene an hour and a half to explain everything they didn't know. The victims didn't correlate at all: old, young, male, female, pretty, ugly, rich, poor. The killer's profile was limited to Male, Caucasian, twenty-four to fifty years old, and a childhood history of arson, bed-wetting, and cruelty to animals, just like almost every other organized serial profiled by the FBI's Violent Criminal Apprehension Program.

Forensic linguistics on early phone calls indicated the killer grew up in the Plains, 65% probability. All they really had were anonymous fingerprints on murder weapons and cellular phones, black hair, and some skin cells from many of the crime scenes. They knew he was Caucasian and male from DNA, and that was about it.

By the end of the meeting, Gene felt like he needed a shower. Captain Stukly obviously didn't care much about the poor woman blown to pieces only sixteen blocks away, except insofar as it affected his bid for mayor. Gene left the office with Stukly staring holes into the back of his head.

He made it down the hall, past rows of cubicles, barnyard pens for human cattle with crummy jobs, and saw a lean, young man in an LAPD uniform hurrying toward him. He looked familiar. *Right. The guy from the crime scene yesterday. Anderson.*

The smiling young man had his hand out and an expectant look on his face. Gene took his hand and shook it. *Too hard again. He probably wants a job with the FBI.* "You here to keep me out of trouble, Officer?" Gene asked, his attempt at levity murdered by his scowl.

Officer Anderson's smile faded to a constipated grimace. "Wasn't very good at it yesterday, Agent Palomini. Not sure what good it'd do today." He looked even more chagrined as the implications of his statement caught up to him. Gene didn't give him the chance to back out.

"It didn't do any 'good' yesterday, and it wouldn't do any 'good' today, because we're the 'good' guys, and getting the 'bad' guys is our job. Why is it your job to get in our way, Officer? Aren't you supposed to be catching the bad guys, too?" He jerked a hand up to stifle a reply and added, "What can I do for you, Officer Anderson?"

Anderson flushed and looked out the window. "Detective Rodriguez told me you were with Stukly. I thought you'd want to know we've got preliminary analysis on the explosive back from the lab. Ammonium nitrate. Fertilizer. We're working on a source now, but that could take weeks."

Gene softened his tone, embarrassed. "Sorry, you didn't deserve that. Thanks for the info. Let me know if…. Let me know when you get the results back." He took out a business card and handed it to the policeman. "My cell's the second number. Call any time, day or night, if something breaks." Officer Anderson took the card, and it disappeared into a pocket.

Inwardly, Gene sighed. Timothy McVeigh used ammonium nitrate to blow up the Federal Building in Oklahoma City. It was as common as anything and could have come from anywhere. In a month anyone could buy enough of the stuff from a garden supply store to make a car bomb without tripping a Department of Homeland Security threshold on dangerous substances. *That's if you didn't just pay a farmer for a truckload of pig crap and make it yourself.*

Anderson's irrepressible smile reappeared. "No problemo. You just let me know if there's anything else we can do. I don't have much pull around here, but I'm well-liked, and Marco—that's Detective Rodriguez, homicide—might be able to help you cut through any bullshit Stukly throws in your face. And call me Jimmy."

Maybe this cop was one of the good guys. "I'll do that, Jimmy. I'll do that." His mood lightened ever so slightly, Gene headed to his car.

Chapter 2

July 17th, 2:25 PM EST; Wegmans Supermarket; Fairfax, Virginia.

Three weeks later, Gene pushed his cart up and down the aisles of the supermarket, trying to stick to his list as much as possible in light of all the temptations offered. He caught a whiff of the in-store Chinese buffet and his stomach growled. *Why do I always come here hungry?*

Every other weekend he drove to Fairfax to get "the good stuff" from Wegmans grocery store. *More like the Taj Mahal of eats.* He wandered aisles packed with everything he could ever want for his kitchen, whether he felt like cooking or just wanted something to take out. Even if it wasn't crowded, it took at least an hour to get out of there, and he always spent more than he meant to. *Why do I come here, again?* By way of reply, his stomach tried to convince his brain that, yes, he did need a two-pound bag of jumbo shrimp to go with the cocktail sauce already in his cart.

His FBI-issued cell phone rang and jolted him out of his reverie. He looked at the caller ID. *Unknown name, Unknown number.* And on a Saturday. He frowned and hit the green "talk" button.

"Hello, this is Gene."

"Hello, Special Agent." The voice on the other end was filtered through a computer scrambler, with no discernible accent. He hoped it wasn't Marty. His childish older brother hadn't met a practical joke he didn't like.

"What can I do for you, Mr. Scrambled-Voice Guy?" He cradled the phone on his right shoulder, grabbed the shrimp, and tossed it into his cart.

"Missouri," the voice said.

"Missouri?" Gene asked. The only reply was a dial tone.

He hung up and moved to dial just as it rang again. It was Samantha Greene's desk.

"Sam, I just got a call...." He didn't know why he bothered. All of their work phones were tapped. Their home phones probably were, too, even though that wouldn't be legal. And Sam was always listening. Even at two-thirty on a Saturday.

"Yeah, got it," she interrupted. "NetPhone. New account. This is the first time it's been used. Um, hold on."

Gene pushed his cart toward the front of the store, his mood obliterated along with his free weekend. *So soon after the Sykes murder, and that case dead in the water.* The explosives hadn't panned out to anything. The ammonium nitrate came from a Home Depot in Fresno that sold thousands of pounds of fertilizer a week. The case was idle, Officers Rodriguez and Anderson had been tasked to other investigations, and Chief Stukly was making "the incompetent feds" a campaign point in his bid for mayor. Sam spoke up as he reached the checkout.

"The account is tied to a new phone purchase with prepaid minutes, activated 2:18 PM July 3rd. Bought at, let's see...."

He loaded the heavy stuff onto the belt as Sam pulled up the information. The cashier started scanning his items.

"Yeah, okay. Maybe an hour out of town. The Wegmans Supermarket in Fairfax, Virginia."

Gene went cold. He looked around. No one seemed to be paying him any particular attention. He stepped out of the line and scanned the crowd. There were hundreds of people in the store. At least twenty blabbed away into handheld and Bluetooth phones.

The cashier gave him a concerned look. "You lose something, sir?" Gene looked through the cashier, not seeing her.

"Um, no, I—" He held up a finger. "Hold on a minute." She

rolled her eyes.

"Crap, Sam, that's where I am now. I mean, crap. I was *here* on the third, in the afternoon! CRAP!" He slammed his hand down on the conveyor. The woman in line behind him glared and pointed at the toddler in her cart.

* * *

July 17th, 8:48 PM EST; Wheelan Air Services Flight 827; somewhere over the Eastern United States.

Gene grinned and looked out the window. Everyone laughed over the droning roar of the twin-engine airplane. Marty clapped him on the shoulder while talking both into the COM and to the rest of the team.

"Yelling 'crap' in public…. Would it kill you to just say 'shit' like a normal person?"

Gene's glare focused on nothing. *Thanks, Sam. How do you glare at someone who isn't there?* "I was freaked out. You would have been, too. I thought the guy was right there. I mean, like right next to me or something." The team sobered and got down to business.

Gene briefed them on what little they knew. Missouri. A phone call instead of a text message. The D Street Killer hadn't done that in years. Sam had accessed the security tape of register three, from which the I-590 NetPhone was purchased on July 3rd. Some guy had paid an eighty-nine-year-old World War Two veteran twenty dollars to buy it for him. A store regular, he couldn't describe the guy. Of the hundreds of people who entered and exited the building about the same time, none triggered as suspicious on the video feeds. Many were store regulars or townies, identified by employees and the local police, but many were strangers. Parking lot cameras didn't catch the exchange. Interviews had gone nowhere. They had nothing, again.

And yet, here they were at fifteen thousand feet and heading to Missouri at over three hundred miles an hour to try to catch the D Street Killer before he killed again. The problem was, as usual, that states are awfully big.

* * *

July 17th, 9:12 PM CST; Terminal G, Lambert-St. Louis International Airport; St. Louis, Missouri.

Gene grabbed his bag and looked out the window. A hodgepodge of suits, uniforms, and five-o'clock shadows waited for them on the tarmac. The men stood in a half-circle at the bottom of the retractable stairs, sheltered under umbrellas from the thunderstorm.

First were two Missouri state troopers, two St. Louis County deputies, and a member of airport security, all of whom looked nervous. Lurking behind the uniformed men stood a sandy-haired man in his early thirties wearing a tailored business suit. Next to him stood a short, black-haired man in a fed-issue suit whom Gene recognized as Special Agent Robert Barnhoorn. Barnhoorn was the local FBI liaison, one of Doug's former classmates from the academy, and the brother of Doug's long-time girlfriend.

Gene half-stumbled down the stairs, legs stiff from hours of sitting. Doug's face was green. He sighed when his feet touched the asphalt and he looked ready to kiss the ground.

They shook hands and introduced themselves. Mr. Tailored-Suit, an attaché to the mayor's office, was concerned about a potential killing in his city. Gene forgot his name the instant he'd heard it, then blew him off as diplomatically as possible to talk to the policemen.

Twenty minutes later, Gene found himself in a private suite reserved for airline executives. It had a fully stocked bar that no one was allowed to touch while on-duty. Marty sauntered over and poured himself a Glenlivet on the rocks, then got trapped in the role of bartender. Everyone but Gene and the mayoral suit ordered a stiff one.

Once comfortable, Gene got started. "Thanks, everybody, for coming down, but I'm sure Agent Greene has already briefed you." Sam chirped a "yup" into his earpiece. "The D Street Killer is going to kill someone in Missouri this week unless we stop him." He held up his hand to prevent the suit from interrupting. When the man closed his mouth, Gene continued. "What we don't know is who, or where in Missouri. Or why. Or by what method. Basically, all we know is that we're in the right state."

Robbie Barnhoorn let out a low whistle. "Y'all have your work cut out for you, that's for sure." He handed Gene a folder. "We're getting you set up with a full suite down at the Marriott. Computers, beds, doughnuts, coffee. The works. The place is booked up with the big tech conference this week, but we managed to squeeze you in." He inclined his head toward the sandy-haired gentleman. "The mayor's office is covering food and coffee as a gesture of good faith, as well as Mr. Gardner here, to help cut through any red tape. You tell him anything you need that I can't get you, he'll make sure to get it done."

Sam spoke in Gene's ear. "Tell them we need access to the hotel's security tapes for the past week and a direct feed ongoing while you're there. We can try to face-match anyone from the store camera back here. He knew where you were shopping, so he might know where you're staying."

Gene looked up to see the others staring at him. He smiled apologetically. "Sorry, that was Sam Greene on the COM. She wants security tapes from the hotel, dating back at least a week, and their video feed ongoing."

The mayoral attaché patted his briefcase. "I can pressure them to release the tapes and patch you in without letting them know why you're there. Hotels are pretty cooperative with open investigations."

Gene nodded, grateful for the assistance. Political appointees to investigations were usually more of a pain in the butt than a help. He opened his mouth to reply when his phone rang. The caller ID said *D Street Killer. Unknown Number.*

"It's him." The background chatter in the room came to an immediate halt. "He's spoofed caller ID, identified himself as the D Street Killer." He put his hand on the button and spoke into the air. "Sam?"

"Tracing," Sam said. "Keep him on as long as you can."

Gene hit "speaker." "Hello?"

The voice was the same, mechanical and without inflection or accent. "Did you have a nice trip, Agent Palomini? I've always hated those tiny little planes. They suck in this kind of weather. Is Agent Goldman keeping his supper down okay?" Everyone looked at Doug, who flushed with anger.

"I—" Gene began. D Street cut him off.

"I can't have you tracing this call past Singapore, so I'll keep this short. I'm feeling feisty and wanted to give you a bit of a head start. J.Z.B." The phone went dead.

Sam's voice spilled out of it. "DAMN IT! I had him in Singapore, where I hit one hell of a glitch. The trace went in eight directions at once. Not sure if it's hardware or what, but we'll see if it's physically there, then call their government. I bet I could have cracked it with a few more seconds."

Carl frowned. "This guy knows too much, Gene. Way too much."

Jerri pursed her lips, pensive. "What I don't get is, why is this one different? The call instead of the text, the two calls in one day. He's even changed his M.O. on timing."

Marty looked annoyed. "Yup. Gave us the state, and now the initials. He didn't give us the city."

"I think he did," Doug said. "Maybe." He pointed at the TV, where a meteorologist droned on about the weather. A little dot of dark green surrounded by a larger wash of lighter green covered the St. Louis area. The rest of the Doppler screen showed nothing. "He said 'this weather.' He's in St. Louis, right under our noses." He sighed. "Maybe."

"Fuckin' A," Marty interjected. "Good catch."

Gardner swore under his breath. "I have to tell the mayor." He stood to leave and dropped a business card on the table.

In response, Agent Barnhoorn yelled, "NO PRESS LEAKS!" Gardner waved him down as he headed for the door.

"Got it, got it. Secrecy's the game, even though this guy already knows you're here. Whatever. You need something, you call me." He walked out.

Gene put his head in his hands, rubbed his temples, and spoke. "Sam?"

She already knew the question and had an answer. "There are only six J.Z.B.s in St. Louis on public record. There are another nine statewide. I'm sending the addresses to your phone right now."

Gene smiled. "You know I love you, don't you, Sam?"

"Who wouldn't, babe?"

Jerri raised her hand, like a teenager in high school. "Hey, Gene?"

Gene smiled. "Don't worry; I love you, too, Jerri."

She frowned and looked at the floor. "That's not it, Gene." She paused.

Never a patient man, Marty glared at her. "What?"

"My middle name is Zoe."

* * *

July 23rd, 7:58 AM CST; The Hotel Marriott Pheasant Room; St. Louis, Missouri.

Gene's heart pounded as he stared at the phone. This could be the day. The loud mid-morning traffic had a hard time competing with the noise coming from the lobby. The Innovators of Tomorrow technology conference, sponsored by the State of Missouri, had the whole city jammed to peak capacity, and the Airport Marriott was no exception. Gene blocked out the noise. This just had to be the day.

With help from the Mayor's office, they were staking out every J.Z.B. in the greater St. Louis area. The state police covered the rest of Missouri. It was a huge expenditure of police power dedicated to one and only one goal—catching the D Street Killer before he killed again.

Special Agent Jerri Zoe Bates bided her time in the basement of the J. Edgar Hoover building back in D.C., surrounded by the best security in the world. Gene couldn't think of a safer place. Even though she was out of the state, and thus shouldn't be the D

Street Killer's target, she'd been closed in for six days, under constant guard like a prisoner, and she was suffering for it.

Jerri had begged Gene to allow her to do something, anything, useful. Gene hadn't budged, so there she sat. Gene knew he'd catch holy heck for it later, but it beat getting her killed. Even if he could forgive himself, Marty never would.

Gene paced back and forth in the Marriott conference room that served as their headquarters. His cell phone sat idle in his hand. He checked his watch. 7:58 AM, day six. The D Street Killer always took his victim within six days of calling the FBI. Always. It was day six. So today had to be the day. But then again, he always gave them a city after two days and initials the morning of the kill, before 8:00 AM. The call with the full name and street always came too late.

This time was different. He hadn't called the second time with the city, and they'd already known the initials. Gene looked at his watch again. One minute to go.

The phone rang. *D Street Killer. Unknown Number,* taunted him on the Caller-ID. Gene hit "talk."

"Hello?"

The mechanical voice greeted him. "Hello, Agent Palomini. I'm just calling to say that you missed one. You have a good morning." The phone went dead.

Gene hit autodial and spoke, his message patched through to the unit commanders in charge of surveillance. "This is Special Agent Gene Palomini. We got the call, I repeat, we got the call. Look sharp." He hung up and spoke into the air. "Sam?"

She replied immediately, an edge of hurried panic in her voice. "I know, I know. If I knew about it, we wouldn't have missed it. Let's hope it's him missing a surveillance team and not us dropping the ball."

He speed-dialed his team. "Go, Gene," his brother said, echoed by the others.

"D Street said we quote-unquote 'missed one.' Sam's looking into possibilities." Marty swore. "Ideas?"

Nobody said anything.

Gene walked to the door. "I'm going to check and see if the

front desk—"

The caller ID beeped in Gene's hand. *D Street Killer. Unknown Number.* Gene stopped dead in his tracks. *Oh, no,* he thought. He pressed "talk" to jump lines. "Jui Zhou Bai, Airport Marriott, lobby. Better luck next time, Agent Palomini."

His phone forgotten, Gene ran to the end of the hall. He took the stairs three at a time, flew down two flights, and slammed into the crash bar on the door with both hands. As it flew open, a crack of thunder and the sound of shattering glass cut through the din of traffic and babble of people. A woman shrieked. Gene pushed through into the lobby and entered complete chaos. Panicked people screamed and trampled one another. The revolving doors stuck in place, jammed with a tide of flesh. He dodged to the side as part of the crowd rushed his position to escape up the stairwell.

Near the front window, a dead man in a crisp tweed suit sat on a sofa. Most of his head was missing, the newspaper in front of him splattered with blood and brains. He still held a large Starbucks and had a brochure for the tech conference tucked under the briefcase in his lap. Blood fountained from the remains of his head, splattering the area with gore. Gene's eyes followed the coffee as it fell to the floor, the brown liquid staining the cream rug already awash in red. An Asian woman in a grey skirt-suit kneeled next to him, screaming.

Gene pushed the victim from his mind. The bullet had exited into the lobby, and blood, bones, and brains were spread in a tight pattern on the coffee table and floor. That meant the shot came from outside, at a high angle. A thirteen-story apartment building towered across the street. It had hundreds of windows, most of which were open to take advantage of the cooler morning air. The shooter could be anywhere inside.

Gene scanned the facade and tried to process the ocean of reflective panes, window air conditioners, and balconies. *There. Seventh floor.* A small black tube protruded from a window, well hidden by the shadow of an air-conditioning unit. Gene took off at a run, calling into his headset. "Shooter used the seventh floor across the street! I'm going in!"

In his heart, he knew he was too late. The D Street Killer had killed again, and this time less than fifty feet from him while most of the police presence was spread elsewhere in the city, watching other J.Z.B's. Gene knew they'd find the gun and little else.

In an anonymous panel van four miles away, outside the apartment of Jason Zimmer Bogandovich, Marty couldn't breathe. The D Street Killer had just murdered someone, an innocent victim's life snuffed out for no good reason, but he only felt relief. Jerri was safe.

Back in Washington, Gene stared at his report. Jui Zhou Bai, a Chinese diplomat sent by his government to scope useful technologies, had been killed on American soil right in front of his personal assistant. The FBI had information on the victim but nothing new on the killer.

Bai's itinerary had been public for weeks, but the guest roster had misspelled his name "Jui Pai." He wasn't a high-profile target, didn't have bodyguards or any serious party or industry connections. He was a non-entity, a nobody. They had no clues on why D Street chose him, except perhaps the similarity in initials to Jerri Bates. Even that was a guess.

They'd found the bolt-action .50-caliber sniper rifle in the apartment, set up on a robotic tripod with a high-quality digital video scope. The tenant was at work at the time of the shooting and seemed to be an upstanding citizen. The lock had been forced earlier that morning, and the killer had left the crowbar at the scene. There were fingerprints everywhere that matched D Street, but no phone.

A diplomat killed on American soil. The FBI had known that there was a killer loose and the initials of the intended target. The political firestorm had kept Gene and his team occupied for the next several weeks.

Gene clicked "Send."

Chapter 3

August 14th, 3:52 AM EST; Gene Palomini's Apartment; Washington, D.C.

Nothing moved. Not even rats scurried about, in spite of the stink of rotting food coming from the dumpster behind the Chinese joint. Gene crept up the alley, pistol ready, and froze in the shadows. The break had come suddenly, a thunderbolt from a clear sky, and he'd be damned if he was going to mess this one up. The Voice of Reason killer had been haunting Richmond for two months and was a tabloid celebrity. The press fed into the man's megalomania, but at least they could be used to flush him out. The bait was out; the trap set.

Gene smiled in the shadows. His first major case as a Special Agent, his first big payoff after all his training. He took another careful step and checked the safety on his service pistol. Marty appeared from nowhere, and looked ready for anything. Gene's phone rang.

Gene snapped awake. His phone rang again. He licked his upper teeth and cringed at the slimy, cottony feeling left by too many gin-and-tonics the night before. He fumbled for the phone. *Stupid retirement parties. Everyone always drinks too much.* He blinked away the fog of ninety minutes' sleep, then lifted the receiver to his ear. He responded with his first semi-coherent thought. "What?" His voice groaned out, thick and sloppy.

Sam sounded wide-awake and cheerful, as always. He held the phone away from his ear, just close enough to hear. "Would you be interested to know that forty black NetPhones were mail-ordered to a P.O. Box in SoHo almost a year ago?" He squinted at the clock and lamented his coordinator's ability to work at all hours.

His brain spun as it tried to process human speech through a haze of sheer hell. "Did you say forty?" His head throbbed with every syllable.

"Yeah, like days and nights in the desert, Gene. Forty. Know anyone who might have need of forty NetPhone I-590s, paid for with a credit card linked to a fake Social Security number?"

Gene sat up. This killer, this dead-end, this invisible man who followed no patterns and killed without conscience, this monster who taunted his team for fun, had just made a mistake. "Do we know who picked them up and when?"

"The bad news is that the post office won't release that information. Right to Privacy and all that."

He hated it when Sam played with him. Why couldn't she just spit it out? Why hadn't he become a dentist, or a hula dancer—something, anything, other than an FBI agent? On the other end of the phone, Sam said nothing. She always made him ask. "What's the good news?" He stumbled into the kitchen, poured himself a glass of water, and drank it as she replied.

"The good news is that they were picked up by one Bradley Jones. Bradley is a small-time hood with a long rap sheet of minor consequence—possession with intent to distribute, stuff like that. He just got busted on federal weapons charges and aggravated assault with a deadly weapon, and trying to plea he copped to a whole lot of weird stuff both legal and not, including this delivery. Thought it was a mob thing, phones fell off a truck or something. Anyway, he delivered them to a warehouse in Queens for a hundred bucks.

"I asked the super to check his records. He said the warehouse was rented by some guy who paid in cash, dropped his lease right after the delivery, just ate the security deposit. They're faxing over the lease so we can get the handwriting analysis guys on it. The local office is already fingerprinting everything they could find. If it was him, we'll know by noon or so."

"Great. What's the name on the lease, Sam?" Gene said.

"Um, here it is, Paul Renner," she said. "Guy's a ghost. He's got no record, no known place of employment, no known address. Social security number's fake."

Sacred Mother, Gene thought, not sure if it was sacrilege or prayer, *let this be the guy's big screw-up.*

"What do we know about these phones?"

Sam replied, "Well, that depends on how much you love me."

"Right," Gene said. "I love you very much. Now spit it out or I'll have you fired, then set on fire for messing with me at four in the morning."

Gene could hear the smile through the phone. "Well, we know that one of them came online last week."

"Great. So how do we find him?" Gene asked.

"Well," Sam said, "we don't. Not really."

"What does 'not really' mean?"

"It means that what we've got is a phone that's currently active, somewhere on the Lower East Side of Manhattan. That's all we can get tracing through cell towers. It's not nearly granular enough to be able to find him, but at least we can track his movements."

"All right," Gene said. "Do it."

* * *

October 5th, 2:30 PM PST; Los Angeles Public Library; Los Angeles, California.

Paul Renner sat in the public library disguised as a homeless man, his body tight with anticipation underneath filthy clothes. He looked at the text message again, then at the computer screen. *Larry Johnson, Jr., 8473 Eagle Crest Drive, Salt Lake City, Utah.* It was downright scary what you could find on the Internet these days.

Mr. Johnson was in his mid-sixties and had found God more than thirty years before when he'd met Mormon missionaries in a NYC park, who saved him from a life of addiction. He went from junky to janitor to union garbage man to shift supervisor in that time, had a lovely wife and seven children, and had retired two years ago. His rambling blog spelled out his typical day in far too much detail.

He spent most mornings doing the crossword and Sudoku in the paper, afternoons sitting in his front lawn sipping coffee—decaffeinated, of course—and waiting for his first grandchild to be dropped off after daycare. He spent his evenings babysitting until his eldest daughter got home, usually just in time to make him miss *Final Jeopardy*, then updated his blog from eight to ten.

It amazed Paul that anyone would write such shit and that anyone else would read it. Well, anyone who wasn't studying Larry Johnson, Jr.'s routine to find the best way to kill him, of course. Whistling, Paul committed most of the blog to memory, booked an American Airlines business-class ticket to Salt Lake City for "Scott Gleichauf," hacked through to gain administrative privileges, and formatted the hard drive.

He swore under his breath and pounded the keyboard, earning a look of reproach from the elderly woman next to him. He stood and flagged down a librarian. "Hey, that computer's broke. Just, like, turned off and shit, man."

Without waiting for a reply, he stumbled out into the afternoon.

* * *

October 18th, 11:27 AM EST; Deck of the *MaryAnne*; off the coast of Virginia.

This stinks, Gene thought as he looked into the choppy water. The boat rocked under his feet. He reeled in and inspected his hook. The four-pound jackfish stared at him with dead eyes, still perfectly intact. He sipped his beer and cast an accusatory glance at his sunbathing brother.

"Marty, I thought you said sharks love these things."

Marty shielded his eyes from the sun and squinted at Gene. "They do. Maybe they're not hungry. Just wait." He closed his eyes.

"Sharks are always hungry," Gene said. "They seem more interested in the mackerel than the jackfish." He cast the line back into the water.

Marty smiled and pulled his hat down over his face, muffling his voice through the fabric. "Give it time, bro. There's like four big makos down there, and the chum's got them all riled up. They'll bite."

Gene took one last look in the water, then sat. "Fair enough." He looked out across the ocean at a massive cargo ship passing in the distance. "You ever think about changing the name of your boat?"

Marty shook his head, making the hat jiggle on his face. "Nope. That's bad luck."

"You don't believe in luck," he replied.

"True," Marty said. "But that doesn't mean boats don't. You don't fucking mess with maritime tradition."

"But isn't having a boat named after your ex-wife a little weird?"

"Not as weird as it could be. She's hard to steer, stubborn, built like a brick shithouse, and just about perfect...." He trailed off.

Gene smiled. "Which MaryAnne are we talking about, here?"

Marty chuckled. "Not sure, bro. I love them both, and never spent enough time with either one."

"This job's hard on relationships," Gene said. "Maybe not as hard as the Navy, but the long hours, unexpected travel, the danger...I don't know how the two of you lasted as long as you did." The left pole dipped. "Hey, we've got a bite!"

Marty flipped to his feet in one fluid motion, an impressive feat on the rocking boat, and grabbed the pole with both hands. Eyes sparkling, he gave it a heave. His muscles strained as he dug in his feet. "That's a big one!"

Gene's phone beeped. *Oh, great,* he thought. He pulled it from his belt and cupped his hand over the screen to block the glare. It said, *Utah.* The caller ID read *D Street.*

"If that's work, tell them we're fucking busy," Marty said,

giving another pull and reeling in a few feet of line.

Gene sighed. "It's work, but it's not Sam. It's D Street."

Marty snarled. "I'm on vacation."

"Not anymore," Gene said. He grabbed the other pole and started reeling. "We need to get these lines in and get to port, ASAP." He hit his speed dial as Marty dragged the shark closer to the boat. The phone rang once.

"On it, Gene," Sam said in his ear. "He's in Salt Lake. Flew there from Des Moines three days ago. I'm putting calls out to Carl and Jerri as we speak. Doug's in California, might be a little harder to track down. You'll have a plane waiting. SLC?"

"Yeah, that's fine. There's no point in trying to be sneaky about it. It might tip him off that we know something. Notify the SLC field office that we're coming."

"Will do. I'll have Doug meet you there. What's your ETA to Dulles?"

"Um...." Gene looked around at the open water. "Give us two hours."

"You got it, Gene." Sam hung up.

Gene patted Marty on the back. "You've got ten minutes to land that shark or let it go."

"Yes, sir."

Chapter 4

October 18th, 12:43 PM PST; San Jacinto Mountain; San Jacinto
State Park, California.

Doug smiled sadly at the love of his life. Maureen Barnhoorn
was a classic beauty, a tiny little thing with raven-black hair, high
cheek bones, smooth skin tanned to milk chocolate, and soft
brown eyes. They lay naked under the sleeping bag, bundled
against the cold.

Doug watched the tears form in Maureen's eyes and stifled a
flash of hatred for Gene Palomini. "I'm sorry," he said, "but I have
to go." It was one thing to be on call. It was another to break her
heart. To be fair, it wasn't Gene's fault. "This guy's going to kill
someone else if we don't stop him. Something might break this
time. We might get him." He brushed his fingers down her back.

"I know, baby," she said. "Robbie tells me you've got the FBI
dream-job, the one everyone shoots for. Special Operations Units
get the big guns, the big budgets, the big toys, and only the best
get in. He's jealous, you know."

Doug nodded but didn't interrupt.

"But Robbie doesn't have to be on call 24/7. His office is ten
minutes from his house. He works forty hours a week and gets
two weeks a year. Two *uninterrupted* weeks. He gets to spend
evenings with his family. Every night." She rolled over and bit his
shoulder. "While you, Mister Glamorous-Too-Good-for-a-Desk-

Job-Superman, disappear for weeks at a time, following Palomini around, trying to catch this guy, leaving me at home with the kids. When was the last time we had two weeks off together?"

Doug grinned at her. "Last year. We went camping in the mountains. Sound familiar?" She widened her eyes and shook her head in false denial. "And we don't have kids, Maureen."

She grinned back. "Seven months."

"What?" he asked.

"Seven months. You. Me. Babies. Seven months."

He pulled back and searched her face with his eyes. She was beautiful, and ten times more so when she smiled. "You're serious."

She beamed. "Ultrasound confirmed it two days ago. I'm nine weeks along."

"We're having a baby—wait, babies?"

"Twins." She giggled.

Doug beamed. "Really? Boys or girls?"

"Too early to tell." She rolled off him, took his palm, and slid it down to her belly. "Two little peanuts, right here, just growing away."

He kissed her, long and slow. Pulling back, he looked into her eyes. "Why didn't you tell me sooner?"

She looked outside. "I wanted to be sure. After trying for so long, and nothing. I didn't want you to be disappointed."

He enveloped her with his arms, careful not to crush her tiny form. She smelled like butterscotch. "You'll never disappoint me, Mo. Never. You're my rock."

"I love you, too, Doug."

They lay together a while, listening to the sounds of nature. An owl hooted in the distance. Some critter foraged in the brush. Song birds chattered in the trees.

Doug realized he'd been dozing, Maureen draped across him like the world's loveliest blanket, her head on his chest. He squeezed her, gently. "You awake?"

"Yeah," she said, but didn't look up. "I'm telling Branson when I get back next week. The firm has a great maternity leave program, and they'll cover my clients while I'm gone."

He chuckled. "Right. As if they could stop you from working at home. You'll go nuts in two weeks without badgering some bank or another into a multimillion-dollar deal." He moved his hands down her body and gave her a playful double-squeeze.

"Quit," she said.

He jerked his hands up to her lower back. "Sorry."

"Not that." She paused. He waited. "I want you to quit. Transfer. Something, anything, as long as it's safer and doesn't take you away from me. From us. I make enough money to support a family. You could do anything you want."

He opened his mouth but nothing came out.

"Not now. After. Catch this guy first. You don't have it in you to leave in the middle of a job. I know that. But nail this guy, then quit. Transfer to another department, leave altogether, whatever. We can move anywhere you want. I don't care. But quit. Be a dad to our babies."

Doug tried again. "I'll talk to Gene," he said. "But right now I need to go."

She squeezed him. "I know. Come home safe, or I'll kill you."

"Love you, too, babe," he said.

She let him go.

* * *

October 20th, 8:04 AM MST; FBI Field Offices; Salt Lake City, Utah.

"Here we go, people," Gene said as he flipped open his phone. He read the message. *Salt Lake City.* "Go figure. We're already in the right city."

"Great," Marty said. "Now all we need to do is interview everybody in the city and see who's feeling homicidal." Jerri rolled her eyes and looked at Carl. Doug waited for Gene to continue.

Gene gave his brother a grim smile. "Well, we can do a little better than that. Sam, tell them what you've got."

"Well, kids," Sam said through the speaker phone, "one of the new toys we've been working on for some years is face-matching software. DHS first field-tested it at an Oakland Raiders game back in '01, comparing football fans with mug shots."

"I remember that," Jerri said. "Almost a quarter of the Raiders fans were ex-cons, but only five percent of the 49ers. It was totally a Big Brother play. Really irked the civil libertarians."

"That's the one," Sam said. "It was pretty accurate, and they've been refining it since. We've got the traffic camera data and several phone shots from the Jenny Sykes murder, which we can compare to the security tapes from both SLC and Des Moines airport terminals. We got great shots of everyone as they boarded and exited the plane, and we know that D Street's phone was on that plane.

"DHS has some guys vetting the passengers as we speak. Once we know what he looks like, we can search for him on Salt Lake traffic cameras and maybe pin him down. It's needle-in-a-haystack work, but we might get lucky."

Marty grunted.

"We've been through this before," Gene said. "A city simply isn't enough to go on. We give the face-matching program a chance to work, and, failing that, we work like the dickens when we get the neighborhood and the initials. Any other ideas?" Nobody replied. "Questions?"

After a moment, they all shook their heads.

"All right," Gene said. "Keep your thinking caps on. Marty, Jerri, you're on liaison work with the Municipal PD. Carl, Doug, you're with the local Feds. I'll cover the State Police. Go."

He closed his notebook and left the room.

* * *

October 22nd, 10:20 AM MST; FBI Field Offices Training Facility; Salt Lake City, Utah.

Gene grunted in pain as Jerri ducked the jab and delivered a solid kick to his ribs. He grabbed her ankle and twisted, hard. She dropped to the ground and spun free, sweeping his legs out from under him in the process. He hit the mat and rolled left as she flipped to her feet. She hit him four more times when he tried to stand. In theory she was pulling punches, but her fists felt like cast iron. He stumbled to his feet and backed up.

He blocked an open-hand slap and threw himself at her, trying to wrap her in a bear hug. She dropped to her knees and delivered a one-two punch right to his groin. The cup absorbed most of the damage, but the impact knocked him off-balance. He stumbled sideways, twisted, and fell on his rear. Jerri stood and leaned casually against the post on the side of the ring.

"That wasn't right, Jerri!" Marty said from the other side of the ropes.

She smiled, took out her mouth guard, and put out a hand to Gene. "We done?"

He removed his own guard. "I think that's enough getting my butt kicked by a girl for today." She helped him up. "That last move wasn't very sporting."

"Jujitsu isn't sporting. It's about putting the hurt on people."

"That would've done it."

"My turn! My turn!" Marty cried from the sidelines, hopping up and down to get his adrenaline flowing. On the floor next to him, the phone in Gene's duffel bag rang.

"Give me that, would you?" Gene asked Marty.

Marty dug into Gene's duffel, peeked at the phone, and walked over. "It's Sam." He handed it to Gene.

He hit "talk."

"Gene."

"Hey. We got a hit."

"What kind of hit?"

"Traffic camera, last night. Seven-thousand block of Eagle Crest Drive. Physical description looks right, and it matches a face ID'd on both the airport cameras and two of the crowd shots from the Sykes murder at ninety-two and eighty-six percent probabilities. Statistics says it's the same guy. Here are the pictures." Gene's phone beeped and an image appeared. Marty stopped hopping and peered over his shoulder.

The first black and white photograph showed a Caucasian male with dark hair driving a dark Nissan Sentra. The next was a full-color shot of the same man boarding the plane in Des Moines. The third showed him dressed in a nice suit, hurrying away from the Rodeo Drive car bombing. The fourth was the same scene shot at a different angle.

"Tags?" Gene asked.

"Rental," Sam said. "Rented ten days ago by a Paul Renner, paid with cash but with a credit card on file. Hertz doesn't have a security camera at their counter, but the name's too much of a coincidence to think it's not our guy. I can't find a good reason for the alias. The only vaguely famous 'Paul Renner' was a twentieth century German typographer. Nice fonts. Anyway, his social security number belongs to an eighty-three-year-old named Bruce Hutchinson, who lives in a nursing home in Houston. I haven't notified them of the identity theft yet, and I've got a passive credit alert on the card. If he uses it, we'll get him."

"Sweet," Marty said, eavesdropping.

"Great, Sam," Gene said. "Put out an APB on that Sentra and on 'Paul Renner,' but under no circumstances should law enforcement apprehend. If they see it, tail him, but only if they can do it covertly, and notify me. And get a warrant for that rental paperwork. We might be able to confirm prints off it."

"Got it," Sam said.

"Look into that typographer. The alias might not be a coincidence. It might tell us something about him."

"Sure thing."

"And Sam?"

"Yeah?"

"Tell Carl and Doug to be ready to move at a moment's notice."

"Will do."

He hung up the phone and looked at Jerri. "Shower up. If they find him, we go get him."

Jerri sized up Marty. "Next time, Marty."

Marty grinned. "It'll be my pleasure."

Chapter 5

October 24th, 8:08 AM MST; Sheila Jones' Apartment; Salt Lake City, Utah.

Sheila smiled and stretched languorously on the bed, listening to the shower as last night's e-date got ready for the day. Some kind of business meeting or something. She ran her hands down her naked body and shuddered in remembered pleasure. She fought back the cloud of Ecstasy and alcohol of the previous night to grasp at his name. *Pete? Pat? Something like that.*

Good fuck, whatever his name was. She'd have to ask for his number. She got up and strolled to the kitchen to rummage through the fridge for some milk. As she reached in, she noticed a small scratch on her wrist. *Now where did I get that?* she thought, mentally reminding herself to get some Neosporin once the guy got out of the shower. *Or maybe I should join him?* She frowned. *Maybe I won't ask for his number,* she thought, glaring at the half-gallon as if it were the milk's fault that she had bad taste in men.

She chugged a couple of gulps from the carton and was putting it back when the front window shattered. Her mouth open in an "O" of shock, she stared at the little hockey-puck-like object that skittered across the floor. Her brain had just enough time to register that she should probably duck or hide or at least close the fridge door or something when the flash-bang grenade went off.

Sheila found herself sprawled naked in a widening pool of

milk, staring at the ceiling. Her head felt like a popped balloon, and she tasted blood. The milk felt cold on her back and soaked her hair. She hadn't realized there were so many cobwebs in the corners of her kitchen. *Maybe I ought to dust more.*

She tried to clear her thoughts as sound rushed back in. Boots thumped everywhere, and she heard a man shout, "CLEAR!" Only then did she realize that a short black kid stood over her with some kind of machine gun. He had *F.B.I.* emblazoned on his bulletproof vest and jacket.

"Can you hear me?" His eyes were cold. She nodded. "Sheila Jones?" he asked again, wasting no time on superfluous talk. She nodded again. She felt like a marching band was drumming its way around her skull. "Where's Paul Renner?" *Fuck, that was his name. Paul.*

"Um. Shower." She pointed toward the bathroom. He took off at a dead run. Sheila fainted.

The bathroom door was ajar. Carl pushed it open with his left hand while Jerri covered him. Fog billowed from the muggy room. Condensation covered both the tiny window and the large mirror. Hot water streamed down in the shower. Carl crept forward, both hands tight on the fully automatic MP5. The safety was off. He inched forward. One hand on the trigger, he reached with the other and yanked back the shower curtain. The water sprayed on empty porcelain.

Carl stepped back. "Master bath's clear," he said over the COM. "Jerri, check the bedroom closet."

"Got it," she said from behind.

Carl took a doubtful look at the window, cracked to let in a breeze. *No way a guy could fit through there, even if it were wide open.* He peered out, his weapon raised and ready to fire.

The burst of pain as his elbow dislocated was the first indication that he wasn't alone. Carl tried to cry out, but a strike to the throat silenced him. His mouth worked like a fish's, gasping for breath that wouldn't come. D Street wrenched his arm behind his back. Carl felt ligaments tear and tendons rupture even as the killer plucked the MP5 from his hand.

Ah, shit, this guy's fast, was the last thing Carl had a chance to think before another blow dropped him like a sack of meat. He squirmed on the ground but couldn't summon the mental energy to do anything else. His eyes rolled into the back of his head.

Paul Renner inspected the submachine gun while Special Agent Carl Brent twitched at his feet. There was a round in the chamber, a fully loaded magazine, and the safety was off. He kicked the downed man in the temple, hard, with his steel-toed boot. *Should have looked up,* he thought. With an amused smile, he stepped through the doorway and into the bedroom.

Special Agent Jerri Bates had a fantastic ass. Paul took a moment to admire it as she rifled through the closet, pounding on the walls with the heel of her hand. His grin got bigger as she called out to her partner, her voice muffled by the clothes.

The closet was a dead end. There weren't any secret hidey-holes, nowhere for the perp to go, nowhere to hide. *I hope Marty and Gene are having more luck in the front.* Jerri banged around a bit more just to be sure, then called out, "Carl, he's not in the closet. There's no escape route here!"

"I know," said a man's voice. It wasn't Carl. "Nice guns, these HKs."

Jerri's fingers twitched on her weapon, and she readied herself to turn and fire.

"Don't," the killer said, his voice full of contempt. She froze. "Slowly, drop the gun and put your hands in the air." In spite of herself, she did so. *Oh, God, who's going to tell my mom that I'm dead?*

She turned around, a tear forming in her eye, and looked at the killer. The D Street Killer was so ordinary that he would blend into any crowd. Almost six feet tall, black hair, brown eyes, handsome but not enough to stand out in any given company. *Jesus,* she thought, *I could walk right by him a thousand times and never recognize him.* Even so, she scanned him for anything that might be useful later. A tiny scar on his right eyebrow. A slight asymmetry to his smile. *Not that it matters. I'm already dead.* She glanced at the boots protruding from the bathroom door. *Poor Carl.*

Images flashed through her head. Her mother, laughing as she tried to blow out the five candles on her first real birthday cake. Her friend Angela pushing her on the swing set in third grade. Her first kiss. Her last kiss, only two weeks before. She closed her eyes, filled only with regret. The killer's voice was as soft as silk. "There's no money in this," he said, almost sadly, and her world went black.

*   *   *

October 24th, 8:31 AM MST; Sheila Jones' Apartment; Salt Lake City, Utah.

Gene looked around the apartment, his head throbbing in spite of the cocktail of Benadryl, Advil, and Sudafed he'd downed an hour before. Between a brutal sinus infection and being the Special Agent-in-Charge of this botch-job of an operation, he had good reason for misery. He glared at Marty with unbridled anger, his red face turning redder with the exertion. "How can a guy just disappear out a window barely big enough for a cat?"

"Don't know, Gene," Marty said. "I don't think he ever got in the fucking shower in the first place. Probably wasn't even in the bathroom when Carl went in there." Marty sneered and held up his thumb and index finger. "We were *this fucking close* to nabbing that motherfucker, Gene. *This close.*" He dropped his hand. "Still, we didn't come away entirely empty-handed. Whoever LRJ is, he's safe. For now." With a glance at Carl he continued. "Hey, Carl, show him what we got."

Carl limped over with two sealed plastic bags, the latex gloves a sharp contrast to his dark brown skin. He held up the bags with the arm not in a sling and winced at the effort. The left side of his face was a swollen, purple bruise. Gene almost felt bad for whining to himself about his own head. Almost.

Carl sounded confident, though he looked ready to collapse. "Two wallets, four IDs, six credit cards, two debit cards—both local—and a cell phone, prepaid I-590, same one Sam was tracking, and the same one that sent the text this morning. *LRJ, Poplar Grove.* We're monitoring the account—these things have 'net-accessible mailboxes—even though we know he's too smart to use it again. Sam's checking the balances on the bank accounts so we can seize them."

Sam broke in. "Yeah, not much. A couple grand in each account. The credit cards are all identity-theft. The aliases are all bunk. We're sending some people to check on the addresses, though."

Darn it, Gene thought. *The addresses never check out.*

Carl continued. "I think the woman's worthless, met him through one of those online dating services. Last night was their first date. Jerri and Doug are interrogating her now."

Carl inclined his head toward the bedroom where Sheila Jones sat in a flimsy nightgown, flanked by Doug and Jerri.

Gene's headache was relentless. "Yeah, okay, Carl. Let me know what Sam turns up. In the meantime, get some rest." He turned to his brother. "Marty, talk to local and have them set up interviews with all our LRJs. How many of them do we have?"

"Eighteen," Marty said. "I'm on it." He walked out of the apartment and down the steps to the car.

Gene entered the bedroom and glowered at the woman they'd found in the kitchen. Doug spoke while Jerri stared at the wall. Gene motioned to her, and they stepped into the hallway for privacy.

"Sorry, boss," she said.

"Not your fault, Jerri. It was a clean Op. We were just outsmarted." They'd been outsmarted for three years, and the team before them for another seven.

Jerri sighed, her face doubtful. "If you say so."

Gene's expression, already worried, became downright grave. "What exactly does that mean, Agent Bates?"

She snarled. "Guy had me cold, Gene. I was dead. Dead." She frowned at the tile floor where they had found Carl. "He didn't do me, didn't do Carl. Hell, he barely even touched me." She gave an apologetic look through the doorway. Gene followed her gaze to

Carl, leaning against the wall in the next room. Carl might never regain the use of his arm. "It doesn't make any goddamn sense. Why let us live, especially now that he knows that we know what he looks like?" Her eyes shone with such ferocity that for a moment Gene could see what Marty saw in her.

"Shouldn't surprise us, Jerri. The only M.O. this guy's got is that there isn't any M.O. No serial in the books would have let you or Carl live."

Jerri looked at the floor and said, "There's no money in it."

"What?" Gene asked, confused.

She repeated herself with more certainty, looking him dead in the eyes. "'There's no money in it.' That's what D Street said just before he took me down. What's it mean?"

Gene grimaced. "I don't know, Jerri. But I think we ought to find out."

Over the next three days, two text messages were sent to the phone recovered in Sheila Jones' apartment. They were encrypted, and both a single line in length. Sam knew they were gibberish code-phrases. Phrases that, even if they hacked the encryption, wouldn't mean anything unless she knew what each word represented. "Blue moon sits on the hen's egg" or some crap like that. Even if they weren't gibberish, they were too short to bust open. She'd sent them to cryptanalysis anyway.

Chapter 6

November 14th, 5:18 PM EST; J. Edgar Hoover Building; Washington, D.C.

Gene sat at his desk, working on the Salt Lake City report. He'd been staring at a computer monitor for six hours straight and felt like it. His team, along with countless behind-the-scenes forensics experts, had been working sixteen-hour days for two weeks straight. His phone chirped, and he hit "speaker."

"Palomini."

"Hey," Sam said. "We have our LRJ."

"Fantastic. Who is it?"

"Lawrence Reginald Johnson, Jr., retired garbage man and grandfather."

Gene put his head in his hands and rubbed his temples. "Any pattern matches?"

"None so far. No correlation between Mr. Johnson and any of the other victims."

"No surprise there," Gene said. "Why do we think it's him?"

"We *know* it's him," Sam said, "because Larry has a blog that almost nobody reads. But he was logged six times in the past three months through municipal firewalls. Once from Los Angeles; once from Syracuse, New York; once from Rochester, Minnesota; again from Los Angeles; and twice from Des Moines. In that order. Do those locations sound familiar?"

Gene played dumb. "Gee, Sam, they almost sound like D Street's travel patterns. I assume the dates match what we have from the phone?"

"Yup. Sure do!" Sam's enthusiasm matched his own.

"Awesome work, Sam. Double-check the rest of our LRJs, and let PC know they'll be able to let them go soon."

"Will do. FYI, I'm still trying to crack the encryption on those text messages, but I'm not hopeful. Chad DelGatto from crypto has an idea about using area-code iterations and an Apex-Lucinda approach to break the—"

Gene cut her off. "Sounds good, Sam. Let me know how it goes." He'd never studied cryptography, and she'd never stop explaining once she got rolling.

"Right." She hung up.

Gene turned back to his paperwork. Another hour or two, and he'd be done for the week. But first, he had to figure out what to do with Larry Johnson, Jr. An idea came to him, and he picked up the phone.

* * *

November 16th, 8:20 AM CST; Home of Agent Robert Barnhoorn; St. Louis, Missouri.

Doug walked up the sidewalk, hand in hand with Maureen, to the yellow, two-story colonial. Maureen opened the door and called out, "Hi, Robbie!" A cute little projectile in the form of Evan Barnhoorn flew across the living room and leapt into the air with a gleeful cry. Doug intercepted the squirming child and flipped him upside-down. Holding him up so that they were face-to-inverted-face, Doug gave his best bad-cop face.

"Who are you?" Doug asked, digging his fingers in just enough to tickle with every word.

Evan squirmed and giggled. "Uncle Doug!" he said reproachfully. "I'm Evan!"

Doug gave him a thoughtful stare while Maureen suppressed a smile. "Can't be. Evan is a little tiny thing. You're all grown up!"

Evan giggled again. "How old are you now?" Doug asked.

"Six!"

"Six? That's impossible. You can't be six yet."

"Can, too!" Evan said. "Someday I'll be as old as you! As old as Aunt Maureen!" Marcy Barnhoorn stepped into the living room, smiling. A plump woman in her mid-forties with disheveled strawberry blonde hair framing her face, she had a vitality about her that outshone her appearance, even through her flour-dusted hands and apron. She raised her eyebrows and mouthed the word *coffee*?

Doug flashed her a smile and a quick nod, then flipped Evan right-side up. Maureen stepped around him to greet her sister-in-law.

"And how old is your Aunt Maureen, little man?" Doug asked.

"Old!" Evan said.

Doug set him down and tousled his hair. "Brave little guy, aren't you? Now where's your dad?"

"Robbie's out by the garage," Marcy said. "Why don't you go find him, and I'll brew the coffee and catch up with my favorite girl?"

"Sounds like a plan, ma'am," Doug said. He gave Maureen a quick kiss and headed for the back door.

"For how long?" Robbie asked as he flipped the steaks on the grill.

"We're not sure," Doug said. "We're assuming he's in danger until we catch D Street, so think of it like witness protection." The steaks smelled fantastic, but Robbie always overcooked them.

"And this guy is how old?"

"Sixties. Retired. Wants to get back to his grandchildren. Wants to not get murdered even more."

"Good plan," Robbie said. "It'd probably ruin his year."

"Yeah. Can you do it?"

"Yeah," Robbie said. "We've got a couple of apartments we use as safe houses. There's no reason we couldn't put him up for the foreseeable future. I'll make it happen."

"Great," Doug said. "I'll let Gene know."

"Speaking of Gene, how did he take the news?"

Doug froze. "I haven't said anything yet."

Robbie held up a finger. "Wait a minute. You haven't said anything to him about leaving the team, or you haven't told Mo you aren't?"

Doug looked uncomfortable. "I haven't decided yet." He turned to face Robbie directly. "I'm kind of hoping I can talk her out of it. I can't imagine doing anything else."

Robbie let out a low whistle. "I'll pretend we didn't have this conversation then. Let you deal with Big Sis."

"Good idea," Doug said. "Because if I have to hear it from her that she heard something from you, I'll have to kill you. And then Marcy will kill me. And then Mo will kill her."

Robbie smiled. "So are you excited?"

"Thrilled," Doug said, taking a sip of beer. "Terrified. She's an amazing woman. I can't imagine the forces of nature her kids will be."

Robbie rolled his eyes. "With your luck they'll have her temperament and your size."

* * *

November 16th, 9:55 AM CST; Glenview Manor Apartments; St. Louis, Missouri.

Robbie Barnhoorn parked the car in the back lot of a gargantuan white building, one of ten just like it scattered across the landscape. He killed the engine and looked at his passenger. Larry Johnson was bald, heavily wrinkled, and grotesquely tan. He looked like a shriveled apple in a heavy sweater. "Well, Larry, we're 'home.' Apartment 4B is yours. We've got guys in 4A, and the rest of the floor we keep empty in case we need them."

Larry looked out the window and sighed.

Robbie patted him on the shoulder. "It's just until they catch this guy."

He sighed again. "I know. Let's take a look."

Upstairs, Robbie knocked on the door to 4A. After a few seconds it opened, revealing a stocky man with a bristly gray beard, wearing nothing but green boxer shorts. The man's eyes widened, and he stepped back. "Sorry, Robbie, I didn't realize we had company."

Smirking, Robbie stepped into the apartment, revealing a kitchen to the left and a small living area straight ahead. "Larry, this disgrace to the Bureau is Josh Santee. Josh is an undercover who needs to lay low for a while. If you need anything, just ask. He looks like a wild boar even with clothes on, but he's a pushover. Josh Santee, Larry Johnson. Larry is staying across the hall for a while."

Josh stuck out his hand. "Pleased to meet you."

Larry shook his hand. "Likewise."

"Put some pants on," Robbie said. "It's almost ten in the morning." As Josh ducked into a bedroom, Robbie called out, "Hey, where's Nick?"

"Shopping. He'll be back in a while."

"Nick Faughn is Josh's roommate," Robbie said to Larry. "He's a VICAP guy in town to help us with a case." Larry raised his eyebrows questioningly. "Violent Criminal Apprehension Program, similar job description as Palomini's team, but he does kidnapping, not mass killers." Robbie helped himself to a cup of coffee. "Coffee?"

"Herbal tea if you've got it," Larry said. "Or just water."

Robbie rummaged through the cupboard and emerged victorious with a box of Chamomile. He put a cup of water in the microwave and started it.

Josh emerged from the bedroom in jeans and an Arizona Cardinals T-shirt. "Better?"

"Much," Robbie said.

Josh raised his chin at Larry. "You from Jersey?"

Larry smiled. "Orange. Way back. How'd you know?"

"Newark." He thumbed his chest. "I could hear it in your voice. Not much, but there's a little in there, hiding under all that Southwest."

"Huh," Larry said. "You'd think a couple decades in Utah'd

take care of that." He shrugged. "You're good."

"I can mimic most accents pretty good, and hear them better than just about anybody in the Bureau. When I'm not undercover, I do some forensic linguistics stuff."

"Wow," Larry said.

"Don't let him fool you," Robbie said. "He's every bit as dumb as he looks."

"Thanks, Rob," Josh said. He knocked on the counter twice. "You guys want some breakfast? I'm starving."

Chapter 7

May 17th, 12:28 PM EST; Kendall Memorial Park; Washington, D.C.

Gene rolled his eyes and shoved Marty left-handed, careful not to burn him with the cigar. His brother pinwheeled his arms, lost his balance, and fell off the picnic table. He landed on his back in a spray of scotch and ice, his red plastic cup tumbling out of his hand on impact. Carl stopped the music, laughing. While Marty dusted himself off, Gene puffed on the cigar and stepped down. He walked up to Doug and wrapped him in a hug.

"I love you, man," Gene said. He pulled back and clapped Doug on the shoulders.

"You're drunk," Doug replied, the barest trace of a smirk tugging at his mouth.

Gene nodded and took another puff. "You're a dad."

Doug grinned. "I am."

Gene looked at Maureen and the girls, who sat under the giant parasol that Sam had brought. Jerri and Sam fawned over the pink bassinettes. "Those are some beautiful girls you've got there. And Maureen looks great." Doug caught her eye, and she waved. Her eyes were all for the father of her children, but flickered to Gene and away before she turned her attention back to the babies.

"Yeah." Doug's tone turned serious. "Can we talk?"

"Sure, Doug. What about?"

They walked toward the swing sets as Carl re-started the music. Marty had poured himself another Glenmorangie and was back on the table, dancing badly. Doug looked out across the city. "It's been six months, Gene. No sign."

Gene groaned. "This is about work?" He looked wistfully back at the picnic.

Doug stopped in his tracks and looked Gene in the eye, forcing him to shift his attention back to the conversation. "No. This is about me. I'm quitting the team."

Gene blinked. "What?"

"After we nail D Street. Maureen wants me out, and I want...." He trailed off. He looked up at the sky, thinking. Gene waited. "I want her. And she can't handle this. It rips her up every time I leave, because she doesn't know if I'll be coming back."

Gene stared off into the distance. "What are you going to do?"

"Not sure. Maybe I'll be a stay-at-home dad."

Gene smiled. "You wouldn't last a week. Those girls will eat you alive."

Doug replied softly, "So you're okay with this?"

Gene puffed on his cigar. "I'm not going to try to talk you out of it. You've got different priorities now. Good for you. And if you want it, your job will always be here."

"Thanks, Gene."

They walked back to the group in silence.

* * *

June 22nd, 12:59 PM PST; Paul Renner's Apartment; Los Angeles, California.

Paul was at his computer when the phone rang. He put on his headphones and clicked "answer."

"Hello?" he said.

"Paul Renner?" asked a digitally scrambled voice.

The trace program confirmed the encrypted call came from a recently activated, prepaid cellular phone.

"Yes."

"Your standard fee is fifty thousand dollars American?" The fake Russian accent was pretty good. The way this client said "fifty thousand" never quite changed enough to disguise his identity.

Paul grunted in surprise. Business had dried up after the Larry Johnson fiasco. He never expected another contract from the same employer. *Might as well play dumb*, he thought. *Fifty grand is fifty grand.*

"Plus expenses," he said.

"And to where do I send the information?" He said it like "'info-mission." *Definitely the same man.*

"I'll send you a phone," Paul said, playing along. "You'll get a text with an e-mail account. You reply to that address, which will report that the message bounced. I'll retrieve it from there. I need an address."

The man gave him a P.O. Box at the main Postal hub in Baltimore, Maryland.

"One week."

Paul hung up the phone, frowning. In the past two years, this client had paid fifty large a pop to have seven people killed. He used different phones, different accents, and different accounts, but it was the same man. There were a lot of reasons why any given person would be willing to pay fifty grand to see another person dead. Jealousy, blackmail, cheating, irrational hatred. They all made sense, and Paul was happy to provide the service if the price was right. But so many people hated by one man?

A retired policeman, a nursing assistant, a second grade teacher, an unemployed derelict in public housing, the mother of a celebutante known for getting drunk and screaming at her entourage, a community college ombudsman, and a retired garbage man.

Weird. Paul took out a brand-new NetPhone I-590, fresh out of the box. He went online, activated it, and packaged it for shipping.

A week later, Paul stared at his phone in utter disbelief. He couldn't tear his eyes away from the screen. His mind wouldn't accept what he saw.

> *Kevin Parsons*
> *271 Hawkes Drive*
> *Lincoln, NE 68508*

He read it again, for the hundredth time.

This can't be a test. They don't know who I am.

Research time gave him a few months to figure this out. He could invent a delay if he needed to. He read the name again.

This can't be a coincidence.

He read it again.

If I turn it down, they'll send somebody else.

He read it again.

This can't be a trap. It can't be a test.

The phone shattered against the wall. Paul closed his eyes tight and took several deep breaths. His heart rate slowed. His mind went through the litany.

Kevin Parsons. Age 66. Retired. Widower, lives alone. One child, 36. No grandchildren. No security on the house, no guards, no dog, no frequent visitors. Clockwork schedule: goes to service on Sundays, then out to breakfast at the Easy Peasy; bowls on Tuesdays, 7:30 PM; jogs every morning at 6:15 AM. An easy kill. *But why would anyone want him dead?*

* * *

June 26th, 10:45 AM CST; Home of Kevin Parsons; Lincoln, Nebraska.

Paul Renner pulled the rental car up to the driveway of a quaint, 1950s-style split-level, painted a generic off-white with a gray-shingled roof. A plastic trout served as the mailbox, emblazoned *Parsons* in bold white on the side. He gathered his thoughts, suppressing the façade of Paul Renner into background noise.

He got out of the car, patted the fish-box on the head, walked up to the door, and rang the bell. A familiar chime sounded inside the house, followed by his father's gruff voice. "Just a minute!"

The door opened to reveal a man in his mid-sixties. He held a cup of coffee in one hand, a newspaper in the other, and had an enormous grin on his face. His dad had long ago lost the battle to a receding hairline and had only wisps of white above his ears. Despite the hour, he wore white boxer shorts and an undershirt stretched comfortably over a bit of a gut.

"Steve!" his dad cried out and wrapped him in a giant hug, almost spilling his coffee in the process.

"Hi, Dad," Paul said, his voice sounding chagrined.

His father pulled back, his face sly. "What're you doing here, after so long with no visits? Need money?"

It was a long-standing joke. Whenever he visited, Paul tried to give his dad money, or a car, or a new TV, or tickets to the theater. Every time, Dad turned him down. His dad had taken to asking him if he needed money before he could offer anything.

"No, Dad. I'm set for cash."

"Have you talked to your cousin Ryan lately?" his dad asked, leading him to the kitchen.

"Not in a few months. We're both busy, I guess." Paul helped himself to a cup of coffee and pointed at the old, battered toaster oven next to the pot. "Hey, where's the one I got you?"

His dad smiled. "That one works just fine. Pastor Jenkins needed a new one for the hospitality room. Theirs died."

"Huh," Paul said. He took a tentative sip. "Sheesh, Dad, you could strip paint with this." He set the cup on the counter and opened the cupboard, looking for some sugar.

His dad chuckled and took a swallow of his own. "Does the body good." He paused. "You should call Ryan, though. Family's important. The most important thing you've got."

Paul smiled, blanking his thoughts. "I will, Dad, I will. I met his new girl, what's-her-name, not too long ago. We saw a show and caught up a little. She seems nice."

"She *is* nice, Steve. So's that Courtney you brought around that time. I wouldn't mind seeing her around a bit more."

Paul frowned. *That time* was three years ago. Long-term attachments didn't mesh well with his line of work.

His dad hadn't noticed. "You could use a lady in your life, you know? Your mother...."

Paul looked at his dad, startled. Dad never talked about Mom. Never.

"Your mother...." He smiled sadly. "She was the best thing that ever happened to me. The best."

"I know, Pop," Paul said. He blinked. *A blonde woman lay on beige carpet stained red with blood. He pressed his palms into her neck. His hands were too small; he couldn't stop the bleeding. Hot and red, it filled his nostrils, metallic and cloying. Rough hands on his shoulders dragged him to a navy-blue van emblazoned with three yellow letters: FBI. He couldn't breathe. He couldn't stop screaming.* He blinked again. "I wish I'd known her."

They drank their coffee in silence. After a few minutes, his dad clapped once. "Well, enough moping about the past. What say we go work on that crawl space?"

"Ooh, goody."

They put their dishes away and headed to the back of the house.

That evening Paul sat at the kitchen table, a cup of rotgut coffee in one hand and a powdered doughnut in the other, and stared at his father's incredulous face. It felt discordant looking at his dad with the façade of Renner in place, but this wasn't a job for the real him. *Man up,* he thought. *A little cognitive dissonance never hurt anybody.*

"You want me to do what?" Kevin Parsons asked.

"I need you to hide for a while," Paul said. "I have a cabin, fully stocked, isolated. Nobody knows it's mine. Nobody could trace you there. I need you to get in the car I've got outside, go there, and not tell anybody. Anybody. And don't use any credit cards along the way."

"But.... Why? For how long?"

"I don't know. Probably a few months, maybe longer. I can't tell you why, but it's very important."

Kevin frowned out the window, then at his son. "This is ridiculous. Are you in danger?"

Paul shook his head.

"Am I?"

Paul took a sip of coffee, stalling. He looked at the ceiling, then at Kevin. "Yes."

"From who?"

"I don't know, Dad," Paul said. "But they're going to kill you, and I need time to figure out who they are and how to stop them."

Kevin blinked several times, then pinched his own arm. "Am I dreaming?"

"No," Paul said. Kevin paced in front of the window.

"Steve, this is ridiculous. People are trying to kill me, but you don't know who they are, or how long I'll be hiding, or why they—" He stopped dead, then approached the table. A giant grin split his face as he leaned on the back of a chair. "And where is this cabin?"

Paul didn't like the look of that grin. "Near Lake Tahoe."

His dad flopped into the chair. "Jesus, Son, you really had me there. If you want to buy me a vacation, you don't need to scare me to death. The answer's still no, though. We've been through this, and it's not like I don't appreciate the thought." One look at his son's face and his smile faded.

Paul leaned across the table and grabbed his father's hand. He looked him in the eyes and willed him to understand. "Dad. I'm not kidding. This isn't a vacation. This is hiding, from very bad people."

Come on, Paul thought. *Just believe it.*

"You're serious," his dad said.

Paul squeezed Kevin's hand, then let go. "Yeah, I'm serious." He picked up the doughnut and took a bite.

"But...who on Earth would want me dead?"

"My thoughts exactly," Paul said, leaning back in his chair. "It doesn't make any sense."

His dad frowned. "And how do you know? How are you mixed up in all this, Steve?"

Paul looked into his cup. "You trust me, don't you, Dad?"

"Yeah, of course I do. But this. This is nuts."

"Yes, it is," Paul replied. "Will you do it?"

"Do I have a choice?"

Paul folded his hands over his head and looked at the ceiling. "Yeah, Dad, of course you have a choice. You can stay here until they get you, or you can run somewhere else while I sort this out. Or you could go to the cops, but they won't believe you." He looked at Kevin. "They'll just think you're crazy."

Kevin stared at him across the table. "Son, you have a lot of money, more than a mid-level programmer should have. I've known that for a long time. I raised you better than to be a crook, so I always figured you have to work for the government. CIA or something."

Paul kept his face blank.

"Anyway," Kevin continued, "I know you've been protecting your innocent old dad from it for a long time. Thank you. I've never asked before, but I need to know. Are you a criminal?"

"No," he lied. "I do what I'm paid to do. It's…complicated, and classified, but it's on the up-and-up." Paul kept his eyes locked on Kevin's. Finally, Kevin looked down.

"Okay, son. Okay. I believe you."

"But?" Paul asked.

"But can't you do something about this guy? Like, I stay here, and, when he comes to get me, you and your buddies get him instead?"

Paul sighed. "They'd just hire somebody else. Whoever 'they' are."

"So I go hide in a hole somewhere, and you find out."

"Yup," Paul said. "But it's a nice cabin, Dad. You'll like it. You can hunt and fish, and there's plenty of food, satellite TV and radio, a small library. It'll be nice. I'll give you a cell. I'll call every week, and, once I figure this thing out, I'll come get you."

"So be it. When do we leave?"

Paul picked up the keys. "Right now."

Chapter 8

Sam's phone rang. She touched the "answer" icon on her computer screen. "Sam Greene, hold please," she said without taking her eyes from the monitor. She pressed "hold." The satellite video feed showed a truck pulling into a warehouse. She relayed this information to Team Bravo, then hit the "hold" button again.

"Yes?" she asked.

"Would you be interested in a lead on the D Street case?" Chad DelGatto asked.

Sam smiled. Almost a year had passed since the near-miss in Salt Lake, and D Street had gone gun-shy. Palomini's team had been tasked to "supplementary investigations support." They were desperate for a break. "Very," she said.

"Well, then, look what I've found, Sammy," Chad said. A ten-digit number popped up on the screen.

"That is?"

"That's the phone number of the guy who sent those text messages to your I-590 last October. We still can't break the messages themselves, but we managed to crunch through the numerical with Apex-Lucinda and an area code regression Jim wrote. A-L is hot shit, Sam. You should see it in action. Beautiful."

"Chad, I could kiss you," she said.

"Happy hunting."

The line went dead.

The area code was D.C., the exchange Georgetown. She searched for details on the number. Beaming, Sam hit the COM button for Gene Palomini.

* * *

September 19th, 10:38 PM EST; Georgetown; Washington, D.C.

Jerri surveyed the complex. It was brick, one of a million just like it in cities all over America. According to Sam it contained nine small apartments, three per floor, each over two thousand dollars a month, plus utilities. They were considered cheap for the area.

Remind me not to move to Georgetown, Jerri thought as she crept up the stairs toward the door labeled 3A. A typical American pre-fab panel, all it would take would be a good kick from a trained martial artist to open it, deadbolt or no. Doug stood behind her, service 9mm pointed at the door. Carl whispered through the COM. "Fire escape clear. Back entrance clear."

"Approaching entrance," she whispered back, her senses at maximum alert.

With grim determination, she motioned to Doug. Infrared surveillance showed one person, awake and in the kitchen, with a stove burner on.

"Entrance in three, two, one!" Doug Goldman body-slammed the door. The flimsy wood shattered against not one but two deadbolts and a security chain. Doug smashed right through the cheap door and into the room, rolling left to give Jerri a clear field of fire.

"FBI, FREEZE!" she yelled, stepping through and panning her sub-machinegun toward the kitchen. The place reeked of sautéed garlic and unchanged litter box. An unattended pan crackled on the stove, the source of the more pleasant of the two smells. *Where is he?* she thought. Paul Renner had gotten the jump on her once, and she swore to herself it wouldn't happen again. Carl still didn't know where the hell he'd come from in that bathroom.

She covered Doug as he moved into the kitchen. Staccato gunfire rang out from the fire escape, the high-pitched ricochets louder than the muffled shots of Carl's automatic. "He's got a gun!" cried Carl over the COM as Gene eased up behind her. Jerri tracked her weapon left and right. Nothing moved.

"You're surrounded," Gene yelled. "Come out with your hands up!" His voice filled the small apartment, making the following silence that much more silent. Five seconds passed. Then ten.

A shape emerged from the bedroom on the right, hands folded on top of his head like a good little criminal. *Great, career perp,* thought Jerri. Keeping his assault rifle trained, Gene ordered him into the living room. The man did as he was told and stepped into the light. About 5' 10", he was in his mid-twenties, with brown hair and eyes to match. His stupid grin made Jerri regret not shooting him the moment he came into view. He wore a wife-beater and plaid boxers, with black socks that matched the spit-shined dress shoes by the door.

"Sit on the couch and keep your hands where we can see them," Gene said. The man complied. Jerri wanted to bash the grin off his face with the butt of her gun.

Instead she asked, "ID?" The man reached slowly toward the wallet on the end table. He seemed oblivious to the danger posed by three high-strung and heavily armed FBI agents. *Cool cucumber,* Jerri thought.

"CLEAR!" sounded from the bedroom, and a few seconds later from the bathroom. Gene still stood in the doorway, weapon pointed at the man's head, finger on the trigger, a bead of sweat trickling down his temple. The suspect tossed the wallet to Jerri. She found a D.C. driver's license for Brian LaMonte, whose picture matched the man in front of her, sleazy grin and all.

"Do you know why we're here, Mr. LaMonte?" Jerri said. She kept her voice calm in spite of the adrenaline pumping through her system.

LaMonte shook his head and didn't even look around as

Doug came back into the room behind him. Doug held up a small pistol. "This was on the bed," he said.

Jerri sneered at LaMonte. "Can you guess?"

He shook his head again.

With a sigh, Gene began the Miranda litany. "You have the right to remain silent...."

LaMonte's voice shook, but not as much as it should have. "Don't bother. You're in over your head, agent whoever-you-are, and you're not getting a life preserver from me." A nervous giggle punctuated the remark.

Gene's jaw clenched tight as he spat the rest of the words through his teeth. "Does 'don't bother' mean you are waiving your rights?"

Jerri glanced at her boss with serious concern. *Just don't kill him, Gene.*

LaMonte looked from Gene back to Jerri. "Nah, not waiving. I just think you should talk to my boss instead of me."

Gene waited, but LaMonte just let him wait. "And who might that be, Mr. LaMonte?"

"I'm not at liberty to say."

Jerri put her hand on Gene's shoulder and thanked God that Marty was with Carl. Gene held his temper in check, one of several reasons he had "In Charge" after "Special Agent" on his title, while Marty didn't.

Jerri broke in, holding a slip of paper in front of LaMonte's eyes. "What does this phone number mean to you?" She ignored Gene's annoyed look.

The man said, "You'll have to ask my boss."

Time for bad cop, she thought. LaMonte gasped in pain as Jerri grabbed his hair and wrenched his head back.

"I SAID WHAT THE FUCK DOES IT MEAN TO YOU, ASSHOLE?"

LaMonte's grin returned. "Get your hands off me or I'll have you up on charges."

"Well then," Jerri said, "we might as well get our money's worth." Her hand tightened on his hair and bent his head back farther. LaMonte looked desperately past her. Gene left the room.

Doug cracked his knuckles and formed a pair of ham-sized fists. It was time for "bad cop, worse cop."

Brian LaMonte broke immediately. "Don't. Please. I work for Central Intelligence."

* * *

October 2nd, 7:53 PM EST; J. Edgar Hoover Building; Washington, D.C.

Marty pulled off 9th Street toward 935 Pennsylvania Avenue, the J. Edgar Hoover Building. He eased the government-owned Ford Taurus four-door through the tourist-choked traffic, cursing the existence of every car in his way. The building ahead of him was awe-inspiring, both in size and in modern hideousness. It was everything that the White House was not.

The squat edifice covered a city block and comprised 2.8 million square feet of cubicles, offices, training grounds, and even a gun range. It housed more than six thousand employees of the Federal Bureau of Investigation. Hoover himself was rumored to have called it "the ugliest building I've ever seen." Rumor or no, Marty agreed. The thing was grotesque. He waved his pass at the security guard, parked, and went inside.

Brian LaMonte was in FBI custody at an undisclosed location, and once he realized that, no, he wouldn't be given a phone call, and, no, he had no rights except what they chose to give him, and, no, it didn't matter that he was a CIA spook, he'd finally given them the name of his boss and a promise that he'd "clear everything up."

LaMonte's boss, Ernest MacGowan, was in a conference room in the Hoover building, waiting for Marty and the rest of his brother's team to show up. He'd already told Gene by phone that there was nothing he could do for them. He'd also agreed to meet with them, if only for the sake of professional courtesy, and on the condition that they released Brian LaMonte into his custody. According to Sam, Mr. MacGowan had been stalling, hedging, and hiding behind the "classified nature of the subject." Marty couldn't wait to shatter his illusions.

Marty lumbered down the hall to Conference Room Magnolia. Why the FBI would name their rooms after flowers of all things he'd never know. *Fucking flowers.* He opened the door without knocking, the sneer on his face unrelenting. The rest of the team sat at the table, and every one of them looked annoyed as hell.

MacGowan was a short, fat dude, obviously of Scottish descent, with a mop of curly red hair and pasty white skin that would rival that of any vampire. *If Moby Dick got drunk enough to fuck Carrot Top...*, Marty thought. He hated him on sight.

Carl and Doug glared at MacGowan with naked hostility. Carl's bad arm rested on the table. *Poor bastard will never heal completely.* The thought infuriated Marty. Jerri lounged against the wall while Gene frowned across the table at the pasty, fat little man.

With a momentary glance at Marty, whale-boy continued talking. "Like I said, Agent LaMonte is on special assignment, and his involvement with Mr. Renner is classified." He crossed his arms in a matter-of-fact, "so that's that" sort of way.

Gene opened his mouth to speak, but Marty never gave him a chance. He lunged, grabbed the fat little puke by the chin, and hefted him to his feet. The CIA-man's pale face flushed with anger, and he blustered in protest. Marty slammed him against the wall one-handed, adrenaline cooperating with corded muscle in one fluid motion.

He leaned to within inches of MacGowan's stinking little freckled face and spat out in barely-controlled rage, "You realize we have a fucking serial killer on our hands? You realize this guy's killed at least two dozen people over the past ten years?"

Pointing at Carl's wounded arm with his free hand, he seethed through clenched teeth, "You realize he crippled my fucking partner, you fat fuck? If you think you're getting your man back without some kind of cooperation—"

Gene laid a hand on his brother's arm. Marty's eyes flashed in anger. "Let him go, bro."

Marty shook with rage, ready to pull MacGowan's head off

with his bare hands. After a long moment, he dropped him with a shove into the wall. The recoil propelled Marty backward and into the table. With a sneer he spat, "Okay, then, CIA-man, what the fuck is the problem? You going to tell us to just walk away from this?"

To Marty's surprise, Ernest MacGowan calmly straightened his clothes, even though his hands were shaking. "That's exactly what I'm telling you to do. This man isn't a common criminal. He isn't even an uncommon criminal." He sat down, picked up a powdered doughnut, and added, "In fact, you might not be able to call him a criminal at all." He took a small bite, white powder coating his double chin.

His eyes narrowed to dangerous slits, and Doug blurted, "What does that mean, Agent MacGowan?" Doug's face was blotchy from the effort of remaining civil under the circumstances. Marty was right there with him. "I may be just a dense G-man, but how is a serial killer not a criminal, exactly?"

MacGowan sucked powdered sugar from his fingers and looked up at the ceiling while he formulated his reply. "What I'm about to tell you can't leave this room." He looked at Gene, eyebrows raised in question. Gene looked at Jerri, Marty, Doug, and finally at Carl. Carl gave a quick nod. Gene looked back at the CIA agent.

"Okay, shoot."

"Over the past ten years, the CIA has employed Paul Renner as a part-time employee. He's useful when certain elements need to be removed in a permanent manner."

Gene snorted. "You mean the CIA paid him to kill people."

MacGowan idly scratched his forehead. "Who do you think we use, Boy Scouts?" Gene and Jerri shared a knowing look. Carl clenched his fists.

Marty interrupted, shaking his head in anger. "Now wait just one goddamn fucking minute here. You're telling me that the guy we've been chasing for the past three years, this motherfucker who crippled my fucking partner is a motherfucking CIA *Agent?*" A gentle hand on his arm—Jerri's—calmed him down just a little. He shook his head in disbelief and added, "No fucking way." He sat down, deflated.

For the first time, MacGowan looked uncomfortable. "Not exactly. He's more of an...entrepreneur. A, shall we say, contractor. Part-time." Marty wanted nothing more than to wring the neck holding up his flabby head.

Gene fingered the file in front of him. "What reason would the CIA have to kill Jenny Sykes? Eugenia Klammen? Darrell Eaton? What reason would they have to kill half of these people? They're nobodies. There's no correlation between any of them."

MacGowan shrugged, then jerked his hands up defensively when Marty lunged toward him. "Wait!" Marty stopped short, inches from crippling the man with his bare hands. "I don't mean that I won't say. That's not it. Several of these people weren't CIA targets."

"So he's a professional and a hobbyist?" Carl asked.

"No," MacGowan said. "I don't think so. I think he does a lot of freelance work."

Carl looked at the victim file. "That explains why we couldn't figure out the M.O. or how he chooses his victims. Or why his psyche profile didn't make any sense."

Marty scowled. "If he's not a serial killer, why does he taunt us?"

"We don't know," MacGowan said. "I don't know what this current killing spree is about. We haven't even tried to contact him since last October."

"How do we contact him?" Gene asked.

MacGowan shook his head. "'We' don't, Special Agent Palomini. I do. If we have a job, I have Brian call a number. It gets forwarded through an online messaging service. A few days or weeks later, we get a cell phone through the United States Post Office. We get a text message within forty-eight hours that tells us where to send a name and address. It's always some kind of Internet relay, totally untraceable. You cannot find this man."

You've got to be kidding me, Marty thought. *We have a lead we can't use.*

Jerri interrupted his thought. "Yeah, but we don't have to find him."

Every eye turned to her. "We use you to set some bait, then you get your agent back." She raised her eyebrows at Gene.

"I'm game," Gene said.

MacGowan took another bite of doughnut. "Done."

Marty smiled ear-to-ear. *Here we come, motherfucker.*

* * *

October 24th, 11:28 AM EST; J. Edgar Hoover Building; Washington, D.C.

This second meeting was almost too much, even for Gene. The wry smirks on MacGowan and his toady LaMonte's faces were enough to drive the most stable of men right over the edge. From the look of Marty and Doug, they weren't feeling too stable. If it weren't for the black I-590 NetPhone that sat on the table in front of them, Gene would have happily let them beat both men into unconsciousness.

Gene unlocked LaMonte's handcuffs and shoved him toward the table, just as Jerri picked up the phone and hit the "messages" button.

She found a single text message, a Gmail address of random letters and symbols. She typed in the name and address of Mr. Mark Burton.

Staff Sergeant Mark Burton was a former Marine sniper from Camp Pendleton, California, who had volunteered to be bait, no questions asked. They needed a real person for a decoy, not someone connected in any way to Gene's team or the FBI. It had to be someone whom Paul Renner wouldn't suspect and a man whom someone in the CIA might want dead.

Ten years prior, Burton had destroyed the drug empire of a rogue agent. He'd come clean on some unauthorized black ops, testifying before Congress at the cost of his own job. None of it hit the media, but the agent went down, and so did Burton's career. Those in the know described it as "taking a lot of balls." Almost as much as it took to be bait for an assassin the FBI hadn't been able to catch for ten years.

Chapter 9

December 2nd, 1:42 AM EST; Times Square; New York City, New York.

Under an orange night sky devoid of stars, Paul Renner walked along Times Square like a tourist. He wore a *Rent* hoodie and blue jeans, and took his time. He gawked at the billboards. He wasn't acting. He'd never paid much attention to the new, commercialized New York created by Mayor Giuliani. Sure, his time had passed, but the changes wrought by his predecessor had endured.

Gone were the titty bars and porno theaters. Walt Disney had replaced Peekaboo Theater, the world's largest Toys 'R Us instead of the Bunny Hop Lounge. Even at this hour, tourists lined the streets instead of the winos and drunkards Paul was accustomed to. He was so used to the run-down Manhattan of earlier days he couldn't quite believe the pleasant environment that awaited the modern New Yorker.

He ambled south toward downtown. He took his time and enjoyed the sights. Art galleries, upscale eateries, trendy cafés. Throw in a couple Starbucks to supply the city with five-dollar coffee and you get a New York Paul could just about live in full-time.

He wandered through the half-empty streets, marveling at the lack of horn-honking and general litter. Bored, he wasn't sure what he was looking for, and was leery of using Internet dating sites since the near-miss with the Feds in Salt Lake. He wasn't sure how they'd found him, so he needed to be careful.

He caught a midnight showing of some action flick, a spy thriller starring Matt Damon. It was grotesquely unbelievable but fun nonetheless. He left the theater and was buying a Pop Tart from a news stand when he noticed a man following him. He turned north, toward Central Park, and picked up his pace. It was never truly dark in New York, but the park was as close as it got.

The guy was a good tail. He changed his appearance every few blocks with different hats and a reversible jacket. Paul kept track of him by the length of his stride and pattern of his gait. *Goddamn Feds,* he thought.

Walking north past Central Park, Paul cut east. He found the perfect observation post, a below-ground entrance to an ugly cinderblock apartment building. The stairs went down a full story to a lime-green door and were shielded on both sides with short concrete walls.

Crouched a third of the way down, he waited to see if his quarry would walk past. He made no sound that wouldn't be masked by the slight breeze through the streets and the general noise of the city. Paul wasn't used to being stalked and found the sensation uncomfortable. *At least I have the courtesy of killing my prey while they're clueless,* he thought. He waited five minutes, then peeked out from his hiding place.

A blinding flash of pain screamed through his head and spun him to his knees on the stairs. Hot, wet blood streamed down his scalp in a river, the pain a burning reminder that he was both alive and lucky to be so. The concrete battered his body as he rolled to the bottom of the stairs. He accepted the bruises as payment for his continued life. He hadn't heard a gunshot. *No Miranda rights. No warning shot. This asshole's trying to kill me.* Survival instinct was no stranger to Paul. The righteous anger that accompanied it was.

Paul pulled the snub-nosed .38 revolver from his ankle holster and wished he had something with more punch on hand. He wiped at the blood that flowed down his face and into his eyes. *I've got to be able to see.* He knew it was a losing battle; head wounds bled too much to control without a serious bandage. Without taking his eyes from the street, he backed into the door of the basement apartment and tried the doorknob.

A slow but frantic turn to the left met resistance, and a turn to the right verified the fact. *Shit. Trapped.* The safety-glass window was imbedded with chicken wire.

He ducked into the corner, his eyes closed tight to adjust them to the new level of darkness as quickly as possible. He then stood to his full height and snapped his eyes wide open. He scanned the street, just barely visible above the top of the steps, and looked for any sign of movement. He grunted at a sudden impact to his right shoulder. The revolver fell from his hand, clattering to the pavement at his feet. The wound didn't hurt, per se. Not yet. He knew it would later, though, when the adrenaline wore off. *If there was a later.*

The little .38 was no good outside of ten feet. Paul fell on the pistol and played dead to bait the man closer. A red blackness threatened to consume his vision, and he fought against the shock that pulled him down into a sleep from which he would never wake. He gripped the gun left-handed, willed himself to alert stillness and waited for his killer to approach. *Hopefully, I can kill this bastard before I pass out.*

Twenty seconds later, the silhouette of a man appeared at the top of the stairs. The silenced pistol in his right hand was blackened to avoid any unwanted reflection from the streetlights or the moon. The man didn't waste any time trying to explain, to ask questions, or to get him to beg for mercy. He raised the pistol in one smooth motion.

Paul gritted his teeth against the agony in his arm and squeezed the trigger.

Two shots shattered the relative silence of the deserted street with the double-tap all too common in neighborhoods farther north. A small hole appeared in the assassin's left eye. Paul knew there wouldn't be an exit wound from the tiny, low-power round. The second shot followed right behind, blazing through the hole bored by the first bullet. The man collapsed in a heap as Paul crawled up the stairs, scanning the street for any backup as he did so.

Aside from the wind, nothing stirred. A car passed by on the cross-street, followed by another. With a grimace of pain, Paul pulled his emergency oxycodone out of his pocket. He couldn't open the cap; his right hand wasn't responding properly.

He used his teeth to hold the bottle and cranked off the cap with his left hand. He chewed up three of the narcotics dry. His face contorted against the harsh taste. He slapped the lid back on, then stood. He swooned but caught himself on the wall. He stumbled toward the street and dropped to his knees in front of the corpse.

Paul winced at the pain in his shoulder. *That's going to bruise.* Feeling slowly returned to his right hand as the narcotics kicked in. He looked down at the small hole in his hoodie. *This is why we wear our bulletproof vests, kiddies,* he thought. As far as he was concerned, "unhealthy paranoia" was an oxymoron.

Paul tore the man's shirt in half and yanked it off the body. He twisted it into a makeshift bandana and used it to bandage his torn scalp. He pulled it tight, then put up the hood to cover the bandage.

A quick search of the body revealed a backup 9mm, which he ignored, and a complete lack of identification. Whoever he was, Paul didn't recognize him. He left the silenced pistol on the sidewalk and rose, steadying himself against the light pole.

Paul stumbled off toward the lighted street to the east, his thoughts ablaze.

* * *

December 12th, 6:18 PM CST; Glenview Manor Apartments, Apartment 4A; St. Louis, Missouri.

Larry Johnson stood in the neighbor's apartment, cutting tomatoes on the tiny kitchen counter. Every night he'd cook, Josh would clean up, and they'd commiserate about the "joys" of being confined to witness protection for over a year. *At least Josh gets paid for it.* He chided himself for the un-Christian thought. He didn't need the money, anyway. What he needed was for Palomini's team to do their jobs so he could go home. Smuggled, middle-of-the-night visits from his loved ones weren't enough.

Agent Barnhoorn was coming over to check in and inform him of the lack of progress, just as he did every couple of weeks, so sausage-stuffed tomatoes were on the menu. "Hey, Josh!" he called.

"Yeah," Josh replied from in front of the television.

"Can you come in here and get me down the bread crumbs?"

"No problem," Josh said. He came into the kitchen and opened the cupboard, took down the can of crumbs, and set it on the counter. Larry looked at Josh's neck. Something was wrong, something missing. Something out of place. He looked harder, searching.

"What?" Josh asked.

Larry thrust the seven-inch knife into the side of Josh's neck. *That's better.* Josh stumbled backward, his eyes open wide in shock. Larry kept a firm grip on the knife, and it came free with a wet rip. Bright red blood spurted from the wound, splattering the kitchen in a shower of gore. Josh pressed both hands to his neck. He tried to speak, an inarticulate, wet, burbling sound. *That doesn't sound good.* Larry stabbed him in the chest and the sound stopped. *That's better.* He pulled the knife free, and Josh Santee's body dropped to the floor.

The apartment was quiet. Something was missing. Larry stepped to the door and opened it, searching the hallway. There was nobody there. Downstairs, a TV blared. He walked down the stairs to the third floor and knocked on the door to apartment 3A. There was something out of place. *Why is my hand wet?* He absentmindedly wiped his hand on the front of his shirt, then knocked again.

A woman's voice responded. He didn't understand what she said. The door opened a crack, revealing a wide-eyed woman in jeans and a tank top. She looked familiar. She babbled something. There was something wrong with her. He thrust through the crack in the door, burying the knife in her abdomen. *That's better.*

He threw his weight against the door, shredding the security-chain housing and forcing his way into the apartment. A fat man sat on the couch, holding a beer, his eyes wide with shock. There was something wrong with him.

Robbie pulled into the parking lot, grabbed the Italian rolls off the front seat, and headed for the back door. A woman shrieked. He took the stairs two at a time, his service revolver drawn. The screaming stopped as he reached the third-floor landing.

He listened at the fire door. Behind it, he heard panting. He grabbed the handle with his left hand and pulled. He rolled his body around the door, weapon-hand leading. At the end of the hall, Larry Johnson sat on the floor with a young woman. She lay on her stomach, but her head rested face-up in his lap, her eyes wide open. They were both covered in blood, as were the walls and floor. Naked feet stuck out from the doorway to 3B. A pool of blood spread into the hall.

"Jesus Christ, Larry," Robbie said. "What happened?"

Larry looked up at the sound of his voice, a puzzled look on his face. He staggered to his feet, dropping the woman to the floor, then bent over and picked up a kitchen knife.

"Larry?"

No response.

Larry walked toward him, holding the knife with white knuckles.

"Larry?" Robbie choked up the revolver. Larry took another step. "Put the knife down, Larry." He took another step. He was ten feet away.

Robbie aimed the revolver at Larry's right thigh. "One more step and I'll have to shoot you, Larry." Larry took another step. Robbie pulled the trigger. The bullet entered and exited the leg in the blink of an eye, a clean shot straight through the muscle. Without reaction, Larry Johnson took another step. *Oh, shit,* Robbie thought.

Robbie shot him in the other leg. Larry fell to the ground without so much as a whimper. He stabbed the knife into the floor and used it to pull himself forward an arm's length, dragging his face across the floor without bothering to lift his head. He did it again. Robbie got out his handcuffs and stepped on Larry's wrist to pin the knife in place.

Larry grabbed Robbie's ankle with his other hand and yanked him off his feet. Robbie hit the ground hard; the handcuffs clattered across the floor, but he managed to keep hold of the gun. Kicking frantically, he tried to dislodge Larry's hand. Larry didn't react, as if he didn't even feel it. His scratched face still looked befuddled as he yanked the knife from the floor and looked from Robbie's face to the ankle he still held.

"Don't," Robbie said. He aimed the pistol down the length of his body, right at the top of Larry's head. "Please." Larry raised the knife. Robbie shot him through the cranium at point-blank range. Larry's head dropped to the ground, and his body relaxed. The knife clattered to the floor. Blood gushed from the wound, thick and red.

Robbie scrambled to his feet and took out his phone. He stared at the body as he auto-dialed his office. A pleasant male voice answered the phone, "FBI St. Louis, Agent Barnhoorn's office."

"Chet, we have multiple civilians and maybe some officers down. I need an ambulance, police, and forensics at the Glenview safe house. Send a team, maybe two. I'm not sure this is over." The calm of his own voice surprised him. He couldn't stop shaking.

"Got it, Robert," Chet replied.

"And Chet? Contact Gene Palomini and Doug Goldman."

* * *

December 24th, 6:28pm CST; Home of Agent Robert Barnhoorn; St. Louis, Missouri.

Doug wiped up the juices from the Christmas ham with a piece of bread and shoved it whole into his mouth. He dumped his plate in the sink and returned to the living room.

Robbie's house was an explosion of holiday cheer. Wreaths

hung from every wall, electric candles sparkled in every window, and the Christmas tree dominated the living room. A mound of presents spilled out from beneath it in perfectly orchestrated chaos. Seven-year-old Evan Barnhoorn lurked nearby, never too far from the tree.

Maureen sat with Marcy, nursing little Christine while Grace squirmed in her bassinette. Doug scooped her up one-handed and tickled her belly. She giggled.

He sat on the couch and grinned at Robbie. "I can't believe it's their first Christmas already."

Robbie grinned back. "I can't believe it's Evan's seventh. They get so big so fast." Marcy beamed at him from across the room. He leaned in and frowned. "Marcy wants to try for more."

Doug avoided looking at Maureen. "Mo's exhausted all the time. I don't know how she does it, between the kids and her clients. But she's already said she wants more. We'll have to see."

The phone rang. Robbie hopped up and grabbed the phone from the cradle. He looked at the caller ID, frowned, and walked out of the room. Marcy looked at Doug. He shrugged, then rubbed noses with his daughter, cooing.

Robbie walked back into the room and put the phone back on the charger. "Work," he said. "Nothing that can't wait." He nudged Doug with his foot. "Help me with these dishes, will you?"

Subtle, Doug thought. He stood and followed Robbie into the kitchen. "What's up?"

"Larry's toxicology came back negative."

Doug frowned. "That's impossible."

Robbie grabbed a sponge and turned on the sink. "Maybe, but it's true. Clean as clean. He had some needle scars, but they were old. Very old." He washed a plate and handed it to Doug, who grabbed the dish towel off the stove handle and dried it. He put it in the drainer.

"No brain tumor, no chemical imbalance, no drugs. How the hell did Renner do it?"

"I don't know," Robbie said. "I don't know."

Marcy let Evan open one present, an Optimus Prime action

figure the size of Doug's arm, then put him to bed. Marcy and Maureen headed upstairs to tuck in the girls while Doug and Robbie stuffed stockings. The house smelled of cinnamon.

Robbie looked pointedly toward the stairs. "Does she know?"

Doug shoved a handful of Tootsie Rolls into a red-and-green sock. "No, not yet."

Robbie sucked air through his teeth. "What are you going to tell her?"

"I don't know. The truth. We have to catch this bastard. We have to."

"Right. But she already knows that. What about after?"

Doug leaned his head against the wall and squeezed his eyes shut. "After that, there are ten thousand more just like him." He opened his eyes and stared at the ceiling. "The world is full of monsters, and if men like us don't catch them, what happens to our children?"

"Men like you," Robbie said.

"What?"

"Men like *you* catch monsters. I push pencils. I'd never fired my weapon, never even drawn it, on duty. It's...." He looked at Doug, stricken.

"It's not what you think," Doug finished for him.

Robbie shook his head. "It's the most terrible thing I've ever done. And God help me for saying it, that's why we need men like you. To do what the rest of us can't."

Doug said nothing. He picked up another handful of candy and shoved it into a stocking.

"Hey, Doug?" Robbie asked.

"Yeah?"

"You need to tell her soon."

"I know," Doug said. "I'll get to it. Just as soon as I know what I'm going to do."

On the staircase, Maureen listened silently and wept.

* * *

January 1st, 7:02 AM EST; Gene Palomini's Apartment; Washington, D.C.

The ring of Gene's cell phone shattered through the bars of *Auld Lang Syne* that ran through his dream. He sat up with a start, spilling leftover popcorn all over the floor. He lay on the couch in his boxer shorts, surrounded by empty pizza boxes and an enormous pile of beer bottles. He'd shut the TV off six hours earlier, ten minutes after the last guest had left. The phone rang again. He knocked over several empties and fumbled for the phone he knew was somewhere on the coffee table.

What kind of monster calls at 7 AM on New Year's Day? He found the phone and managed to pick it up. He stared at the tiny screen with sleep-bleary eyes and tried to read the caller ID. It snapped into focus, and he smiled. *Finally!* It had been almost two months since they'd sent the fake job to Paul Renner.

The entire team feared for Burton's life. Paul might not alert them to every job that he did, and Gene feared he would try to kill the man without ever calling. That thought had occurred to Mark Burton, but he'd signed up anyway. Gene worried that six undercover bodyguards might not be enough.

Gene had no idea where he'd put his micro-bead. He cleared his throat and hit "send."

"Hello?"

The voice wasn't even disguised. "Hello, Special Agent Palomini. How's Carl's arm?"

"Go screw yourself," Gene replied.

"California," was all he said. And then the line went dead.

Gene smiled to himself. *Hook, line, and sinker. Got him.*

Gene stumbled to the shower.

Chapter 10

January 6th, 3:12 PM PST; Shady Grove retirement community; San Diego, California.

Gene savored the salty air of a beautiful winter's day in southern California. The temperature was seventy-eight degrees Fahrenheit, the humidity near zero, and twenty-eight FBI agents had staked out the entire area surrounding Shady Grove senior living facility, Mark Burton's home just outside of San Diego.

Shady Grove wasn't shady, and it wasn't a grove. It was a gated community complete with every luxury a retired person might want. It had its own tennis and squash courts, an eighteen-hole golf course, a gym complete with a massage service and personal trainers, four fine-dining restaurants, and even its own yacht club. It housed almost eight hundred men and women over the age of sixty-two, and was much like a town in its own right. Gene didn't want to know how a former Marine sergeant could afford the twelve thousand dollars a month it cost to live there.

Renner's timeline put the hit on Thursday, when Mark went golfing with some of the other residents, so they found themselves staked out around the course while Mark and his friends worked their way down the back nine.

Agent Atkinson's team was disguised as a group of Pacific Gas and Electric employees working on the power line, complete with an authentic PG&E truck. Their best sniper stood in the cherry-picker with a good view of the surrounding area. Doug was in the club house basement, watching everything on the security feeds and relaying information to the team.

Go time, Gene thought.

Man, it's nice around here, Paul thought as he hefted his golf bag. He'd hooked up with a couple of proctologists who'd been drinking in the club house. Today he was Dan McLawry, a psychologist from Connecticut in town on business. He'd chatted about problematic patients and let the doctors reminisce about their worst problems.

Like any good kill, the plan today was simple; play a few holes of golf, slip away with a medical emergency, remove the rifle from the golf bag, and shoot Mark Burton through the head. "One shot, one kill" was the marine sniper saying. *Today, this guy's going to learn what it really means, up close and personal,* Paul thought. He chuckled, coinciding with the punch line of Dr. Odan's dirty golf joke. The doctors laughed along with him, but at the wrong joke.

"Nine holes. Nice," Dr. Ryan said. They all laughed again, and with more horseplay than was seemly for their professions, headed out to the links.

"Cart or hoof it?" Paul asked.

Their replies were incredulous; of course they would walk. Paul sighed. *These Californians are a little too gung-ho about exercise.* He endured some good-natured ribbing about "lazy east-coasters," hefted his bag and followed the doctors onto the first hole.

He sliced the first ball hard and landed it in a bunker. He was off the lead by twelve at the fourth hole, his mind more on the job ahead than on the game. The doctors bemoaned his bad luck and offered their sympathies. Behind his back they bemoaned Stein's bad luck for finding such a bad partner, and Paul pretended not to hear them. He put his hand in his pocket and pressed a button. His phone rang.

Paul stepped aside and answered it with a curt "Hello." Keeping his voice low, he argued with the dial tone. Amid tepid protests, he begged off the rest of the game, and headed for the clubhouse. The doctors watched him go with a mixture of annoyance and relief.

Doug sat in the clubhouse basement, basking in the light of a bank of black-and-white monitors. He was grumpy about being stuck in the basement doing Sam's job, especially on a day this beautiful, just because the filthy rich owners of this "resort retirement community" didn't want to pony up the bucks to update their security system. He comforted himself in the knowledge that he wasn't stuck in a hot, sticky van like Gene. He scanned the images again. *Man, there's a lot of people out there today.*

His eyes flicked across the screens. He'd taped a picture of Paul Renner to the desk, courtesy of MacGowan at the CIA. He sipped his coffee and watched as Sergeant Burton finished his bogie on the sixteenth. *They're not bad, but I think I could take them,* he thought. Motion on the fourth hole caught his eye.

A man left a foursome, hefting a bulky bag of golf clubs, and headed to the clubhouse. He was of average height, average build, and walked with the confident grace of a martial artist. Doug looked at the picture of Paul Renner, then zoomed in, leaning toward the screen. He set down his coffee and fingered his COM ear-bead.

After a moment it was clear. *This isn't our guy. Right height, right hair color, but the face is all wrong.* The guy had an aquiline nose, like the pictures of Caesar on old Roman coins. Doug took a sip of his coffee and sighed. Mark Burton teed off on the last hole. If the hit was going to happen here, it would have to happen soon.

Once in the bathroom, Paul took a handicapped stall. He stripped off the ridiculous golf outfit, stuffed it into his golf bag's front pocket, then changed into the khaki shorts and green polo shirt of a Shady Grove groundskeeper's uniform. He tore off the prosthetic nose and dropped it into the toilet, rubbed his face to remove the remainder of the latex adhesive, then slid the disassembled rifle out of the bag. Within forty seconds it was complete, except for the barrel attachment. That he would save for the roof.

Paul stuffed the mostly assembled rifle back into the bag, flushed the toilet, and exited the bathroom. A quick sidestep brought him into the kitchen, where an access door led to the roof. He opened it and recoiled, squinting.

The terra-cotta tiles blazed orange in the sunlight. Heat radiated off them in waves. Pausing to let his eyes adjust, Paul crouched and waited at the open door. He used the time to attach the barrel to the 30.06, which he did by touch. He clucked peevishly and thought for a moment that not bringing a scope was a mistake, but once he attached it, he didn't have a way to calibrate it anyway, so he let the thought go. He could shoot well enough without one.

"One, this is three."

"Go ahead, three," Gene said into the COM. He couldn't see anything from the back of the panel van and relied on Adkinson's team for recon.

"Someone just opened the access door on the roof of the clubhouse. Whoever it is, he's crouching down."

Gene triggered the COM to hit all frequencies. "This is *go*, people. Stay sharp. Possible shooter on the roof of the clubhouse."

Sergeant Mark Burton's gravelly voice rasped over the COM, "Just get him before he gets me. I don't want to miss meatloaf night."

I knew we shouldn't have wired him for COM, thought Gene. "Do you have visual confirmation of the target, three?"

"No, one. Someone's up there, but we can't tell who."

Something glinted in the sunlight in Paul's peripheral vision. A lens flashed from the bucket of the PG&E cherry-picker. Binoculars! Looking right at him.

Ah, shit. Setup.

Paul dropped the rifle and rolled off the roof. His body tensed as he fell to the wooden deck twelve feet below. A pair of servers on their cigarette break jumped in alarm when he landed in front of them. They were still gawking when he disabled their voice boxes with a pair of stiff-fingered strikes to the throat.

Marty heard Adkinson's sniper curse through the COM. "Gig's up! He made me!"

Marty bolted from the van, running for all he was worth toward the clubhouse. "DOUG! HE'S ALL YOURS!" he heard Gene scream into the COM, all sense of stealth obliterated. Two cars full of well-armed and highly trained FBI agents screeched onto the curb behind him. Men spilled out and broke into a run, rapidly catching up to the larger but slower Palomini.

The sound of assault rifles cocking was music to Marty's ears. *Maybe we'll get to kill this motherfucker instead of arresting him*, he thought with grim anticipation. Senior citizens cowered on the sidewalk. They dove to the ground from their café tables as fast as their old bodies would propel them.

The older Palomini slammed through the front door while

Mathis' assault squad surrounded the building. Shouts of "Clear!" rang over the COM as they searched the rooms. Two civilians—service staff—were reported down but conscious. They couldn't speak yet, but both pointed into the clubhouse.

Within two minutes they'd searched every room but the pantry. Marty, machine gun held ready, sidled up to the door as Doug reached a massive hand toward the brass knob. Marty listened at the door and heard nothing. He stepped back, re-readied his weapon in both hands, then nodded. Doug opened the door and Marty charged in, Doug right behind him.

Shelves filled the room, packed with every non-perishable foodstuff imaginable: canned vegetables and soup starters, bags of flour and sugar, boxes of pasta, bags of potatoes, and a complete lack of killers that needed killing. "FUCKING CLEAR, GODDAMN IT!" Marty bellowed into the COM. He barely restrained himself from upending a shelf of canned goods. He took a deep breath, then said in a calmer voice, "He ain't in here, Gene."

* * *

January 6th, 3:32 PM PST; Shady Grove retirement community; San Diego, California.

Gene exhaled for the first time in forever. He hadn't realized he'd been holding his breath, and his lungs hurt. He got out of the van. He scanned the area for anyone, anything out of the ordinary, anything that might indicate where Paul Renner had gone. His eyes caught the shed on the edge of the golf course where two of Miller's squad guarded the service tunnel that led from the clubhouse. The door stood ajar.

He jogged in that direction and spoke into his COM. "Five, one, what's your twenty, over?" In civilian speak: *Hey, guys in the shack, this is Gene. What's going on?*

No response. He tried again, speaking clearly in case of interference.

"Five, this is one. What's your status, over?"

Nothing.

"FIVE, REPORT!"

Nothing.

He broke into a run and heard Sam in his ear. "No response on five, Gene. They last checked in four minutes ago, just after Renner was spotted by three."

Agent Mathis chimed in, "We just got confirmation from the service guys. The guy on the roof matches Renner's description. Suspect is wearing a groundskeeper's uniform, khaki shorts, and a green polo. Repeat, suspect's outfit is khaki shorts and a green, short-sleeved, collared shirt with *Shady Grove* embroidered on the front."

Gene stopped and looked around. Just across the property, not two hundred feet away, a man of average build and average height walked unhurriedly toward the yacht club and the beach, directly away from the maintenance shack. He had short-cropped black hair and wore khaki shorts and a green polo. Gene broke into a run. "Got him, got him, got him, headed west! Backup!" He kept his voice low and tried to maneuver behind the man to keep from being spotted.

Paul Renner broke into a run. Gene's pistol cleared its holster as he sprinted after him. His COM sprang to life.

Sam's voice was crisp and clear in his ear. "We have a foot pursuit moving down the boardwalk toward the Shady Grove Yacht Club. Request immediate helicopter assist."

A deep male voice Gene didn't recognize responded. "Air support is inbound." Gene hit the boardwalk and slid on the sandy wood, almost crashing into an elderly couple enjoying their ice-cream cones. He closed on Renner, but not fast enough. The boardwalk stretched a half mile along the ocean, and it looked like the assassin knew where he was going.

Sam continued in his ear, "All units respond to the Shady Grove boardwalk. Agent in pursuit of suspect considered armed and extremely dangerous." A gray-bearded man in a loud Hawaiian shirt noticed the foot-chase and tackled Renner as he went past. They went down with a crash onto the boards and slid a good eight feet before Renner regained his feet, scrambling away. Now he was less than fifty feet ahead, and Gene saw where he was going.

Agent Miller's voice rang out in his ear. "Jesus. Agents down! Get an ambulance up here, now! Agents down!"

Gene replied breathlessly, "Pier! Pier! Maybe a boat!" Sure enough, just ahead Paul Renner broke right and ran down the pier. Gene lost sight of him amid the crab-shacks and tourist-trap souvenir stands but heard the heavy footsteps as they reverberated on the boards.

Sam replied in his ear, "This is the FBI requesting immediate Coast Guard support. Suspect is a white male, thirties, bl–" Gene slammed full-force into a white-haired woman with a walker. The aluminum frame tangled in his feet and sent him sprawling to the ground. His pistol scattered across the pier and into the water. The boards dug slivers deep into his palms. He scrambled to his feet and took off down the pier.

The crowd was thicker here. Renner pushed people out of the way and shouldered his way to the end of the pier. This partially cleared the crowd for Gene, so the FBI agent had the advantage. Twenty feet away. Fifteen. Ten. A burst of adrenaline brought Gene forward just as Paul Renner dove toward the water fifteen feet below. As Paul cleared the wooden planking, he hooked a rope to the safety fencing, then held on with both hands.

In mid-dive, Gene slammed into him. Gene's Kevlar vest took the bulk of the impact, and Paul Renner grunted in pain as they sailed out over the water. Renner held onto the rope, and they switched direction, swinging in under the pier, where he let go. They fell. Gene saw the deck of a speedboat rushing toward their entangled bodies.

The impact blasted the air from his lungs, but Renner took the worst of it. All two-hundred-twenty pounds of agent and gear slammed Renner into the deck. Even so, the man recovered quickly and rolled to his feet. The killer had apparently avoided breaking anything. Gene wasn't sure he was so lucky, given the sudden, sharp pain in his right ankle.

Gene stood and lifted his fists. Renner kicked him in the chest. He stumbled backward, favoring his good leg and trying not to pitch overboard. Renner moved with blinding speed and danced on his feet in the rocking boat. Gene knew he was in deep trouble, with the Kevlar vest hindering his mobility. But he'd fought small, good guys before; he could take one hell of a beating and dish out a lot more. He kept his head and spoke into the COM. "Under the pier, two-thirds down."

Paul Renner smiled and circled, looking for an opening against the injured agent. His voice was calm, his breathing steady. He tapped his ear and his grin widened. "Who you talking to, Agent Palomini?"

Gene reached up and touched his ear. His ear bead wasn't there. *That's not g–* Renner's knuckles crashed into his nose. Blood sprayed across his face, but he took the punch and wrapped with his arms, crushing Paul Renner in a vise-like bear hug. Renner punched at his abdomen viciously, hitting the areas that were least protected by the Kevlar vest. Gene ignored the pain and squeezed harder. He felt rather than heard a rib shift, then crack. Fists rained down like a rockslide, and his entire body burned. He squeezed harder, trying to crush the life out of the killer. Another rib cracked. Renner gasped in pain.

Renner stomped on Gene's injured foot. The FBI agent's strength left him as pain shot up his leg. He stumbled to one knee and was rewarded with a snap-kick to the face. He rolled with it, and through bloody eyes saw a harpoon gun on the deck just a few feet away. He scrambled across the deck and almost had it when Renner stomped on his fingers. He barely managed to flatten his hand before the shoe slammed down. The agony threatened to overwhelm him. He pulled his hand in, and suffered another kick to the face for his efforts. This time his nose broke, and he saw stars.

Gene tried to shake off a delirious haze. *Get up or get beaten to death.* He could barely see. He tried to stumble to his feet, and Renner clubbed him across the back with something heavy and wooden. He fell back to his knees. Another swing clipped him across the back of the head, but he managed to turn the blow with the meat of his wrist. He stumbled to the side of the boat, trying to get overboard.

Renner smashed the stock of the harpoon gun into Gene's ankles. Gene went down again, hitting his head on the aluminum railing on the side of the boat. He fought to stay conscious. The world blurred. He wasn't sure where he was. Sound distorted, as if he were under water. He had to get up, had to move, but his body wouldn't respond. He wanted to fight but mumbled instead.

Something dragged him, half-crawling, to the stern of the boat. He tried to swat at whatever had him, but his arms wouldn't respond. Knees on his back forced him to his belly, and his head went under water.

He tried not to breathe; he tried to roll over. His fingernails scrabbled across the wooden deck for support, but found nothing to hold on to. He tore into the hands that held him, trying to detach the insane grip. There was no mercy in them, and they didn't move.

Blood streaked through the water. Knees dug into his back, and his legs wouldn't respond. At last his body could take no more.

He breathed in.

Paul Renner frowned at the body beneath him. He'd never drowned anyone before. It was just a mean thing to do, but he couldn't trust that he could take a man as big as Gene Palomini in anything approaching a fair fight. Every breath brought searing agony and if Palomini didn't bite his nails, Paul's hands would be tatters. He didn't let the pain touch him. He drifted to that blank place where his mind lived at the moment of a kill and held Gene's head down with both hands.

He shook his head as the big man's struggle faded. After a few more seconds, Gene's pathetic struggles weakened further. A few more and they stopped altogether.

Twenty seconds later a maroon speedboat shot from under the dock and into open water. In seconds it skimmed the water at close to one hundred nautical miles per hour. Behind it a helicopter closed in, screaming out to sea from several miles inland. Ahead of the boat, the Coast Guard cut it off.

The cutter hailed the boat, but got no response. Faced with no real choice, Captain John Ash ordered the ship to fire. The tripod-mounted heavy machine gun obliterated the boat's engine, bringing it to rest almost two miles out. The FBI helicopter caught up and circled overhead. Before agents could rappel down and search the boat, it exploded.

The chopper veered left to avoid the rising fireball. Shrapnel pinged off the fuselage. Captain Ash ordered lifeboats deployed, though he knew no one could survive a blast of that magnitude.

Marty heard the blast from the country club. He stared numbly at the rising fireball. He spoke into his COM. "Gene?" Gene didn't reply.

He tried again. "Sam? What the fuck was that?"

Her voice was soft. "Marty, that was Renner's getaway boat. We had him surrounded. It almost took out the helicopter."

His voice was thick as he replied. "Gene?"

Sam replied. "Witnesses saw him tackle Renner onto the boat."

Marty forced out the words. "But where is he now?"

"Dive teams are en route, Marty."

Under the dock, Paul Renner tossed the remote control and the detonator overboard. He paddled the small sailboat into the harbor, ignoring the pain in his chest as he unfurled the sail. The beach was crowded, both in and out of the water, and despite the odd excitement, people were enjoying the beautiful southern California weather.

Paul lay back and let the sun warm his face and chest. Every breath hurt, but it was tolerable. A new wig crowned his head with long, blond, surfer-dude hair, and light blue contacts changed his eye color. A few hours sunbathing while the feds combed the area, and then he'd be headed home, or what passed as home these days. *Not a bad way to spend an afternoon, given the way the day almost went. Not bad at all.* He closed his eyes and smiled.

Chapter 11

January 6th, 5:53 PM PST; Unknown location; San Diego, California.

Gene knew he was conscious by the dim haze of red-filtered light. He sucked air into his lungs, then performed a mental checklist of body parts. *No torso wounds, right ankle hurts, not broken. Left foot hurts like heck, might be broken. Nose feels as big as a grapefruit. Hands tied, feet tied, and there's something over my head.* A quick strain at his bonds brought pain. *Wire.*

He explored his options. His chair wouldn't budge. Any serious struggling would cause the wire to slice into his flesh. He didn't know how long he'd been under, and he didn't know where he was. It was deathly quiet. His heart hammered in his chest as claustrophobia crept in.

Calm down, Gene. A few deep breaths got him started, then he relaxed his hands. *Breathe in.* Then feet. *Now out.* Then arms. *Breathe in.* Then legs. *Now out.* He soon had control of his heart rate. His mind cleared while his chin sank to his chest.

"Okay. I give up," Gene said to the room in a voice more calm than he felt. "I'm not gagged, so I assume screaming isn't going to do me any good. What do you want? Why am I here?"

In response, Gene heard a soft ring, like a wet finger running along the top of a wine glass. It was the unmistakable sound of a blade sliding across metal. He clenched his teeth as renewed fear clawed into his gut. He wouldn't show a reaction.

Gene jumped as Paul Renner spoke from the darkness less than a foot in front of him. "I haven't decided yet, Palomini." Cold fear like he'd never known threatened to throw him into panic.

Marty's voice spoke in his head. *Don't you give that motherfucker the satisfaction, boss.*

Paul yanked the hood off his head. He sat at a dining room table in what looked like a typical, middle-class, American house. Gene looked into the eyes of the man he'd been hunting and realized he wasn't a predator anymore; he was prey. Renner held a large hunting knife in his left hand and scraped the blade up and down his blue jeans.

"Any idea when you're going to decide?" Gene said. *Atta-boy, boss.* Even though he knew it wasn't there, he took comfort in Marty's voice.

"You see...." Paul cleaned his fingernails with the knife. "I've got a bit of a problem to deal with. You've devoted most of the past few years to bringing me to justice, which is just cop talk for throwing my ass in prison. I've spent a lot of time spitting in your face and laughing at your efforts."

Gene didn't comment. It was better to let someone ramble rather than to interrupt. This was especially true if you're the one who's tied to a chair, and he's the one with the big knife.

"That's got to piss a guy like you right off, huh, Palomini?" Paul pointed at him with the knife, then went back to his nails. For all his cool, Paul didn't extend his arm all the way. Renner was hurt.

"Anyway, the reason that's a problem is that I need your help." Paul winced a little every time he breathed in.

I definitely cracked a couple of his ribs.

Gene coughed, incredulous. "I would never help a killer like you."

Paul's eyes brightened. He slid the knife back into its sheath and grinned. "I think you're going to take some convincing. My motives are pretty simple, Gene-o. Clients give me money, and I kill who they want dead. I think you figured that much out. What you don't know, though, is that more often than not I'm working for the same U.S. government you are. I've got way less rules tying me down, and I get my hands a lot dirtier than you're allowed to, but that's just the nature of the beast.

"Just like a Navy SEAL, for example, might have a different set of rules than a common soldier. When a SEAL kills for his government on a black op, it isn't always strictly legal, is it, Lieutenant-turned-Special-Agent in Charge Palomini?" Paul let the question hang in the air.

Gene kept his voice carefully controlled. "I wouldn't make that comparison, Mr. Renner."

"At what point does a paid government killer become a criminal? Just because the illegal work he does for the government is now illegal work he's doing for somebody else? You've killed people for a paycheck. You've ordered it done." He looked Gene in the eyes. "A job's a job, and this is mine. I'm not some crazy psycho. I even work hard to minimize collateral damage, especially when I'm using something flashy like a car bomb. You and I are not so different."

"Wonderful story," Gene said. "Do you have a point?"

"Gene," Paul said with a raised eyebrow, "you're tied to a chair, so hush up a second, and you'll hear the point." Paul groaned slightly as he stood. He paced while he talked. "Where was I? Oh yeah.

"After a point I started to recognize patterns, to see the reasons behind the hits. This guy's cheating on his wife, that guy's a commie spy, this lady slept with the Secretary of State, whatever. Every now and then, not knowing is no big deal.

"When your superiors ordered your unit to fly to God-knows-where on a black op, did you ask questions? Of course not." Paul took a step toward Gene, his eyes wide.

Gene started to think that Paul really wanted to be believed. *That's not the same as telling the truth.* "Umm. Sure. I'm not saying I agree, but I see where you're coming from."

"Okay, good," Paul said. "So over the past couple years the same guy contacted me for multiple jobs. I don't know who he is, but I'm pretty sure he's a private citizen. But here's the fucked up part. He doesn't have me kill some cheating wife, or a businessman he's in competition with, or a bookie. There wasn't any obvious motive behind the job.

"For one hit, it's no big deal. If I can't figure out why, whatever. It happens sometimes, like I said. So anyway, he calls me up again pretending to be someone else, and offers me another job. And then he does it again." Paul waggled his finger at Gene, hissed in pain, and pulled his arm back. "Now that's fucked up. If someone wants multiple people snuffed and you can't find the pattern, it gets your brain churning, and you can't help but get curious, you know?"

Gene almost suppressed a snort. Pain shot through his broken nose. "I know all about victim patterns not making sense, Mister Renner."

"*Touché,*" Paul said. "So I end up with a series of targets, all from the same guy, in all different parts of the country with no rhyme or reason. To make a long story short, I call this one off. Tell him I'm done, give him his money back. No big deal, I've done it before." He spun around, both fingers pointed like kids' guns at Gene. "And then, you know what?"

Gene didn't reply.

"The next thing I know someone tries to kill me."

Paul knelt inches from Gene's face and pushed his hair back with his palm. A mostly-healed scab adorned his scalp, the scar pink and glossy. All of the enthusiasm leached out of Paul's voice. "He shot me in the head, Gene, but I got him before he could finish the job."

Gene looked at the scar and said nothing.

"Look, I know you cops cut deals with the little guys if it'll help you catch a big guy. All the time. What I want is a deal. You use your resources to help me find the bastard who put the hit out on me, and I give you the information I have on the victims. You bust the real bad guy, the guy who hired out at least seven killings. This fish is bigger than me. Way bigger."

Gene laughed harshly. "You've been messing with the FBI for a decade. Why would I possibly believe you now?"

Paul took a step back, frowning. "I've never lied to you, Agent Palomini. Never once."

Gene raised his eyebrows. "Perhaps not, but you toyed with me. With us."

"That's true," Paul said. "But I've never killed anyone who someone else wasn't going to kill if I didn't. I'm not a random murderer. I'm a weapon. What I'm offering you is the chance to catch the killer."

Gene tugged at the wire on his wrists and ankles. "Mr. Renner, you're crazy if you think I'm going to negotiate while tied to a chair."

With an exaggerated roll of his eyes, Paul moved behind Gene and out of sight. He heard the knife clear the sheath. At the metallic ring of wire being cut, Gene felt immediate relief from the pressure in his feet. A spike of pain followed as blood flowed to the battered bones in his left foot. *That's got to be broken.*

"You fucked up my chest," Paul said from behind him. More faintly he continued, "I'm going to let you out of the chair now. If you attack me this go around, one of us isn't walking out of this room alive. I can guarantee that that person will be you. Got it?"

"Got it, Mr. Renner."

"Good. And call me Paul."

Another quick snip and the wire pressure relaxed on Gene's wrists. He flexed his hands to restore circulation, staying seated as Paul moved back in front of him. He wasn't sure he could stand yet anyway. Paul grabbed a chair, dragged it across the room one-handed, and set it so the back faced Gene. He let his arms take the brunt of the effort as he lowered himself into a sitting position. "I think you cracked some ribs."

Gene chuckled. "I think you broke my foot, and I know you broke my nose." He continued flexing his hands, wrists, ankles, and toes. The pins and needles were almost unbearable. "Paul, you know I can't trust you."

With a flick of his wrist, Paul tossed a cell phone to Gene. "Call your team and tell them you're not dead. They think we both are, so I could kill you and walk away now and the case would be closed. So as a gesture of good faith, call your brother and tell him you're alive, but keep it under ten seconds." A compact pistol appeared in Renner's hand, then disappeared. The man moved so fast it might as well have been magic.

Gene's eyebrows rose.

"And," Paul added, "even if you say 'no' to the deal, I'll let you go. Safe and sound, with no more injury than you've already got."

Gene dialed. Marty picked up with a string of expletives and threats he couldn't quite decipher. "It's me, Marty. Not him. I'm alive, he's alive, and I'll call you later. Got to go." He pressed the "end" button. The sound of his brother's voice being cut off made Gene's chest tighten. He wanted to redial, but instead he tossed the phone back to Renner.

With a quick look at the phone, Paul put it back in his pocket. "How's that? You're untied, your brother and your team know you're alive, and they can hunt me until the end of my days if something happens to you."

Gene sighed. "There's just no way I can offer you a deal. You're a serial killer, for crying out loud."

"I don't need a long-term deal, and I won't ask for immunity," Paul said flatly. "I just want help finding who's behind this, who's trying to kill me." Paul leaned forward. "I'll put myself in your custody."

Gene wanted to spit in Renner's face. He wanted revenge for Carl's arm and Jerri's concussion. Still, while Renner was an awfully big fish, whoever this other man was, he was bigger. "No immunity, no pardons, and we keep you on a *very* short leash," Gene began.

"No arrests, no kicking the shit out of me."

"And when it's done?" Gene asked. "What?"

"I walk away," Paul said.

"We just let you go?" Gene asked.

"That's right," Paul answered. "I walk off into the sunset a free man. Chase me down all over again if that's what it's got to be. Just give me a day to lose your team; something tells me they're going to want blood."

Gene looked the killer in the eyes as the saying *there's no honor among thieves* popped into his head. *I'm sure the same applies to paid killers. Sometimes, it applies to the FBI.*

"So you'll let me go, and if I want to deal I can, what, call you?"

"Drive away. In five minutes, when it's obvious you're free, come back and pick me up. Just you, though."

"So what do you want from me? Something in writing?"

"Nah," Paul said. He pulled out a set of car keys. "If your word's no good I'm screwed either way."

"I'll have to clear it with the Assistant Director." Gene couldn't believe he'd just said it.

Paul held out the keys. "Car's in the driveway."

* * *

January 6th, 6:27 PM PST; FBI Building, 880 Front St; San Diego, California.

"He hasn't called back." Marty's eyes were still red. His voice was hoarse from screaming.

"But we know he's alive," Jerri said, putting a tentative hand on his shoulder.

Marty jerked away from her touch like it burned him. "That's bullshit and you know it. All we know is that he *was* alive half an hour ago. I swear to fucking God I'll kill that motherfucker with my bare fucking hands...." He turned away from her, his hands clenching and unclenching with hopelessness and rage as he hid his tears from the rest of the team.

Jerri turned to Carl. She didn't know what to do with rejected offers of comfort. She worried about Gene as well but still rode the high that came from his call. She had always considered her relationship with her co-workers to be clinical. They were teammates, not friends or family. Carl's sheepish grin told her he didn't know how to handle Marty either. Doug stared out the window.

Today's events put something in perspective. She didn't just respect her co-workers. She loved them. They were her family, every bit as much as her real family. She couldn't love Marty the way he loved her, but she did love him.

Carl's nerdiness, Marty's brutal honesty, Gene's obsessive

determination, Doug's quiet intelligence, and even Sam's stupid sense of humor were all a part of her now. Two and a half hours of knowing that Gene was dead had hurt her more than she thought possible, and his call had filled her with so much joy she couldn't imagine slipping into Marty-esque defeatism.

He'll call, Carl mouthed to her, his confidence cementing the certainty in her head.

"I know," she whispered back as she came close. "But waiting for it sure does suck."

As if on cue, Marty's phone rang. The caller ID glared "D Street Killer." He snatched it from the desktop. He didn't have a chance to hit "send."

"I got it," Sam piped over the COM. "Team broadcast."

"This is Sam Greene," the team heard in their ear-beads, "please identify yourself."

"Hi, team, it's me again." Gene's voice sounded nasal and tired but relaxed. "I'm bringing him in. ETA twenty minutes. I want an interrogation room set up for non-hostile debrief of Paul Renner and a conference room for the crew to meet."

The relief on Marty's face was palpable. "Gene. I—We thought you were gone."

"So did I, bro. I'll be there soon. I lost my COM bead on the dock. Carl, get me a replacement."

Carl piped in with an unsure tone to his voice. "Will do. Um, what do you mean, a non-hostile setup for debrief?"

"Exactly what it sounds like. I'll explain when I get there. See you soon. Bye."

The phone clicked off.

"Back to work!" Doug said, grinning. He clapped his hands together and stood.

Jerri winked at him, beaming a smile of her own.

"We got the son of a bitch!" Marty said.

Chapter 12

January 6th, 6:48 PM PST; Front Street FBI Building; San Diego, California.

Oh, hell, yeah! Marty thought as the car pulled into the parking garage twenty minutes later. He couldn't keep still.

His forehead creased with confusion as the car got close. There was no one in the back, but someone sat shotgun. Gene pulled into a space about eight car-lengths away and killed the engine.

Marty shared confused looks with the rest of the team as Gene got out of the driver's side and the D Street Killer stepped out of the passenger side. No handcuffs. No restraints of any kind. The car door wasn't even locked. *What the fuck?*

A firm look from Gene stopped him from stepping forward, but his hands clenched into fists. "What the fuck are you up to, Gene?" he said into the COM.

Carl held up an ear-bead. "He can't hear you, Marty."

Marty's chin jutted out as they limped closer. Gene leaned on Renner for support. *Like they're best goddamn friends, just helping each other along.*

Marty noted how little Renner moved his arms and how carefully he walked. The killer obviously had some significant pain in his chest. Gene looked worse. His nose was crooked, dark purple, and twice its normal size. Black bruises crept under each eye, and he walked like he didn't know which foot to limp with more.

Gene looked like shit, but the killer's injuries were more limiting. He made a mental note to take advantage of the damaged ribs when the opportunity arose. *But if he's the one who got the beat-down, why the fuck isn't he in handcuffs?*

"Paul Renner," Gene said by way of introduction, "this is Marty Palomini, Doug Goldman, Jerri Bates, and Carl Brent. Team"—the trepidation in his voice was slight but perceptible— "this is the D Street Killer." Gene wore his don't-fuck-this-up face.

Gene motioned to Doug. "Agent Goldman, please escort Mr. Renner to the debriefing area. Gently. Agent Brent." Gene mouthed *Thank You* as he took the replacement ear-bead and inserted it. "Get another ear-bead for Mr. Renner, then have Sam queue him up. Everyone else, come with me to the conference area." Marty helped Gene limp across the parking lot as Doug shadowed Renner.

As the group moved off toward the building, Gene stopped at the metal detector and weapons-check. "Hang on a second," he said to Doug. "Lock this tray up," he said, placing the car keys into a dark-gray screening tray, the kind found at any airport security station. Wordlessly, the guard slapped a lid and padlock on the tray, attached a two-part ticket to the lock with a zip-strip, and handed the ticket stub to Gene. Renner reached for the stub. Gene put it in his front pocket.

Well, that's a good sign, Marty thought.

After a trip through the metal detector and a thorough pat-down, the guard let Paul through. As they stepped past the security station, Marty muttered under his breath. "We've got you now, asshole." He wasn't quiet enough.

Without turning, Renner replied, "I'm here because I want to be, Agent Palomini. Your brother and I have an understanding."

Marty took a menacing step forward, and Paul turned in a defensive stance. Gene jerked up his hand. "STOP IT." He gave his brother a withering look. "This will be hard enough without the two of you at each other's throats."

"Oh, so we're not supposed to be wringing his fucking neck

right now?" Marty said.

"Doug, Carl, get going. We'll meet you in the conference room." He looked at his brother.

"What?" Marty said.

* * *

January 6th, 6:57 PM PST; Conference Room 4, Front Street FBI Building; San Diego, California.

In the conference room, Jerri leaned against the wall as Marty and Gene had it out. Gene leaned on the table while Marty sneered in his face. Gene's eye was swollen half-shut, and the EMT had finished re-setting his nose only minutes ago.

"You're out of your fucking mind!" Marty yelled for the half-dozenth time. "*Work with him?* With that murdering piece of shit? I won't do it. Fuck you! Fuck him! Fuck this! No!" Spittle flew from Marty's mouth.

"Marty, calm down, sit down, and listen," Gene said. "That's an order." Jerri smiled. The word "order" transformed Gene from a misguided younger brother into Special Agent in Charge, whether he was holding an ice pack on his face or not.

Marty leaned back into the wall but kept his mouth shut. He moved to the conference table and pulled out a chair, then eased himself into it. He glanced at Jerri, his blush showing how little he appreciated being humbled in front of her.

"Carl and Doug will be here in a few minutes," Gene said. "When they get here, after I explain to them what I've been trying to explain to you, you may be part of the discussion if, and only if, you keep your temper in check. Are we clear?"

"Yeah," Marty said as the raging anger in his eyes faded to a slow burn. "I'm sorry I blew up, bro. I think you're making a big fucking mistake, though."

"We'll find out, Marty. After we've gotten what intel we can get out of Paul Renner. Do you want some coffee?" Marty shook his head. "Get me some, please, would you?" Marty sneered and opened his mouth to reply, something insubordinate and inappropriate, Jerri was sure, but his face softened as Gene limped on both legs to a chair and sat down. The sneer disappeared, and Marty went to the urn to pour him a cup.

Doug and Carl arrived as Gene stirred in his half-and-half. "Is Mr. Renner situated?"

"Yes, sir," Doug said. "The prisoner is in Interrogation One with a non-hostile setup, as ordered, with four guards posted outside." His face was a mask of wrath. "I never thought I'd have to get that son of a bitch a sandwich and coffee, Gene. We should be cracking his other ribs, not bandaging up the ones he's got. What's going on?"

Gene ignored the question and turned to Carl. "Ear-bead set up?"

Sam answered over the COM. "Yeah, boss. Let me know when you want him piped in."

"Good," Gene said, glad the team followed his orders. "Let's get down to business." He told his story.

Chapter 13

January 6th, 7:12 PM PST; Conference Room 4, Front Street FBI Building; San Diego, California.

Gene sat at the head of the conference room table, flanked by Marty and Doug. Carl leaned his good shoulder against the wall, and Jerri stood next to him. Gene felt like they were interrogating *him*.

"I agree with Marty," Doug said. "That man should never draw another breath of free air."

"Or any air," Marty chimed in. "He's a ruthless killer, and this is going to bite us in the ass."

Doug folded his arms. "I know we cut deals with little fish all the time, but this is a really big fish, Gene. I say we get what information we can out of him by playing nice, then classify him as hostile, squeeze some more info that way, then put him away for good."

"I talked it over with A.D. Adams, Doug—" Gene began.

"So fucking what?" Marty interjected. "We lie to perps all the time. You were under duress, and, in case you've forgotten, your new buddy is the goddamn D Street Killer."

Gene's face turned red. "He's not my buddy, Marty, and he let me go. We can use him to find the man *behind* the killings. As I was saying, I talked it over with A.D. Adams, and he agreed that this was the right move."

"Well, fuck him, too, Gene," Marty said. "*Can* isn't the same as *should*."

Doug took over the tag-team. "For Christ's sake, you've been to the crime scenes. You've interviewed the orphans and widows. We can't just let him wander around. We can't."

"Carl, help us out here," Marty said. "Are you going to work with the ruthless fuck who crippled your arm?"

Carl looked uncomfortable as all of the room's attention turned his way. "He's not ruthless," he said quietly. "He had the jump on me, Marty. I was holding a submachine gun, and he knew I'd kill him if I saw him coming at me. If I were in his shoes, I would have killed me. And Jerri. Especially Jerri. As far as he knew, she's the first person to ever get a good look at his face, and he *let her go*. I don't know if it was compassion or what, but I know it wasn't ruthlessness." Carl's face looked pained as he rubbed at his still-damaged arm. "There are plenty of reasons to hate that man. Don't pick sparing my life as yours."

Marty didn't respond. Doug did.

"This could just be another way to screw with us, Gene. Taking it to the next level."

Jerri threw in her two cents. "I agree with Marty and Doug," she said. "At best this guy is a brutal killer. One of his victims was *strangled*. You've got to be one sick, nasty person to strangle someone. Best case, this guy's a loose cannon that you're putting right in the middle of us. I don't want to be around when he goes off."

Gene looked to Carl, the only person who said anything close to supporting the boss's case. "What's your opinion, Carl? Cut the deal or bust him?"

"Bust him," Carl said without hesitation. "He may not be the worst of the worst, and the guy hiring him may be a hundred times more evil that he ever was, but he's got to pay for what he's done. No question, Gene. Bust him. We'll get the other guy some other way."

"Sam?" Gene asked.

"Opinions aren't my job, boss."

Gene swiveled his chair away from the group and looked up

to the heavens. If the drop-ceiling tiles had any wisdom to share, they kept it to themselves. *Lord, forgive me for what I'm about to do.* He doubted God granted forgiveness-in-advance, and as he spun back and faced his crew, he knew that they wouldn't be forgiving him either. "I'm keeping the deal."

He held up a hand to forestall objections even before they spewed from the lips of his team. "I know you don't like it. I know you don't think it's the right thing to do. I have misgivings myself. But unless and until I say otherwise, this team is going to work *with* Paul Renner to find the mastermind behind the pattern-killings. He didn't have to let me go, much less come here. He'll stick around as long as we've got something he wants."

"What does he want, Gene?" Doug asked.

"Well," Gene said, "he says he wants to find the man who tried to kill him, but I'm not sure I believe him. I think it's true as far as it goes, but it's not enough for him to take a risk of this magnitude. There's something else here, and until he gets it, he'll stick around. We need to find it first, then take him down."

"You can't seriously be thinking about letting him walk around free," Jerri said.

"He'll be on a short leash, unarmed, with a locator ankle bracelet. When we're done, assuming he's cooperated fully, the deal is that we're letting him walk away." Marty opened his mouth and Gene shot him down with a look. Carl scowled. Doug looked at the floor. Gene continued. "That's not going to happen. We'll take him down when the time is right." Marty gave his brother a satisfied smile. "In the meantime, we'll work with him. This is an order. Understood?"

Each team member sounded off in the affirmative, but Gene saw not only distaste but distrust.

He pulled out his boss-voice and gave them orders. "Doug and Jerri, report to Interrogation One for the debrief. Carl, run the recording and the voice analysis. Marty, you're with me behind the glass. Sam, do your thing. Move out."

Marty lagged behind as the team filed out. Gene let the rest of the team put distance between them. With his limp, it wasn't hard. "Say what you need to, Marty, but don't you dare throw another tantrum."

Marty ran his tongue along his teeth. He breathed in, held it, then spoke. "I know you're not going to change your mind. But when that sick fucker kills or cripples somebody, you just remember that every last fucking bit of it is your doing. And when this is all said and done, if Paul-fucking-Renner gets away, every new widow and orphan he makes is because of what you're doing today. You're my brother, and you know I love you, but today you just make me sick."

Gene let Marty shoulder past him on his way out. *I know. God help me, I know.*

* * *

January 6th, 7:22 PM PST; Interrogation Room A, Front Street FBI Building; San Diego, California.

Jerri waited while Carl finished his work. Doug stood at the door.

"So if I stay super-calm, I can fool this thing, right?" Paul asked as Carl attached electrodes to his arms and chest.

"This isn't a polygraph," Carl said. "And besides, even if it was, despite what you see in Steven Seagal movies, you can't fool them. They're highly accurate, and the vast majority of false positives and negatives are a result of user error. I've personally run a number of...." He continued to ramble despite the fact no one seemed to be listening to him.

I wonder what all that stuff is, Jerri thought. Interrogation One was packed with recording devices and sensors, some sort of medical monitoring device, and Carl's ubiquitous Black Box; a battered black briefcase that contained a variety of devices Jerri didn't think she could pronounce much less understand.

Carl left and closed the door behind him.

Gene watched through the glass as Carl exited the interrogation room and stepped into the viewing room. "No video?" Marty asked.

"Don't need it," Carl responded. "First of all, he won't consent to being video-recorded, and as a non-hostile, we have to respect his wishes." His eyes flicked toward Gene, then back. "Second, you can catch all the visual cues you want through the glass, but if he lies, I'll know it." He flipped open his laptop and scanned the displays.

The three of them watched Jerri smooth her skirt and sit across from Paul Renner. After a few calculated moments arranging her notepad and pens, she looked up at Paul. "Mr. Renner, this isn't a standard interrogation, as it's at your request. You claim to have information to provide. Please begin."

Doug Goldman stood near the door. A practiced look of complete boredom as he leaned into the wall typically had even experienced perps assuming he was there for muscle or intimidation. In truth, Doug did provide bulk when necessary, but his keen mind had already begun examining Paul's body language and mannerisms.

"Seven people," Paul said. "A man hired me to assassinate seven different people. He's hired at least one other person to kill two more. He made efforts to conceal his identity, and I don't think that he knows that I know it was the same guy each time, and there is, as far as I can tell, no rhyme or reason to the targets.

"I'm going to give you the targets' names." He paused for a drink of water. Unless Renner was stupid, and Gene had no reason to believe he was, he knew full well that once he gave them names they might change their minds and put him away forever.

Jerri interjected. "How do you know he hired another killer for these other two jobs?"

"That, I'm not going to tell you. If it makes less paperwork for you, pretend I did them," Renner said. Jerri motioned for him to continue. Behind the glass, Marty sneered. Gene put his finger to his lips and kept watching.

"And?" she asked.

"And I need you to use your fancy databases to find the link," Paul said.

"Mr. Renner," Jerri began with her first scripted question. "Sometimes the insane will pick targets at random. What makes you so sure there's a pattern here?"

"No one, not even the richest of the filthy stinking rich, spends fifty-thousand dollars a pop killing people at random. There's no such thing as a psychotic who hires out his killings. That means there's a pattern, and I just don't see it. The only thing I know that they all have in common is that they're all over forty."

Marty, Gene, and Carl shared knowing glances, having plenty of first-hand experience with how difficult it was to find a pattern to Paul's kills. "Let's start with the most recent contract," Jerri's voice came through the glass.

"The most recent contract, or the most recent completed contract?"

"Part of the pattern may be the timeline itself, so let's start with the most recent event and move backward." Gene knew that Jerri deliberately avoided words like "murder'" and "killing." *Let him use them all he wants,* he thought. *But there's no sense putting him on the defensive. Not yet, anyway.*

"The last time I was called I turned down the job. It was for a retired guy in Lincoln, Nebraska," Paul began. He fingered one of the electrodes stuck to his chest and frowned at the mirror. "His name is Kevin Parsons."

Sam broke in through their ear-beads. "Paul, do you know his street address?"

"271 Hawkes Drive," he said with annoyance, though Gene couldn't tell what annoyed him.

"One moment," Sam said. After a brief pause, she rattled off information into their ears. "Okay, got him. Kevin Sean Parsons. Born May 17th, 1945...." Her voice trailed off. "A missing persons report was filed on him seven months ago. He never showed up for church. His house was destroyed. Arson. Is Mr. Renner sure he turned that job down?"

Renner looked even more annoyed. "I'm sure."

Sam was obviously lost in thought, so Jerri jumped back in. "What date were you contacted for this contract?"

"This past June. I think the 22nd or 23rd."

"Do you remember the time of day?"

"Not really," Paul said. "It's just a text to a cell phone. I don't even check it every day."

Jerri continued with question after question. Even though they recorded all interrogations, she wrote down every detail in stenographer's shorthand. "The contract that preceded Kevin Parsons involved whom?"

"Larry Johnson."

It was as if the temperature had dropped by fifteen degrees. "Here we go," Carl whispered to Marty as Gene looked through the glass.

"And how did you eliminate Mr. Johnson?" Jerri asked.

"You know damn well I didn't get him. You interrupted me."

"But...." Jerri hesitated. "What about the psychotic break?"

Paul leaned forward, his eyebrows raised. "I have no idea what you're talking about."

Jerri looked at the mirror, then back at Paul. "You're telling me that you didn't kill him while he was in custody?"

Paul's eyes widened. "No, I didn't even know he was dead. My employer must have found someone else."

Jerri fiddled with her notes for a moment, then changed the subject. "Very well. Who preceded Larry Johnson?"

"Jenny Sykes."

Jenny Sykes wasn't just some victim in a case file. Memories of a charred corpse and scattered body parts still haunted Gene's dreams, as did the text-messaged taunt that erased Jenny Sykes from the earth. Paul Renner had just admitted to first-degree murder. On tape.

"What date were you contacted for this contract?" It was a credit to Jerri's professionalism that she sounded exactly the same as when she had asked about Kevin Parsons.

The debrief took less than forty minutes. At its completion, Sam had starts on dossiers for nine victims; seven, if you didn't count Larry Johnson and Kevin Parsons.

"What about...?" Jerri paused and leafed through her notebook. "Daniel Burnhardt. He matches the age pattern."

Paul's brow crinkled with distaste. "That was a CIA job." His voice went flat. "That contract isn't relevant to this investigation."

Behind the glass, Gene shared a look with Carl. "Why is she

bringing up Burnhardt?" His throbbing foot and nose made it difficult to concentrate, and he was afraid he'd missed something.

Carl shrugged.

Through the glass, Paul looked angry. "What's your game, Agent Bates?" Doug shifted his weight against the wall to draw Paul's attention.

"I'm just validating some assumptions, Mr. Renner," she said.

"Well, I'm not here to validate your assumptions." Doug stepped forward as Paul stood. "You have the information you need. So," he said in a raised voice as he faced the one-way mirror, "Agent Palomini. Time to prove you're a man of your word." Paul walked toward the door and stopped, eye level with Doug's chest. Without lifting his head, he looked up into Doug's eyes and waited.

"Don't do it, Gene," said Marty.

"Let him out, Doug," Gene said through the COM. Paul's lack of reaction showed that Sam had turned off his ear-bead. After a blatantly antagonistic size-up, Doug stepped aside.

A guard opened the door to let Paul out. "Okay, we're done for the day. Everyone check out. We'll see you in the morning. Renner, you're with me. Your security detail will follow us to the hotel."

Chapter 14

January 7th, 8:00 AM PST; Conference Room 4, Front Street FBI Building; San Diego, California.

Carl spent the next day directing the team as they compiled massive amounts of information: birth and death certificates, driver's licenses, passports, and medical and dental records. The organizations that required subpoenas to release information were hacked by Sam. They could get warrants later if they needed them. With Renner's confession to murder one on tape, no one cared if they invalidated some of this evidence.

Newspaper articles, alumni lists, high school and college transcripts. Fingerprints, military service records, library cards, credit records, and business records. Resumes, online forum posts, blogs. All of these things were found, copied, scanned, collated, annotated, and packed into tidy electronic files for each victim.

By midday, Paul was pitching in, feeding file after file into the insatiable scanner. He looked bored out of his mind. Carl walked by him and chuckled. "Lucky you, Renner. Now you get to see how glamorous and exciting real police work is."

Paul returned Carl's grin. "I hope this isn't the fun part."

"Not even close," Carl said. "Next we set up bulk classifications to assign each piece of data to, then spend hour after hour doing the assignments. The computers can do some of it for us, and they'll be instrumental once it's all scanned in, but this sort of thing comes down to a person seeing something that makes a connection. That's the only reason you're here. Something might jog in your memory when you see the data classified and organized properly."

"Great," Paul said without enthusiasm.

By six-thirty that evening, every possible document for each victim had been scanned. Sophisticated optical-character-recognition software went to work converting pictures of documents and hand-written letters into computer-readable text.

"Everyone take your gear with you tonight," Gene announced. He stood and grabbed his brand-new pair of crutches. "Our plane leaves at oh-nine-forty. Get there early. We have to pass through normal airport security. This is a commercial flight, not Bureau."

A chorus of groans answered. Airport security in San Diego was bad enough for civilians. Gone were the good old days when an agent could flash his badge and walk around the detectors. Now there was paperwork, lots and lots of paperwork, and all of it had to be perfect to allow weapons through security.

Marty gave Paul a smug look, which Renner seemed not to notice.

Despite Paul Renner's unwelcome presence, Carl felt pretty good. They had a massive amount of data, and it felt like they were glutted with clues and leads. It was a pleasant change of pace.

At dinnertime most of the team called it a day. While the others went out to eat or to their hotel rooms for some shuteye, Carl stayed behind. He worked with Sam to create bulk classifications for the data. After ninety minutes, Carl yawned and looked at the clock. He hadn't done anything productive in two minutes.

"Hey, Sam?"

"Yeah, babe?"

"I think I'm going to cut out, grab a bite, call my wife, and get some sleep. It's been a long day."

"No worries. We're about past where I need you anyway. I'll wrap the rest of this up in the next couple of hours. Should give you a lot more to do on the plane tomorrow."

"Sounds good. Goodnight, Sam."

Sam giggled. "Goodnight, Ralph."

Ralph? Carl thought. *Whatever.* He shut down his computer and headed out in search of food.

* * *

January 8th, 10:20 AM CST; Central Air Flight 1551; Somewhere over the continental United States.

For all the whining, Paul thought they'd made it through security in no time. The small jet was neither crowded nor cramped and had reasonable legroom even for people using laptop computers. Gene sat in the front, with the most legroom possible to accommodate his swollen feet, the seat next to him empty except for his crutches. Paul found it a little strange how none of the paper files followed the team to D.C. The entire kit and caboodle was now digital. *Soon everything everyone has ever known will fit in a wristwatch,* he thought.

Not a fan of plane travel even without cracked ribs, Paul had dressed for comfort—elastic-banded jogging pants, an overlarge T-shirt in nondescript gray, and a comfortable pair of tattered Reeboks. He looked more like someone out for a morning run than traveling across the country on a plane stuffed with federal agents.

The team spent their time doing data classification, which to Paul seemed a lot like turning a needle in a haystack into thirty needles in thirty haystacks. *Only in this case haystacks are called "bulk classifications."* Apparently there were computers in D.C. that automated much of the process, but it still looked like a never-ending pile to Paul. The manual boredom of the previous day became digital boredom.

After an hour of click-drag-drop *ad nauseum,* Paul stood to stretch his legs and rest his eyes, if only for a moment. A mini-fridge sat at the front of First Class, right next to the cockpit door, so he grabbed himself a can of Coke, flashing his eyebrows at

Gene as he slid past. Jerri looked up when he popped the tab, and, as Paul slurped his first taste, she signaled for him to bring her one.

He grabbed a second can, ignored the look of reproach from the stewardess, shut the fridge with his foot, and walked to the back of the cabin. "Thanks," Jerri said as she took the offered beverage. Paul noted that she didn't look at him with the disgust or disdain of the past few days. At least for this fleeting moment, he had evolved in her mind from pond scum to guy-who-grabbed-her-a-Coke. *Looks like I'm moving up in the world.*

He sat next to her and looked at her screen. She was working on the same thing they all were, sorting data and shoving it into piles. Click-drag-drop. More as a reason to forestall a retreat back to his own private click-drag-drop hell than to start a conversation, he said, "How long is this step supposed to take?"

"Oh, I don't know," Jerri said. "As long as it does. I hope we're done before we land, but probably not. Not too long after, anyway."

"What was that?"

Jerri looked from her screen to Paul's face. "What was what?"

"You just looked at my hands, shuddered, and looked away. Why?"

"I—" She paused. "I probably shouldn't get into it."

"Does it have something to do with why you asked me about the Burnhardt job?" Paul could tell he had hit a nerve.

"Mr. Renner—"

"Call me Paul."

"Mr. Renner, you strangled a man to death with your bare hands." Her shudder was more pronounced this time. "Frankly, I find your hands to be positively creepy."

"Why?" Paul asked, holding them up for examination. "They're just hands. Just like yours, or Gene's, or anyone else's."

"Look, even if I found myself in a position where I was going to kill someone, I could never choke the life out of them. It's too...personal."

Paul grunted as his ribs shifted. "I told you yesterday that was a CIA job." He leaned in a little, almost too close to her. "Let me educate you a little about my industry." He tried not to sound patronizing. "There are three types of contracts. Dead, looks-like-an-accident dead, and CIA dead. Most CIA jobs are just another version of the first two types, but sometimes they insist on a certain method. Daniel Burnhardt was one of those cases." Jerri opened her mouth to ask a question, but he kept talking. "I don't know why, I don't ask why, and Langley doesn't tell why.

"Besides," he said, standing, "I didn't choke the life out him with my bare hands. If it makes you feel better, I wore gloves. It doesn't make me feel any better about it, but if it helps you at all, more power to you. I'll let you get back to your work."

Paul headed back up to his seat. He noted with passing interest the look of pure venom on Martin Palomini's face. *What did I do now?* Paul wondered.

He sat back down, picked up the laptop he'd been assigned, and went back to work. Click-drag-drop, click-drag-drop.

* * *

January 8th, 5:52 PM EST; Dulles International Airport; Washington, D.C.

Just short of six PM Eastern Standard Time, the plane landed at Dulles International Airport. The team exited down a portable flight of stairs to twin government sedans waiting on the tarmac. The vehicles were stereotypically black, with tinted windows and "US GOV" on the license plates.

Gene, Doug, and Paul loaded into one while Marty, Jerri, and Carl took the other. They were awash with new car smell and looked to Doug like they had never been ridden in. The drivers were non-descript Bureau employees, paid to drive safely, observe and react to everything going on outside the vehicle, and ignore everything inside.

Doug continued to click-drag-drop from the passenger seat as the cars started rolling. Even after hours of nausea on a plane, somehow when he worked in a car it didn't bother his stomach. Carl had confiscated Paul's laptop before they left the plane, and

Paul looked down at Gene's laptop sitting at his feet. "Not going to work on the way?" Paul asked.

"No," Gene said. "I'm fine in a plane. In a car it just gives me a headache." He favored Paul with a puzzled look. "Why didn't you pack a bag?"

"I'm not going to reveal where I have bags to pack, Gene. I'll buy what I need here or have one of your guys do it," Paul said. "Speaking of which, it's probably not a good idea for security at the FBI building to find this." A small pistol appeared in his hand from out of nowhere.

Gene had frisked Paul before they'd entered the airport and was positive he was clean. Paul held the gun out to him.

Gene took the pistol while Doug stared with his mouth open.

"Paul, this is completely unacceptable. Surrender all other weapons on your person, immediately, or the deal is off and we're remanding you to custody. Now." Unseen by the others, Doug slid his pistol out of his holster and fingered the safety.

Paul smiled sheepishly. "That was it. Frisk me. I have no other weapons." They pulled over the car and Doug frisked him, with as much attention to detail as he'd ever put into a search. He was rougher this time and took his embarrassment out on Renner.

"One more stunt," Gene said, "and you're done. One. Got it?"

"I got it," Paul said. Doug gave Gene an I-told-you-so look. They got back into the car.

"How did you get this through airport security?" Gene asked.

"Lots of Special Forces troops are trained to do it. Sometimes with much bigger guns."

"Is that where you learned to do it?" Doug asked.

Paul looked out the window and smiled. "Something like that."

"Your prints don't match any military records," Gene said.

Paul's smile widened. "True."

Forty-five minutes later at the J. Edgar Hoover building, Paul Renner experienced the single most thorough frisking he'd ever been through. It didn't include a cavity search, but he still felt that the guard owed him dinner and flowers by the time he finished.

He was then subjected to a metal detector and an X-ray. "I suppose I have you to thank for the extra attention," he said as he walked up to Gene.

"Absolutely." Gene's tone was businesslike, a Special Agent in Charge at the FBI Headquarters sort of voice. He gestured for Paul to follow him down one of the warrens leading into the massive complex and started off on his crutches. "The Assistant Deputy Director who approved our arrangement wants to make sure a confirmed freelance assassin isn't roaming his halls armed. That's what the ankle bracelet is for.

"In addition, the guards have all been issued your photo, and the badge you're wearing gives people permission to shoot first and ask questions later. It's equipped with RFID and a tiny heart rate monitor, just to make sure you keep it exactly where it's supposed to be, so we know where you are at all times. Removing either it or the ankle bracelet will trigger an immediate manhunt, and security won't be concerned with sparing your life.

"You will be escorted by a member of my team at all times, though you shouldn't have any reason to leave our section. As long as you're in this building, the only thing you're free to do is exactly what you're told. Anything else will be viewed as a hostile action and will be responded to in kind." Gene stopped and looked him in the eyes. "Have I made myself perfectly clear?"

"Crystal," Paul said. He wasn't sure he believed all that, but he didn't want to test it.

"Good, because I meant every word," Gene said. He gestured forward, then started off on his crutches. "Let's go find the man who hired you, shall we?"

By the time they reached Gene's section, Paul felt like a tiny mouse in a gigantic maze. There were no colored lines on the wall, no friendly and well-lit directories with "You Are Here" printed on them. On this level there weren't even exit signs. Paul knew that wasn't legal and was sure it was intentional.

Gene's section consisted of a large meeting room, three offices, a single-seat unisex bathroom, and a small kitchen complete with a full-sized fridge, coffee pot, and microwave. A short, fat girl in neon-green stretch pants and an oversized Toby

Keith T-shirt walked out of the kitchen nook, her brown hair pulled back in a ponytail. She carried a freshly opened pint of Ben and Jerry's Chunky Monkey ice cream, the first spoonful already in her mouth. She stopped and looked Paul over from top to bottom. "I thought you'd be taller," said Sam Greene's familiar voice as she waddled her way to a doorway, swiped a key-card, and disappeared into the darkened room beyond. The door shut behind her.

Paul raised an eyebrow at Gene, who motioned him to the large meeting room. A huge, dark-stained table dominated the room. A single desktop computer sat in the middle with adjustable wheeled office chairs around the outside. Circling the table were nine individual desks against the walls. On each desk sat a large stack of papers, a computer monitor and keyboard, and a folded-paper plaque, each with a separate victim's name.

"Listen up," Sam chirped over the COM. A large projector in the middle of the ceiling lit a wall nearly the size of a movie screen. "Data classification will be complete within the hour and we'll start matching. Each station has physical and digital copies of all data compiled for each victim listed. When you're done with your last bit of data, feel free to start rooting. It goes without saying that all files on a desk stay on that desk. PPD has been combing through this data and will add their findings in real-time.

"Keep an eye on the match lists. The converters won't be done until morning, so you can force priority if you want. There's a link in all this data somewhere. Go find it." Sam's voice cut off.

"Does anyone want to translate that into English for me?" Paul asked no one in particular.

"I will." Carl motioned Paul closer so as not to disturb the rest of the team. "PPD is the VICAP Psychological Profiling Department. They've gone over most of this with a fine-toothed comb, and they'll help us create data matches with what they can figure out about victim correlations and a profile on the guy who hired you.

"As the computer finds information that's the same for other victims, it creates a match which it will display on that projection there. We're looking for high-numbered, irreconcilable matches. That is, matches that aren't automatically explained by another factor.

"For example, we're going to get a Match-7 on males, but that's automatically reconcilable because the other two are by default females. So we know these victims weren't killed because of their sex. Hence, sex will be discarded and will come off the screen. Sam will be poring over matches as the data shows up, flagging them as reconcilable or irreconcilable.

"The converters change non-computer-recognized text into computer-recognized text. That's just a fancy way of saying it turns handwriting into computer-readable text. A separate but similar program converts photos of text. That is, everything we could only get paper copies of and some of the file-types for the electronic stuff doesn't show up like a web page or a word processor document. Imagine having to re-type every one of the documents we scanned yesterday. Yeeesh."

Paul shuddered at the thought. Scanning alone had taken hours. Carl was way too excited about the process.

"Yep," Carl continued. "It's a lot of boring work, but because we did it, what would take weeks or months will be done tomorrow. The *really* cool thing is that Sam wrote both converters. I don't think your buddies at Langley have anything anywhere near as good. Commercial OCR's have come a long way in the past decade, but they still haven't caught up to her stuff. The really *un*-cool thing is that she wrote the code on Bureau time, so instead of being able to patent it and sell it, it's proprietary to the FBI.

"Anyway...," Carl moved back to the topic at hand, "forcing priority means you can put something in front of the others for the computer to dig for matches on. So, if we see that five of the nine people went to Rutgers University, we can tell the computer to complete all of the alumni-record conversions first to see if that's our link. It'll drop everything and try that, then go back to what it was doing before.

"Ideally, when it's all said and done, we'll have one and only one irreconcilable Match-9."

"And that means?" Paul asked with raised eyebrows.

Carl stopped his lecture to explain the term. "Irreconcilable Match-9 would mean that all nine people have something in common, a perfect coincidence. It's doubtful we'll get one, but if we do, we have a massively high chance that that's our link, odds at least in the high 90th percentile. Does that all make sense?" The little man was actually smiling.

"It does," Paul said. "You're an extraordinarily nerdy man, you know that?"

"All I'm missing is the pocket protector," Carl said. He turned back to his computer. Paul noted that although Carl didn't have full range-of-motion with his injured arm, he could type with blinding speed.

"How's your arm?" Paul asked.

"Not so bad anymore," Carl said and rotated his shoulder in a practiced stretch. "I had to have a couple surgeries to repair some tendons, but with a few more months of physical therapy, it should be good as new." He grinned. "Fuck you very much."

Paul chuckled. "I'm glad it's healing okay," he said and turned back to his work. He started looking for matches as the grin faded from Carl's face. Carl rubbed his arm self-consciously and turned back to his computer. *Poor guy*, Paul thought.

Chapter 15

January 9th, 8:12 AM EST; J. Edgar Hoover building; Washington, D.C.

After another pornographic frisking and an escort through the endless hallways, Paul found himself back in the same conference room with the same piles of papers, the same nine computers, and the same large display on the wall. The team was busy rooting through documents. "Why does everybody look so pissed off?" Paul asked.

Carl jerked his head toward the wall display, and Paul had his answer. A list was projected on the wall in digital clarity:

Match-2 (276) Rotator cuff surgery, lived in CA, allergic to penicillin, etc.

Match-3 (92) Alumni SUNY school, owned a Hyundai, glasses required for driving, etc.

Match-4 (17) MasterCard, patient at South Manhattan Municipal, etc.

Match-5 (3) Lived in NY, Lived in NJ, two children

Match-6 (0) No matches

Match-7 (1) Owned a cat

Match-8 (0) No matches

Match-9 (0) No matches.

Paul looked at Carl. "So what do the numbers in parentheses mean?" Paul asked.

Sam replied in his ear. "Number of matches in that category. Now shush."

He had no experience with this sort of thing but was pretty sure that even though the team wasn't expecting Carl's ideal Match-9, they expected something higher than a Match-5 that was more significant than cat ownership.

They spent the next few hours digging through files. Again. Looking for missed clues. Again. *I'm glad I never wanted to be a cop,* Paul thought.

Every now and then they found something that the computer hadn't recognized. Paul didn't see why upgrading "Owned a Hyundai" from Match-3 to Match-4 was important or relevant, but Carl seemed pleased when he found the typo that threw the computer off track. He supposed that if there was one error, there must be more. They spent the next several hours looking.

"I think...," Doug started to say, then stopped and studied the paper in his hand. The rest of the team exchanged hopeful looks. Doug slid himself over to the next desk and jumped to the medical files. He muttered to himself as he read. "Knee surgery. There it is again. Toradol, followed by Ultram." After a quick scan, he moved to the next victim's information. At each terminal he made a small entry.

The rest of the team looked at each other with restrained excitement. "There he goes," Jerri muttered to Marty, hope painted on her face. *Good God, she's beautiful,* Paul thought.

It took less than five minutes for Doug to complete the circuit of desks. He walked to the center console and typed, his fingers a blur on the keyboard. Paul wanted to ask what he was doing but didn't dare interrupt.

After a minute Doug looked up at Gene, his eyes ablaze with excitement. "Why would you prescribe Toradol followed by Ultram for pain?"

Gene's eyes widened. "I...I have no idea, Doug. Why would you prescribe Toradol followed by Ultram for pain?"

"I don't know. They're both non-narcotic, non-steroidal analgesics. Toradol can mess you up pretty good and isn't nearly as cheap as something like oxycodone or codeine. There were some lawsuits in the mid-to-late nineties about liver damage, even some deaths." He went back to the computer and continued to type.

"How do you know this shit?" Marty asked.

Doug grinned without looking up and shook his head. "I'll never tell."

Marty rolled his eyes.

A minute passed, then another. All work had stopped except for Doug's frantic hammering on the keys. His mutters turned into a coherent statement. "Sam, please put victim nine's autopsy photos on the large screen."

Larry Johnson Jr.'s photos appeared on screen. The body was shriveled with age, a sad, slack-jawed raisin of a man.

"There," Doug said and pointed to the old scars on the right arm. "Does anyone else want to bet we'll find needle tracks on all of the others?"

The whole team dove to the terminals to confirm what Doug already knew. Within minutes, Doug pointed at the updated display.

Match-2 Arrested for drug possession (1,7)
Match-3 No pre-1980 medical records (4,5,9)
Match-4 Pre-1980 patient at S. Manhattan Municipal H(1,3,6,8)
Match-5 Lived in NY City (1,4,5,7,9)
Match-6 No matches
Match-7 Matches deleted
Match-8 No matches
Match-9 Former intravenous drug user (1,2,3,4,5,6,7,8,9)

"That," Doug said, "is not a coincidence."

"Actually, it technically is," muttered Carl.

"Holy shit," Marty said with a huge grin. "They're all junkies!"

In the excitement of the new find, no one noticed Paul Renner brooding at the wall screen.

"Guess what?" Sam said over the COM. "Until 1982 the South Manhattan Municipal Hospital ran an affiliated methadone clinic in SoHo. The building was used for a couple of years as a document storage facility for the hospital. It burned down in 1984. Arson. Unsolved. I'll have RiC look into it."

Paul raised an eyebrow at Carl. "Who's Rick?"

"Research and Information Processing Center. Big 'R,' little 'i,' big 'C.' RiC. They make the phone calls and ask the questions for the Special Operations Units. Us."

"Gotcha," Paul said.

Work continued for several hours without finding any more leads. The familiar frustration known to investigators everywhere set in. Finally, Sam's voice broke the monotony.

"Hey, Gene?"

"Go ahead."

"RiC's got something for us. All of the clinic records were destroyed in the fire." There was a pregnant pause. Gene rolled his eyes.

"But...," he prompted.

"But an old maintenance guy there, Seth Hawkes, says that quite a few of the files were moved to their Records building shortly before the fire, when they started transferring their records to computers. Said he thinks they might still have them in a box somewhere."

"ROAD TRIP!" Carl, Marty, and Jerri shouted at once. The team scrambled to grab laptops, PDAs, jackets, and briefcases. Paul followed Gene out the door.

* * *

January 9th, 6:15 PM EST; Houston Street; New York City, New York.

Less than five hours after Doug's revelation and Sam's find in D.C., the team crawled through Manhattan traffic.

"Oh, come ON!" Carl yelled at traffic from the passenger's seat. Although years of ruthless traffic enforcement kept the intersections reasonably clear, and the now genetically inherited knowledge that a cabbie will run you over if you're not where you're supposed to be kept the pedestrians on the sidewalks and crosswalks, no law of man or God could compete with New York City traffic on a weekday at six PM.

Gene had arranged for a warrant on the plane, just in case they needed it. They pulled up to a five-story brick building that looked a lot more like apartments than a warehouse or office building. A blue-shirted NYPD officer walked up to the passenger side of Gene's SUV. He was already talking, so Carl rolled down the window.

"I'm Officer Mullins. Here's your warrant." He handed the paper to Carl through the window. "Go ahead and double-park right up there." He gestured to a stretch of road a quarter of a block away.

"Leave me the keys so I can let people out if I got to, you know? I'll make sure no one messes with the vehicles."

"Thanks, officer," Gene said. He pulled up to the indicated spot, Marty right behind him. The team walked through the only door into a sparsely furnished lobby. Gene followed on his crutches. Fluorescent lights buzzed above a small security desk, and a bored-looking twenty-something girl with a gaudy gold badge pinned to her dark blue uniform served as a guard.

She glanced at them and continued typing on her phone. Gene stood at the desk for a full ten seconds before he cleared his throat.

"Yeah?" the girl said without looking up.

Jerri held out the papers. "We have a warrant to enter the South Manhattan Municipal Hospital offices located in this building and to examine the documents contained therein. Your cooperation is required."

They waited while the guard called the main office, faxed a copy of the warrant, and received authorization. Gene chose not to point out that the team couldn't legally be denied access. The guard handed Jerri a key-card.

"It's the whole fifth floor. There's no elevator, so you'll have to hoof it," the girl said. She smiled sympathetically at Gene, gestured toward the door to the stairwell and went back to texting.

Doug and Marty helped Gene up the five flights of stairs. As they reached the fifth-floor landing, the stairs continued up to a roof-access door. Jerri swiped the key-card and opened the lower door. Occupying the floor-space equivalent to four large apartments sat rows of four-and-a-half foot high, four-foot deep, three-drawer filing cabinets. The room smelled of musty paper.

"Oh, for the love of Christ," Paul said to no one in particular. "More piles of papers to root through. Your guys' job sucks."

The files were well organized and well labeled, so it took less than ten minutes to find the records for the methadone clinic. The overhead lights weren't that bright, and although a rectangle of orange streetlight beamed through each of the three east-facing windows, they just reinforced the gloom. Carl pulled out files and handed them off at random. There were no chairs, so they leaned against filing cabinets while they flipped through records.

"Okay," Carl said. "It looks like the full clinic records are in these six cabinets, with patient records in these three right here." He patted the cabinet closest to him. "We either need to lug all of them downstairs or bring a scanner up."

"I vote for bringing a scanner up," Marty said. "Why the hell don't they have this shit on microfiche?"

"Fine by me," Doug said. Gene's foot wasn't broken, and he could walk on it if he had to, but it hurt like heck to do it. One quality scanner brought up sounded much better than dozens of trips down.

"Does anyone smell smoke?" Carl paused at the filing cabinets and sniffed the air.

"Yeah." Marty said as he walked to the west wall. Wispy tendrils climbed from under the baseboard. As he passed a window, a small glint of light shone from the top of the building next door. As Gene turned toward it, Marty tackled him. The window exploded inward. The unmistakable sound of a high-velocity ricochet was the only indication that a bullet was the culprit.

"TAKE COVER!" Marty yelled, turning his dive into a roll. Windows shattered and bullets thudded into filing cabinets while the team dove to the floor. Glass rained down on them.

Smoke poured in, faster now.

"We're taking fire!" Jerri yelled into the COM.

"Calling 911," Sam chimed in.

"Stay down!" Gene yelled as he moved to the door and shouldered it open. The stairwell was clear of smoke. "Let's go!" He limped downward on one crutch with his pistol leading the way.

He rounded the half-landing to the fourth floor, caught a glimpse of a waiting silhouette, and ducked back. Automatic weapon fire spattered off the concrete wall, sending jagged chips of concrete into the air. Gene fired several shots down the stairs to discourage pursuit and retreated back up the stairs.

He heard the fire roaring on the other side of the wall, and more automatic fire slapped against the upper landing. "Can't go that way!" he yelled and pushed Doug back toward the fifth-floor storage area.

They dropped to hands and knees to avoid the smoke and crawled to the rest of the team. "There's a gunman in the stairwell, and the third floor is on fire." Gene kept his voice calm and under control.

Marty filled in the details. "The fire escape is on the west side of the building. It and the roof are both covered by a sniper." His face looked grim. "We're trapped, and fucking Renner is missing."

"So's my gun," Carl added.

"Fire trucks are en route," Sam announced. "SWAT teams are scrambling."

"He's missing," Gene said. It wasn't a question.

"He's not here," Marty continued, "and Sam can't reach him on the COM. The son-of-a-bitch set us up, Gene."

Bright yellow flames licked out of the west wall where the first wisps of smoke had come from. The smoke was three feet from the floor and lowering. The room stank of burning insulation. Jerri looked dumbstruck. "We're going to die here."

Doug closed his eyes. "Our only chance is to rush the gunman on the stairs." He opened his eyes. "Maybe I can buy time for the rest of you to take him out." He checked the magazine in his gun and crawled toward the door.

"No need for heroics," Renner's voice crackled over the COM. "The sniper's down. The fire escape's clear. Move your asses!"

Carl yanked a drawer out of a filing cabinet. "We've got to get the files out!" he yelled. He took a deep breath, stood, and ran to the north wall. He threw the drawer into the window. The glass shattered. Most of the papers plummeted with the drawer sixty feet to the ground, while the rest fluttered away in the cold January air.

He did his best baseball slide back to the filing cabinets. He dropped below the smoke level and sucked in air. "Help me!" he cried, yanking out the next drawer.

Marty motioned for Gene and Jerri to get to the fire escape, then yanked out a patient-record drawer and ran after Carl.

The window that led to the fire escape was in flames. Gene dove through a wall of heat and slammed against the black-painted railing. The hard metal did its job and stopped him from plummeting five stories to his death. He did his best to slow Jerri and Doug as they flew through in turn. "Marty! Carl! There's no time! Get the heck out of there!" He sprinted down the fire escape stairs as fast as he could go, gritting his teeth against the pain.

"GO! GO! GO!" Marty yelled, shoving Carl in front of him. After a second trip, they'd saved what files they could, but the air in the room was changing from smoke to flame. The west wall leading to the fire escape was a mass of fire. He yelled into the COM, "Gene!

The fire escape's cut off!" Marty took the lead, and they crawled to the stairwell door. He pushed it open. Half a flight down, the stairs were an inferno. The air was thick with the smell of lighter fluid.

They covered their mouths and bolted upstairs. Smoke stung their eyes and seared their lungs. Marty threw his shoulder against the roof exit, and the pair stumbled out into the blessedly cold air. The tar at their feet blistered from the heat beneath, and acrid smoke extended the building's shape upward into the cold night sky. For the moment, Marty and Carl stood in the eye of the storm.

Marty spun and looked for any way down. The closest building was thirty feet away. The west side of the building was engulfed in flames. The staccato crackling of bursting tar bubbles rippled across the roof's surface. "Carl. I...This is going to be a fucking shitty way to die."

Gene hit the ground at a dead sprint, adrenaline masking the brutal pain in his foot. The fire escape was a lost cause, which meant that Marty and Carl's only chance was the stairwell. He rounded the front of the building and saw fire trucks in the distance. They crawled and blared their way through traffic. *Too late.*

"WHERE'S THAT CHOPPER?" he screamed.

"En route," Sam replied, her voice as calm as ever.

He yanked open the front door and ran in, weapons-ready, Doug and Jerri right behind him. The guard sat in her chair with her head lolled to the side. A small dark circle in the middle of her forehead belied the seriousness of the wound. The small splatter of blood and brains on the wall told the rest of the story. In her right hand, her cell phone buzzed for attention.

Gene ran across the room and slammed his shoulder into the stairwell door. A small gas can sat at the base of the stairs. Gene sprinted up three steps at a time, and as soon as he rounded the second-floor landing, he saw the arsonist.

Officer Mullins of the NYPD, who had greeted them with the warrant thirty minutes before, had a submachine-gun in one hand and a bottle of charcoal lighter fluid in the other. He was coaxing the fire lower with squirts from the bottle when he heard Gene pound up behind him.

He spun to bring his gun to bear, but Gene's was up and aimed. Gene double-tapped him center-mass, then shot him in the face as he ran past. He followed the thin trail of burning liquid around the corner.

At the third floor, the stairwell was awash with flames. He could feel the air as it sucked past him from the lower floors and fed the conflagration above. "Sam!" He threw an arm up to shield his face from the heat, but knew no one could get through that much fire. "Get that helicopter to the roof, now!"

"Working on it."

He sprinted down the stairs. Doug and Jerri dragged Mullins' body toward the lobby. "Marty! Carl! Where are you?" A crash from above was his only answer.

* * *

On the roof, all Carl could hear was the roar of flames and the cracking of super-heated wood. The viscous, sticky tar sucked at his shoes. He backpedaled away as the western part of the roof continued to cave in, Marty half holding him up and half dragging him backward by his shirt collar. The clatter as the fire escape collapsed was deafening.

Marty screamed in his ear, barely audible over the roaring flames. "I think I'd rather jump than burn!"

Carl turned his back to the fire and looked over the edge. It was a long way down to the hard street below. A gawking crowd was already forming. *There must be dozens of cameras down there,* he thought.

"Me, too," he shouted back. "But I'm not jumping. It's one thing for my kids to know their daddy's dead. I'm sure as hell not going to let them watch me die on YouTube."

"I won't let that happen, Carl."

A small object landed in the sticky tar next to Carl's foot. It was a brass baseball nested in a thin, fishnet pouch. The pouch was tied to a long, drawstring-like rope. Carl looked up through the wall of smoke and could see a long, white shape that stretched upward and away. It danced in the wind like a kite's tail.

Carl grabbed the string and dragged it hand over hand as fast as he could while Marty picked up the slack. It was far too thin to support Carl's weight, not to mention Marty's, but whatever else it was, it was *hope.* The wispy, white shape revealed itself through the smoke as a string of bed sheets, blankets, and towels, all tied and retied into a long, thick rescue line. There were even loops for hand and foot-holds at the bottom. Still hauling, Carl started to giggle.

"I'll hold this end," Marty said with a wink. "You go first." Carl grabbed the bottommost handholds and noticed that they were soaking wet. *Smart.* He passed them over to Marty.

Marty wrapped the loops tightly around his wrists. "Climb fast. I don't think this is strong enough to support bo—"

With a huge crack, the roof broke free. Carl dove forward, barely wrapping his fingers around Marty's belt. The pair of FBI agents swung like a pendulum through the burning fifth floor and crashed into the smoking wall. Carl's hair shriveled from the heat. His lungs burned. He couldn't open his eyes.

He tried to ignore the panic clawing at his brain. He couldn't let himself breathe in. He felt the rope shift upward, and he churned his legs against the wall to help Marty support his weight. He could feel the soles of his shoes melting. With a surge of adrenaline, they clamored over the edge of the wall, only to Tarzan-swing into the brick façade of the building next door.

Carl swung wildly as Marty smashed full-force into the wall. Carl's knees slammed into the bricks. His heart jumped into his throat as they dropped. He closed his eyes and braced for impact. They fell less than a foot. Carl looked up in shock. Marty had let go of the makeshift rescue line, but the loops wrapped around his wrists held firm. He gasped for breath, his head lolling back in pain.

Oh, shit, Carl thought.

He breathed a sigh of relief as Marty's hands re-closed around the loops. Marty opened his eyes and met Carl's gaze, a fierce grin on his face. "Still some work to do, Carl. Move your feet. Like this." Marty began to walk up the wall. Carl tried to help, but was facing the wrong direction.

They rose slowly, Carl dangling from Marty's belt. His elbow was in agony. As they neared the roof, Carl heard grunts of exertion echoing from above. He did his best to use his legs to ease the burden, but there were no ledges or sills, and he didn't have any leverage.

Marty made it up over the ledge and onto the solid flat surface of the top of the building, and Carl was dragged to the roof lip. A team of exhausted men and women grabbed the makeshift rope and pulled again. With another heave, he was up. Carl couldn't let go of Marty's belt. His hands wouldn't respond. He collapsed onto the cool stone of the rooftop and just breathed.

A rousing cheer drowned out the inferno as people of all shapes and sizes came to their aid. Strong hands pried his fingers apart and hauled him to his feet. Men slapped him on the back. Women hugged him. Smiling, sweaty faces greeted him everywhere he looked, except for a lone figure in the back of the crowd.

Paul Renner wasn't smiling. He stood with his arms folded, watching them. A few exhausted men stood nearby, congratulating each other on a job well done. A man clapped Renner on the back and hugged him.

"Thank you all, so much," Carl said, shaking hands and taking hugs, tears of relief filling his eyes. "We have to go. We have to go." The crowd pressed in and threatened to smother them with good will.

"People!" Marty barked. He held his hands up to stop the crowd. "I can't tell you how wonderful you all are, and I thank you from the bottom of my heart. But we're on FBI business, and we have to go. Thank you again!"

Marty herded Carl toward the rooftop doorway. As they reached it, another chorus of cheers erupted behind them. They turned and waved one last time. No one was looking at them. Instead, Paul Renner was receiving an adoring send-off.

"I've never seen anything like that in my entire life."

"You're a hero, man."

"That was unbelievable!"

"I didn't think there was any way when you jumped."

"I'm glad men like you are on our side."

Paul shook hands, kissed cheeks, and smiled from ear to ear. He extracted himself from the crowd and approached the two agents, his smile vanishing.

Carl put his hands in his pockets. "Umm…thanks, Paul."

Marty moved in close and leaned down, his lips pulled back in a sneer. "This doesn't change a motherfucking thing, killer."

Paul frowned. "Don't let a little thing like me saving your life get in the way of you hating me, Agent Palomini." He turned to Carl. "Sorry, I had to borrow this. I didn't figure you'd lend it to me." He held Carl's pistol in his outstretched hand. Carl opened his mouth in shock, then closed it.

"Uh, thanks," Carl said and took the weapon.

The trio headed down the stairs with a score of proud apartment dwellers in tow.

Chapter 16

January 9th, 8:18 PM EST; South Manhattan Municipal Hospital storage facility; New York City, New York.

Now confined to a wheelchair just to deal with the pain, Gene had ridiculous amounts of paperwork to fill out. Swarms of policemen gathered scattered files and brought them back to Carl and Doug. They set aside anything that matched one of their victims and piled up the rest to let hospital interns organize at a later date.

They found the body of the sniper on the roof of the western building. He had suffered a single round to the throat and had drowned in his own blood. The man wore normal civilian clothes and had apparently hidden the rifle under his heavy winter coat. He had a USMC tattoo on his right bicep, and Sam confirmed that his ID was fake.

The NYPD had conniptions about Officer Mullins. When he had shown up at the courthouse to pick up the warrant, the desk clerk hadn't recognized him. Following protocol, she had run his ID. His Personnel Record File showed that he was a six-year veteran of the force, but no one had ever heard of him.

With Sam's help, they determined that his credentials had been loaded into all relevant systems less than an hour after Gene had called for the warrant. The e-mail that requested an officer deliver the warrant still sat in the court clerk's "Sent" folder, but had been deleted at the server right after it had been sent.

Meanwhile, Jerri reviewed her notes from her witness interviews. Juan Martinez' Mexican accent was thick enough to be charming but clear enough to be easily understood. She found herself reading and re-reading his testimony.

You're not going to believe this. Hell, I saw it with my own two eyes, and I don't believe it. I'm up on the roof for a cigarillo when I hear the glass break. I see the man with the rifle shooting into the other building. I'm two floors up, si? So the man with the rifle, he don't see me.

I see the smoke, and the roof door, it opens a crack. The rifleman shoots POW-POW-POW, and the door, it clicks back shut. Then the roof door flies open, and Señor Paul dives out. He comes up and POW, the man with the rifle drops.

Now, I see a lot of blood, but Señor Paul I don't think can see it. He don't know if he hit the man with the rifle, si? So he run across and up onto the fire escape and jumps! Hijole! I never seen a man jump so far! He land two floors down on the other fire escape. I don't know how his legs stay unbroken, you know?

So he run up the stairs, and he see the man with the rifle lying bleeding, and he run to the edge of the roof and jumps again! I tell you, Señora, at first I think Señor Paul is just a brave man, but now I know he is touched by God. It's not as far to my building from the other, but when I tell you he jumped again, he jumped again! He's loco.

I don't see where he land, but he come running up the roof yelling "Rope! Rope!" I see you and the two guys get out, but still he yell "Rope! Rope!" So I run inside and he with me, and we get the neighbors and make the rope from the towels and the sheets, and Señor Johnson, he weight the end with his boy's trophy-ball. And Señor Paul throw it over to the other men.

When the roof fell, all we see is sparks and the men disappeared. So we pull, and they come out, and they're okay! I tell you, Señora Bates, Señor Paul is like Spiderman. In all my years, I've never seen such a thing.

"Hey, look!" Carl yelled, distracting her. Though missing eyebrows and oddly lustrous, his face beamed with triumph. He held up an old photograph from one of the files gathered from the street. "It's Jeanette Santiago; victim number four. She matched no pre-1980 medical records, but here she is. She's listed here as *Jane Doe, Name Refused*. I think that pretty much proves Doug pegged the connection." He looked at the burned building and the multitude of flashing red-and-blue emergency lights. "Well, plus someone doesn't want us to see where this trail leads." He trailed off and looked back to the file. "It says she was here for only one week, treated by Dr. Abraham Lefkowitz."

Doug held up a paper. "Larry Johnson, Jr., also with no pre-1980 records. He's right here, treated by Dr. A. S. Lefkowitz."

"Okay," Sam chimed in from HQ. "Here's a resume less than ten years old. Lefkowitz worked for South Manhattan Municipal Hospital's Methadone Clinic as a general practitioner and 'addiction rehabilitation specialist' from 1973 to 1978. Give me a minute to find where he is now." She mumbled to herself over the COM while she dug through data. Her voice rose as she found relevant information and shared it with the team.

"Currently's got a private practice in Manassas. Home info unlisted, I'll find that in a sec. Left the clinic to go work in pharmaceutical development. Started his own lab. Sold some patents for–wow!–seventy million dollars. And his current home address is 132 Alabaster Circle, just outside of good old Manassas, Virginia."

Gene had been shaking hands and passing out business cards when he had paused so he could listen to Sam. To those without a COM it looked like he was staring off into space, listening to nothing. He punched the air triumphantly. "Saddle up, people!"

Carl gave some final instructions to the cops in charge of retrieving the rest of the documents. Doug and Jerri stuffed their briefcases with files, folders, and laptop computers. Marty, his face pink and shiny, missing both eyebrows and most of his moustache, disentangled himself from the local Bureau guys. Paul Renner sat in the SUV, under guard.

* * *

January 9th, 9:52 PM EST; JFK International Airport; New York, New York.

Ninety minutes later Paul found himself on yet another small commercial jet as it taxied toward the runway at J.F.K. Gene and Marty sat near the front, across the aisle from each other. A small Chinese man had offered his front-row seat to Doug. This put him by himself at the front of the cabin, but it gave him a great deal more leg room. Carl was stuck all the way in the back by himself. Jerri switched seats with a businessman to sit next to Paul.

"That was a pretty crazy day." Jerri sighed and sank into the window seat. Paul took note of the frown on her reflection as she looked out the window. "I hate it when all I can see is wing." She turned back and glanced at Paul's hands, then away. "That was an amazing thing you did today."

Paul gingerly lowered himself into his seat. "If you say so. I just did what anyone else would've done, if they could." He sighed in relief as the chair took the brunt of the pressure off his battered body. As if it were waiting for him to get seated, the *fasten seatbelt* sign came on.

"I don't know about that," Jerri said. "Marty *hates* you. He really, really hates you, and you know it. But you put yourself on the line for him. I mean, your ribs aren't even healed from your fight with Gene, and you mangled your hands." The plane rolled away from the gate.

Paul turned his hands palms-up with a chuckle. "I think 'mangled' is a bit exaggerated." His palms were red, scraped, and blistered. The EMTs had washed out as much of the grit as they could, and although it stung like hell and itched like crazy, it looked a lot worse that it was. "Like I said, I don't think I did anything that anyone else wouldn't have done."

"I don't know," Jerri said. "It just doesn't fit with what we know about you. You were a hero today. I wouldn't have expected it."

"Agent Bates," Paul said. "Don't ever make the mistake of thinking I'm not the bad guy. People who get in my way get hurt. We just happen to be headed in the same direction." Punctuating his point, the plane accelerated down the runway.

"You can't be all bad," Jerri said with a tiny smile. "You didn't kill Carl or me when you got the jump on us, you didn't kill Gene after he broke your ribs, and you rescued Carl and Marty today. Why?" she asked. "What makes you tick? What led you down the path to D Street?"

Paul wondered if her curiosity was genuine. "You first. What makes a pretty little Irish girl grow up to be an FBI agent?" The landing gear left the runway, and they were airborne.

"Ugh," she said. "Calling me 'pretty little' should earn you a punch in the mouth. I deal with sexist bullshit twenty-four-seven."

"Well, you're not exactly large, and you're attractive. And I don't buy into people getting offended by the truth."

"I'm not offended," Jerri said. "But being a woman in a male-dominated field means you can't let people call you 'pretty little' anything."

"Fair enough," Paul said. "So what makes a petite, attractive woman want to join a male-dominated field like the FBI?"

Her cheeks colored a touch. "You can't laugh."

Paul affected his best poker face. "I won't." She said nothing for a long moment. Paul smiled at her. "I said I wouldn't laugh."

The words escaped softly from her mouth. "Agent Scully." A crimson rush covered her face.

Paul almost suppressed a grin. "From the *X-Files*?"

She nodded, and her cheeks deepened to nearly purple. She replied through clenched teeth. "You said you wouldn't laugh!"

"I'm not laughing." He laughed. "Tell me more."

Paul followed her gaze to the front of the plane. Gene and Marty leaned toward one another, bickering. Doug had leaned his seat back, and he looked to be asleep. Behind them, Carl sat in the back where he plugged away at his PDA, oblivious to the world. "Paul, I swear if you tell anyone—"

"I know how to keep a secret," he said. "Why her?"

"Scully was just so strong and smart. In the turmoil of the whole show, she grounded everything in reality." She looked sheepish. "I wanted to be just like her."

"And is it everything you thought it would be?"

"It's nothing like I thought it would be. It's better, just in totally different ways. I mean, obviously some parts of it suck. The paperwork is crazy. Dead-ends are frustrating. *You* are frustrating. We took your taunts personally. Why do you do that?"

"Let's just say that the FBI aren't always the good guys they think they are."

"What does that mean?"

"It means what it means," Paul said.

"Uh-uh, not good enough. Scully buys me more than that, Paul."

He looked in her eyes and said nothing. She waited. He grinned. "Maybe you'll find out one day. But not today."

Her petulant frown was more cute than angry.

"Did you ever find any aliens?" Paul's eyes lit up with the jab.

Jerri laughed. "Screw you, Renner." She laughed again. "So anyway, that wasn't an answer, so it's your turn."

"Quite the interrogator, aren't you?" He smiled to take the edge off the question.

"It's my job. How'd you get where you are?"

"Gillian Anderson doesn't buy you a story that long, but it'll buy you a start. I was a normal middle-class kid from a middle-class town. My mom died when I was little, and my father never remarried." He smiled to hide the memory. "My dad's a great guy. I'm an only child, so he and I were best buddies. To make a long story short, I had a choice to go to a community college or into the service for the GI Bill to go to a better school. Well, every bumfuck town in this country is packed full of entry-level workers with community college degrees, so I picked the military."

"Which branch?" Jerri asked.

"It doesn't matter." He smiled at the annoyed look on her face. "I found out that I was real good at violence. Firearms, hand-to-hand combat, explosives, whatever. If it involved killing something, Paul Renner was your boy. Well, when Uncle Sam owns your ass and you have a skill he can use, he's a dirty old uncle who likes touching you in your naughty place." He paused. "I think that's more than enough payment for Agent Scully. Where'd you grow up?"

"Pittsburgh," Jerri said. "All the bad parts of a big city combined with all the bad parts of a rural Midwest town."

"Oh, come on, I've been to Pittsburgh lots of times. It's a great town."

"Yeah? Says you."

"That's right," he said, folding his arms. "Says me." He grinned, amused at himself. "Okay, no home town talk. Inspired by Agent Scully, you dyed your hair red and applied to the FBI. How'd that go?"

She rolled her eyes. "It's natural. And I applied three times before I got an interview. I have a bachelor's degree in Criminal Justice, but so did everyone else. I think the *janitors* at Hoover have a BA in Criminal Justice. Anyway, once they called me for an interview, I knew I was in. I can talk my way through anything. They made me an interrogation specialist. Good Cop, mostly, although I can play bitch queen with the best of them. It's not chasing UFOs with David Duchovny, but it's interesting in its own way.

"They skipped me off to the New York field office for a couple years. Then Gene requested that I join his team, and here I am." She cracked her neck and stretched. "Your turn. You're in the service and found your niche. What next?"

"I traveled the world," Paul said. "Europe, Asia, Africa, South America, Australia. Always outside the U.S., no uniform, no dog tags. They'd give me a target and a deadline, and off I'd go. Sometimes I'd have to plant evidence, sometimes remove it. Sometimes I'd have to make it look like an accident or a random thing like a mugging. Sometimes it had to look like it was on purpose. At times, months would go by and I'd just sit on base doing nothing, getting paid to wait for the next job."

"What base?"

Paul ignored the question. "Sometimes they'd bounce me from job to job so quick I'd barely have time for a shower and a cup of coffee before the next briefing started. So, anyway, after four years of dedicated service to my country, I left to go to college and put that well-earned tuition money to good use."

"Which college?"

"Do you want to hear the story or not?"

"You know I do."

"Then quit asking questions you know I won't answer." The amusement in his voice disappeared as he went back to the story. "So I got an associate's degree in Computer Science and transferred to a great four-year school for my bachelor's. Two months in, after two and a half years of no contact, I get a phone call. A threat to national security needs to be removed, and they need me to do it.

"So I tell them I've been out of the service for a couple years, and the guy says word-for-word, 'civilian contractors are always compensated higher.' I point out that this arrangement is illegal. He counters that, without my uniform or my tags, what I was doing was illegal all along. To make a long story short, we negotiated a fee, and on a warm summer night on D Street in Tacoma, Washington, as a service to my country, I killed a man."

"D Street was a government job?"

"Once I picked up the old trade, the calls flooded in. The money was good, the work was challenging, and at some point I stopped caring if they were traitors or spies or terrorist masterminds. I was more interested in the job than the money.

"So one day I get a call from someone who knew someone who knew that someone important's wife knew that he was cheating on her, and she was going to file for divorce and bilk him for all he's worth. They, of course, needed Paul Renner to resolve the problem. It didn't even occur to me that taking that job crossed some fictional line that turned an honorable soldier into a murderer.

"They needed someone killed, so they called a killer." He felt no remorse and sadness as he said it. It was just a fact.

Jerri stared out the window for a while. Finally she spoke. "That's pretty fucked up, Paul."

"Yep," he said.

"You know, this morning I was afraid of your hands." Jerri set her hand atop Paul's. "But no matter what else you've done with them, at least today they did some good." She smiled at him with sparkling green eyes.

Paul returned the look with interest. "Today they did," he agreed.

She gave his hand a squeeze and pulled hers back, then looked out the window.

It was four in the morning when the plane landed at Dulles International Airport. The howling wind blasted freezing-cold grit in their faces as they assembled on the tarmac. It only took a moment for the government SUVs to pull up. Gene took shotgun in the first, and Renner hopped into the back seat. Jerri took the other side. Marty stepped toward that car, but Doug sidled past him and got in. That left an SUV just for Carl, Marty, and their driver. They got in, and moments later the team was on its way back into Washington D.C.

Carl ran his hand over his mostly-bald head. "I'm going to have to shave tonight. You, too, Marty. We look pretty ridiculous."

Marty didn't reply.

"Listen up, folks," Gene said over the COM. "Sam has confirmed that Doctor Lefkowitz is still in private practice in Manassas, and he's still at the address on file. He doesn't appear to be going anywhere, and we've got the local PD staking him out, so everyone head home and catch an hour's sleep. It'll take forty-five minutes to get there if we leave early, and two hours if we catch the morning rush. That means we're leaving HQ at oh-five-thirty, and you can nap in the car. We'll catch some breakfast once we get there."

Marty checked his watch. *3:47 a.m. Got to get up at 5:00.* Just the thought of the early start brought a yawn. It spread to Carl, who punched him in the arm.

"Jerk," Carl said when he was able to talk again.

Marty killed his COM. "Why do you think he did it?"

Carl looked confused. "Why do I think who did what?"

"Renner. Why'd that motherfucker pull our asses out of the fire today?"

"Well," Carl said, "he probably pulled *mine* out because of the tragedy it would be if my dashing good looks were no longer available to the world. I don't have a clue why he rescued your ugly ass."

Marty scowled. "Be serious, Carl. He's a cold-blooded, ruthless son-of-a-bitch who murders people for a living, and he knows I'd geek him in half a second if I had the chance, and he saves my fucking life? I don't owe that fuck a goddamn thing, Carl. I won't be indebted to that piece of shit."

"Relax, Marty. I don't owe him anything either. I still don't know if working with him is a good idea, but tomorrow we're going to nab the guy who ordered those killings. That's worth something, isn't it?"

Marty looked ready to spit. "I know if it's a good idea, and it fucking isn't. I don't care who else we catch, this fish is big enough for all of us. Fuck him. Motherfucker."

"We'll take him into custody as soon as we have Lefkowitz, you know."

"That motherfucker knows it, too. He's not stupid, and he'll run. You watch, Carl. Someone's going to get hurt tomorrow, you fucking watch. We just got to make sure it's Renner."

Carl let Marty stew in his own juices for the rest of the ride.

Chapter 17

January 10th, 5:27 AM EST; J. Edgar Hoover Building, Parking Garage; Washington, D.C.

Gene yawned into his fist and watched Jerri's car pull in. It was a clear, crisp morning but not as cold as the previous day. With no wind it wasn't that bad outside, and low levels of oxycodone for pain helped his general mood. Paul Renner stepped out of the passenger side of Jerri's car and his FBI escorts out the back. Gene hobbled over to Doug. "Any idea what that's all about?"

"Don't know," Doug said. "I imagine they made arrangements to get Paul from visitor parking to here. So Jerri must have met him there. I'll ask Valiera."

Gene grunted by way of reply. He saw his brother seething at Renner as Paul walked toward the group. "Marty!" he yelled to grab his attention away from Paul. "You're driving car two."

Marty snapped out of his funk and caught the keys that Gene had thrown at his face. "Yeah, whatever." He turned to his assigned vehicle, got in, and slammed the door. Gene turned his attention elsewhere.

Once inside the SUV, Marty looked at the keys in his hand, then realized the car was already warmed up and idling. *What'd he do, throw me his house keys?* Marty dropped the keys into the cup holder as his brother's voice blurted orders through the COM.

"Renner, you and I are riding with Doug. Brent, Bates, you're with Marty. Traffic's picking up; let's move out."

The team piled into the big black SUVs as ordered. In Marty's auto, Carl got in the back, put on some earphones, and settled back to snooze on the way. Jerri hopped into the front seat and smiled. "Morning, guys! Did you get any sleep?"

Carl cracked an eye open and smiled back. "Not much, but I'm going to add to it, starting now." He turned up the volume on his iPod and his eye closed again. Marty couldn't tell what Carl was listening to, but he could hear the bass from the front seat.

"How about you?" she said to Marty as they pulled out.

"Not really," Marty said without looking at her. "No."

"I'm wide awake. Want me to drive?"

As the car stopped at the garage exit, he looked at her with anger in his eyes. "Do you honestly think I don't know what's going on?"

Jerri raised an eyebrow. "Marty, what are you talking about?"

"You and that goddamned killer. I saw the way you were looking at him yesterday." He kept his voice low and kept checking the rear-view to make sure Carl wasn't listening. He appeared to be fast asleep.

"Excuse me," Jerri said, frowning. She counted off points on her fingers. "First of all, it's none of your goddamn business what I do. Second, you're not as smart as you think you are. Empathy is a strong part of interrogation, Marty, and building a bond with Paul might help us nail him. Sam recorded that whole conversation. And third, did I mention it's none of your business?"

"Oh come on, Jerri." Marty scoffed. "It's the whole team's business. If you need a personal life outside of work, by all means have one. But this is the D Street Killer." He emphasized each word with a fist to the dashboard. "You've seen what he leaves behind, the lives he's destroyed. I don't know how you can look at him without wanting to puke, much less want to fuck him."

"You're an asshole, Marty," Jerri said. "Besides, what if I were stupid enough to fall for him? Why would that give you the right to act like a jealous ex-boyfriend?"

"Because...." He struggled to find the words. "I don't have the right. And I am fucking jealous. Of everyone you give your attention to."

"Marty, I don't—" she began, but he cut her off.

"And I know that son-of-a-bitch is going to hurt us, Jerri. I don't know when, and I don't know how, but when you make a deal with the devil, you never fucking win. That motherfucker is a fucking monster, and you hold his goddamn hand and give him a fucking ride."

"Christ, Marty. He saved your life yesterday."

"Don't start with that shit." Marty's lips pulled back in a sneer. "My life wouldn't have been in danger if we'd busted him when we had the chance. Mark my words, Jerri, the second the chance shows up again, that fucker is mine. I just hope it happens before one of us gets killed."

"You're overreacting. Paul's—"

Marty cut her off. "You know what? Just stop talking. We have nothing to say to each other." He punched on the radio and turned it to a morning news station.

Jerri turned to the window. They rode in silence through a darkened landscape.

* * *

January 10th, 7:30 AM EST; Home of Abraham Lefkowitz, M.D.; Manassas, Virginia.

Doctor Abraham Lefkowitz left his house followed by a car that contained a pair of goons in dark suits. Marty was an excellent tail, so Gene let that part of the operation leave his mind. Through Sam, the local police verified that the bodyguards in the house were still there; the guys in the car were new. Gene pulled up to the front of the house, parked the car, and got out.

"Guards have seen you," Sam said.

"Roger that," Gene said.

Gene limped up to the door with Jerri, Paul, and Carl behind him and pushed the doorbell. The door opened. A man nearly as tall as Doug looked down at Gene. "Yes?" he said in a deep baritone.

Gene held up the warrants and his FBI ID. "I'm Special Agent in Charge Giancarlo Palomini of the FBI. I have a warrant to search this household, as well as to detain and search any and all persons found therein. Please have the rest of your crew come to the foyer and disarm themselves."

The man scrutinized the documents, then spoke to someone behind the door. "José, comply." He looked back to Gene, then pulled aside his jacket. He leaned forward so that Gene could remove the handgun holstered inside. He then pulled up a pant-leg and displayed his ankle holster for similar treatment. Gene passed the weapons one-by-one to Carl, who tagged them with bar codes from some kind of handheld widget and put them in a duffel bag.

The man behind the door appeared, a large Latino with an enormous black bushy mustache. He held his weapons by the barrels. Gene took them and passed them back.

The first bodyguard accepted a walkie-talkie from José. "Mike," he said into it, "it's the FBI with a warrant authorizing them to detain us. Come on down weapons-safe, over." His accent was all Virginia.

The device crackled into life. "On my way. Out."

Within minutes, all three men had been frisked and sat on the couch. They had ID, weapon permits, and company cards showing they worked for Old Dominion Security Service, all of which Sam verified. Nonetheless, Gene stood guard with Paul as Jerri and Carl searched the house.

The first guard's name was John Brussard. "So," John said, "what are you guys looking for? Maybe we can just tell you where it is."

"Why does Dr. Lefkowitz need five security guards?" Gene asked.

"Eight. Why does anyone need guards?"

"What do you know about him outside his practice?"

"Agent Palomini, we can't speak to law enforcement without a company attorney present, other than at the request of our client. Now, I know that's a pain in your ass, and it's not how I mean to be. But the doctor told us that someday the authorities might show up. He didn't tell us why; he just told us to let him know if you did.

"If you want to stop him from running, you should let me call my guys so we can make sure this doesn't get ugly. We're a legit security company. We don't assist fugitives or suspects."

Gene weighed his options. "Okay, let's do it that way. It's a good day if no one gets hurt."

"Agreed," John said. "I'll need my cell phone back."

"Let me call my guy first." Gene activated the COM. "Marty, John Brussard is the head of the security detail. He'll be calling the tail car to tell his men to get the doctor to pull over and surrender. They'll disarm themselves and let you take them into custody. Sam, can you put the cell call over the COM?"

"I need the number," she said.

With John's cooperation they made the necessary arrangements. Gene gave his brother the order to apprehend the suspect.

Marty crested a hill to find both cars pulled over. The guards stood outside their vehicle with their hands laced on their heads. Marty pulled up, and Doug hopped out to handle the guards.

"Agent Goldman," the one on the right said, "our weapons are on the back seat. Let us know what you need us to do to put you at ease."

Confident that Doug had that part handled, Marty blocked Lefkowitz in. The doctor had his hands on the steering wheel, but the car was off and the keys sat on the dashboard. Wispy white hair covered his head, disheveled as if he'd been running his hands through it. He stared at the floor.

Marty took no chances. He unholstered his service pistol and pointed it through the windshield. "Doctor Abraham Lefkowitz. Keep your hands on the wheel and do not move them. I am going to approach the vehicle and open the door. When I do, you are to step out slowly with your hands in plain sight, walk to the front of the car, and lean against the hood with both hands. If you understand and will comply, nod your head."

The doctor looked up at Marty and nodded. When Marty looked into his eyes, he expected to see fear, anger, and defiance. The last thing he expected was haunted, horrified relief.

* * *

January 10th, 8:04 AM EST; Home of Abraham Lefkowitz, M.D.; Manassas, Virginia.

Forensics searched the house while Gene's team moved Dr. Lefkowitz to a nearby safe house. Carl had video and audio equipment set up to record the interrogation. Renner looked bored. Gene knew he wasn't. Doug stood behind Paul, prepared to act at a moment's notice. Another pair of agents flanked the doors, focused on Renner. Carl gave Gene the thumbs-up, and he began.

"Doctor Abraham Lefkowitz, you are a person of interest in a multiple homicide case. You have a right to have a lawyer present during questioning. Please call your attorney now."

The doctor looked up at Gene with a haunted expression. "I understand," he said. "I don't want an attorney." His accent was slightly European, a healthy shot of German mixed with a touch of British.

"To be clear," Gene said, "you're waiving your right to have an attorney present during questioning?"

"That is correct."

"Do you have anything to say before we begin?"

"Yes. I have a lot to say. I don't know if you'll believe me, but eventually you won't have a choice." His eyes glossed over as his memory took him back. "I started work at a methadone clinic in Manhattan in 1974, to treat heroin addicts. It was heartbreaking and unrewarding. Even the best patients commonly went back to using within months of finishing treatment. But for one in ten or so, it saved their lives. That made it worth it. Sometimes.

"Then another doctor at the clinic, VanEpps, came in with a miracle treatment. He had *cured* six patients of heroin addiction in a matter of weeks. It was the most amazing thing I had ever seen. I demanded he show me at once.

"He called it Genetic Modification Therapy. Now, you have to understand, what we would today call recombinant-DNA therapy, using a retrovirus or adenovirus to modify human genetics, was scientific speculation back then. Even today, they would tell you this therapy would not work. So, VanEpps showed me his notes, how he cured his patients in mere days.

"Virginia Mullins was my biggest lost cause. She had been mainlining narcotics and opiates for years. It took almost a lethal dose of methadone just to take the edge off. Her husband had brought her in, afraid she would kill herself. So instead of her shooting up in the street, I had her strapped to a bed thrashing in agony, insane for her next fix.

"VanEpps put her on an IV drip of this new medicine, then doped her up. Not with methadone, with heroin. 'Keeping her comfortable,' he called it. He replaced the IV twice a day for three days, reducing the amount of heroin he gave her each day. Then he stopped the heroin altogether, and she recovered. Fully. Her withdrawal symptoms were mild, no more than what one would expect from their first or second high. After that there was no recidivism. No urge. She packed her bags and went home with her husband.

"That was all the proof I needed. I was, of course, a little scared. The cure was from a fledgling company called Bailey Pharmaceutical. They hadn't even been around long enough to apply for human testing, much less prescribed treatment. So this was all highly illegal, you see?

"But they came to us with destroyed bodies and destroyed lives, and we sent them home whole. Thousands of junkies cured.

"For four years we did this, but it was only a matter of time before we were caught. VanEpps and I were threatened with prison by a member of the hospital board. We showed him the data, but he didn't care. He was interested only in protecting the hospital, not helping the patient."

"Gene," Sam interrupted over the COM. "Get a name."

"Doctor," Gene cut him off. "What was the board member's

name?"

Lefkowitz looked thoughtful for a moment. "Bart Jackson, if my memory is correct. It has been a long time."

"Thank you," Gene said. "Continue, please."

"So Jackson cuts off our budget and closes the clinic." A look of distaste crossed his face. "He tells us if we keep our mouths shut, we get a letter of recommendation in exchange for our resignation. Jackson says that any attempt to continue the project or contact Bailey Pharmaceutical will cancel the deal, and he will call the police.

"VanEpps takes the deal, moves to work at a hospital out west. He passed away—what, four, five years ago?—after a successful career as a general practitioner."

"I'm on it," Sam said in their ears. Gene pretended not to hear her as Lefkowitz continued.

"Jackson's threat worked for six months or so. I was too scared to risk it, but the promise of the treatment was too much. I called Bailey, but the number was disconnected. A Norwegian firm bought up Bailey, and all the employees were laid off. That firm sold all of the research documents to a Chinese company, but I was unable to get contact information. I tried for years to track down the cure, but it was buried and gone."

Gene preempted Sam's questions this time. "What were the firm names?"

"The Norwegian firm was Samarbeide Medisin." He spelled the name for them. "But they had nothing. They never even looked at the files before selling them. The Chinese company was only in Chinese. I never knew how to pronounce it. You must understand that this was before the Internet, and such information can be hard to find. I am sorry."

"Go on," Gene prompted.

"I started a lab to do the research myself. Although we mostly research in other fields, as we must to make money, I was always trying to rediscover the cure. Then, a decade ago I got a call from a former patient. He tells me this fanciful tale that the three men he came with to my clinic have all had psychotic episodes."

Gene opened his mouth, and the doctor jumped in ahead.

"Taggart. James Taggart was the man's name."

"Where is he now?"

"He's dead, like the rest. I will show you the records later. May I continue?"

Gene exchanged a glance with Doug. "Please do."

"As—" the Doctor began. Gene interrupted him with a raised hand while Sam's voice broke into his ear.

"Samarbeide Medisin went belly-up in the early nineties. Anything Chinese at that time might be impossible to track. I'll get the corporate research team on both and let you know what we find."

"Thanks, Sam," Gene said to the air. He dropped his hand and looked at Lefkowitz. "I'm sorry. You were saying?"

"As Mr. Taggart told it to me, he used one of those Internet classmate finders to see how his fellow patients turned out in life. Fredrick Grier had killed his mother with a meat cleaver, then threw himself off a building. Iyov Daniels killed three people at a liquor store before the clerk killed him with a shotgun." His hands shook, and he cleared his throat. "Roy Archer's wife found him slamming his newborn baby's head into the floor. He charged at her and she fled. I read the police report. When they handcuffed him, he started crashing his own head into anything that came near.

"It was the treatment. The therapy changed something in them, then it broke them."

"Now just wait a goddamn minute," Marty said. "I see where this is headed. These are mercy killings. You're doing this to save lives. You're not *really* a murderer. You're a *hero!* Spare us the bullshit, doc." Gene gave him a withering look.

The doctor looked up at Marty and gathered his thoughts. "Agent, I murdered over two thousand people in the 1970s. They just don't all know it yet. All I've been doing is trying to save their friends and family."

"Even if all of this is true," Carl said, "you couldn't possibly know that the people you kill will definitely suffer psychotic episodes."

"Of *course* I cannot know," Lefkowitz responded. "In order to know, I'd need tissue samples and DNA maps of multiple patients. Then I'd have to re-create the adenovirus therapy. At that point I'd need to test it on primates, something as close to human as possible. Rhesus monkeys, perhaps. And then maybe chimpanzees."

"Something like that," Carl said.

"Exactly like that," Lefkowitz said. "Ninety-eight percent of rhesus monkeys succumb within a year. Would you like to know the statistics for chimpanzees?" Carl's comment had obviously annoyed him. "Six percent within thirty days. Eight percent within a year. It spikes to eighty-four percent within five years. Only two are still alive, and they try to kill everything that gets near them. They beat themselves against their bars unless under restraint. Would you like to meet them?"

Carl looked incredulous. "But it's been more than thirty years since the last patient, *human* patient, was treated."

"It's slower in humans. Much slower. But it is still inevitable."

"Doctor," Gene said, "how many people are we talking about here?"

"Of the just over two thousand," Lefkowitz said, "six hundred and twelve are still alive. Or they were, as of last night. That doesn't account for VanEpp's patients."

"Jesus," Doug said.

"Over eight hundred of my patients have died while committing murder, attempting to commit murder, or as part of a murder-suicide, six hundred within the past five years. It appears that the longer it takes for the episode to occur, the worse it is. My chimps support that theory, as do the more recent psychotic breaks."

Carl still looked skeptical. "I suppose you have evidence that supports these claims?"

"Evidence?" He chuckled sadly. "I have *proof*. What would you like first? Patient records? A vial of the 'cure?' Newspaper articles showing what happens to my patients when I don't get to them in time? The scientific documentation? Frozen specimens of the monkeys? Video of the chimps? The two surviving chimps? How about Roy Archer? He is in a sanitarium in Maine. I have the address. Which of these do you want to see?"

"We'll take it all," Carl said.

Paul looked antsy. Afraid of what he might do, Gene spoke up. "Do you confess that you hired an assassin to kill Kevin Parsons?"

"I did that, yes, and many others," Lefkowitz said. Paul twitched as if to step forward but restrained himself. Doug grabbed the back of his shirt.

"And you acknowledge that, after accepting the job, Kevin Parsons disappeared and the killer refunded your money?"

"Correct. This will be unfortunate in the long run if he is in hiding," Lefkowitz said. Paul sneered and flexed his hands. Doug tensed.

Gene ignored them. "And you admit to hiring a second killer to kill the assassin who turned you down?"

Lefkowitz recoiled as if struck. "What! Why would I do such a thing?"

"Oh, come on," Paul said. "We already know that the hit man you hired to kill Parsons was attacked after Parsons disappeared. There's no point in denying it."

"Agent," the doctor said to Paul. "With what I have already admitted, why wouldn't I admit if I had done such a thing, if in fact I had? I don't even know the man's name or what he looked like. The only communication I have ever had with him was via phone or text-message."

"What about the fire at the storage facility?" Marty demanded.

"I don't know what you're talking about. What fire? And when?" His voice was puzzled and angry. "I set no fires."

Marty snorted, unimpressed. "So you honestly expect us to buy into the bullshit that you didn't try to kill us?"

"Wait a minute," Lefkowitz said. "A few weeks ago someone made an attempt on *my* life. Or did you think my bodyguards were just for show?"

Gene looked to his team. "Gather the proof. Call in as much help as you need. Let's get the doctor over to PC. We'll continue debrief there.

"Renner, you're with me," Gene said. He walked outside to

clear his head and directed Paul to sit in the car. After ushering Paul to his seat, Doug stood with Gene, looking out across the suburban landscape of innocent-looking pre-fab houses and well-manicured lawns. "What's Renner's problem?"

"Don't know," Doug said.

"Do you think he's telling the truth?"

"He's a lying piece of shit. He hasn't told us everything, and you know it."

Gene held up his hand to forestall the rant. "Not Renner. Lefkowitz."

"Oh. Sam and Carl will figure that out for us, boss. But if he is, who tried to kill us on Houston Street? I'm afraid we've barely scratched the surface of this mess."

Gene exhaled. "What are we going to do about six hundred people who could go insane at any moment?"

"Gene," Doug said. Gene looked at him.

"What?"

"What if there was more than one clinic?"

Chapter 18

January 28th, 2:00 PM EST; CDC Headquarters; DeKalb County, Georgia.

Eighty degrees in January, Samantha Greene thought. *Disgusting.* She ruminated about the many reasons why humankind invented the indoors and huffed her way up the ramp leading to CDC HQ. The Centers for Disease Control Arlen Specter Headquarters and Emergency Operations Center was a great big curvy building outside of Atlanta, Georgia, comprising ten stories of glass atop three stories of brick, and barely a corner to be found anywhere. She clutched her briefcase to her chest and picked up her pace.

Inside the case were several hundred sheets of photocopied paper and a well-chewed ball-point pen missing its cap. The papers weren't marked classified. They weren't on any kind of official letterhead. They weren't even typed. Gene didn't trust Doctor Lefkowitz' handwritten notes to a courier, much less a fax or an e-mail. The only lab in the country set up to analyze this data in anything approaching a reasonable timeframe was the CDC, and the only person on Gene's team with a personal contact at the CDC was Sam Greene.

Air conditioning hit her like the breath of angels. She sighed and leaned against the inner doorframe. The receptionist was cute, blonde, deathly tan, and wore a headset. Instead of the Georgia twang Sam expected, she spoke with the generic accent that infected Middle America nationwide. "May I help you, ma'am?"

Sam nodded, not sure if she was ready to speak. "Yeah. I'm, um…I have an appointment with…." She flashed her FBI badge. If the receptionist was impressed, she didn't show it. "With Doctor Govind Agrawal."

Sam had gone to John Hopkins University with Govind and had suffered through several of the same computer classes. The truth was that she suffered while he found them to be "trivial" and "base." He was the one person in the world who could make her feel dumb in her chosen field. She contented herself with the knowledge that he made *everyone* feel dumb. He had three PhDs— computer science, epidemiology, and viral medicine—as well as his MD. He might possibly be the smartest person on the planet.

"One moment," said the blonde, then she hit a button on her computer and spoke. "Dr. Agrawal, your two o'clock is here?" She made it sound like a question. Perhaps it was, and it was her job to screen visitors. Sam imagined that the CDC attracted its share of raving loonies. The receptionist smiled and said, "Go right up, eighth floor, room eight-oh-six." She hit a buzzer and the elevator opened. There were no buttons on the outside. *Fair share of loonies indeed*, Sam mused.

A minute later she knocked at room 806. A placard on the door read *Dr. Agrawal, PhD, MD.* A rich voice responded in a charming Indian accent.

"Come on in, Sam!"

Sam smiled and opened the door. Govind stood behind an enormous desk. Every inch was covered with journals, newspapers, notebooks, papers, and at least three laptops. It looked like a strong wind would set the poor man back fifty years. Sam smiled as she saw the speckling of gray in the black hair around his temples, standing out like a beacon against his chocolate-colored skin.

He came around the table and gave her a full bear hug, which she returned. Without asking, he poured her a cup of coffee: black, one sugar, just the way she liked it. Sam sat in the chair offered, took a sip, and smiled. They exchanged pleasantries for a few minutes, caught up on a few old friends, then Govind's face turned serious.

"Of course, you did not come here just to reminisce, and I must be going at five o'clock. What is this 'sticky business?' It must be quite a doozy to pry Samantha Greene from her fortress at the FBI and bring her all the way to Atlanta."

Sam's smile faded. She replied as she opened the briefcase, pulled out a stack of papers, and reflexively shoved the end of a blue Bic pen into her mouth. "We're not sure what to make of it, Govey. But we're sure you probably can." She handed over the critical papers and let him read.

After a few minutes he looked up. "I am not certain I can make heads or tails of this in a single sitting, Sam. If you could come back tomorrow, I will have some of my postdocs analyze it and see what is what." He saw the uncomfortable look on her face, smiled, and patted her hand. "Do not worry, these people are as trustworthy as they come. There is no medical secret that they are not cleared to know, and they are experts at keeping their work to themselves."

"I think that's fine. Just don't tell them the source."

Govind narrowed his eyes. "You haven't even told me the source, Sam. Or do you mean that it came from the FBI, or from the great Samantha Greene herself?"

"Yes, Govind," she said. "All of the above. Just ask them to take a look at it."

Dr. Agrawal clasped his hands together. "Come back tomorrow at seven, and I will take you to dinner. Arti and the children are with her mother in India for another week, and I would appreciate the company. We can talk about it then."

"Deal." They shook hands, hugged, and Sam turned to leave. She paused.

"Hey, Govey?"

"Yes, Sam?"

"It goes without saying that your team can't talk about any of this with anyone but me, all right? No one."

"I would not reveal what I learn here should the president himself demand that I do so."

Sam turned and walked out. She called back down the hallway, "Thanks, babe!"

* * *

January 29th, 7:37 PM EST; Hal's on Old Ivy; Atlanta, Georgia.

Sam was ravenous. She'd had a little McDonald's on the way back to the CDC, but that was a while ago. The Oysters Bordelaise made for a delicious appetizer, but they barely took the edge off when shared with a friend. She'd ordered the Steak Oscar. *How can you beat lump crab meat on top of a medium-rare steak?* She'd worried when she realized she was dining with a Hindu. Govind ordered the Veal Piccata, so he was either a bad Hindu or a good gastronome.

The food arrived and was every bit as delicious as promised. They barely spoke as they inhaled their meals. For a small man, Govind could put it away. A satisfied ten minutes later, talk turned to shop.

Their smiles disappeared. Govind kept his voice low. "To quote my lead technician Miranda, the stuff you gave us is 'freaking science fiction.'"

"What do you mean?" Sam used a roll to sop up some of the juices from the steak, then shoved it whole into her mouth. She chewed while he replied.

"Well, it details some kind of recombinant virus therapy we've never seen before, and if we've never seen it here, it doesn't exist. This appears to block mu-opiod receptors in the brain so that a person cannot ever again get high from narcotics or opiates, but my professional opinion is that what you have here is most likely a load of fanciful gibberish."

"Why is that?" she asked around the roll.

Govind's eyes bored into her own as he ticked off reasons on his fingers. "First, because we have yet to get this kind of therapy to work. Second, because someone would have had to do human testing to perfect it. Third, because there is no way that mu-opiod receptors can be so easily blocked by a single drug. We simply do

Patrick & Philip Freivald

not know enough about brain chemistry. Fourth, there is no mention of side effects, and there are always side effects. Fifth, and this is the most compelling, is that if this were real, there would be no reason not to market it. The inventor would be a billionaire." He looked at his hand, all five fingers open and accounted for. "I seem to be out of fingers, but you get the idea. May I ask where you got it?"

Sam shook her head and washed the roll down with a gulp of wine. "All I can say is that it's real, and it's been used on people. Americans."

Govind froze in mid-bite. "You mean that this therapy has been used in human trials, and we have never heard of it? Impossible. Not even the drug cartels could suppress a treatment as incredible as this."

Sam shook her head. "Not trials, Govey. Actual therapy. This was used on people as early as the mid-seventies."

"Impossible." He took a bite and chewed. "While routine in some forms today, recombinant gene therapy was unheard of in the early nineteen seventies, and just an idea for most of the rest of the decade. Whoever your source is for this document is lying to you."

Sam shrugged and shook her head in disagreement. "Believe what you want, babe, but it's true." She took another sip of wine. *Wow, that's good.* "Can you undo the therapy?"

This brought Govind up short. He was about to reply when the waiter rolled up with a dessert cart. They ordered coffee and the chocolate-drizzled cheesecake, which was dense and creamy, with just the right amount of sweetness, then got back to business.

Sam continued through a mouthful of cheesecake. "As I was saying, can the therapy be reversed?"

He furrowed his brow. "What do you mean, can it be reversed?"

"If we give you a sample of the adenovirus, can you reverse the process, change the gene back to the way it was?"

"Why would you want to do that? Assuming this is real, and I am not willing to concede that this is at all the case, why would a person want to become susceptible to drugs again?"

Sam exhaled heavily and leaned forward. "Because of the side effects."

He didn't let her enjoy her pause. "What side effects could possibly be worse than dying of heroin addiction and destroying your family and your children's lives?"

In reply she reached into her purse and dropped three twenty-dollar bills on the table. That wasn't quite Dutch, but he could afford it more than she could. "You tell me if your team can reverse the process or suppress the symptoms, and I'll answer that question."

"But…. To answer to that question could—will—take years!"

So much for quick answers. "Better get started, Govey. This one's a doozy, and you're going to want a cure. I've got to go."

Amid his protestations, she walked out of Hal's and hailed a taxi.

Chapter 19

January 29th, 8:58 PM EST; J. Edgar Hoover Building, Gene Palomini's Office; Washington D.C.

Gene hung up the phone and rubbed his temples. It was nice to be off crutches, but Sam's news did nothing for his mood. Jerri raised her eyebrows in question.

"That was Sam. The CDC might have some answers for us in a couple years."

Jerri leaned forward. "Really?"

"Yeah," Gene said. He took a long pull from his coffee, savoring the bitterness of the dark brew.

"My God, Gene. All those people."

He looked down. "I know, Jerri, I know." He brought his eyes up. "Still, that's not our only problem."

"Finding the bad guys?"

"Yeah," Gene said. "But we don't even know who we're looking for, aside from someone rich enough to afford a team of mercenaries to attack us in New York."

"A guy who can afford it," Jerri replied. "And knew that he needed to do it. That attack wasn't coincidence. Those men weren't just watching the storage facility with orders to take out whoever went inside." She chewed on it a little more. "So why not burn down the building a month ago? Two months ago? Ten years ago?"

Gene looked at her, realization dawning on his face. "They did it yesterday because that's when they found out those records still existed. We have a leak."

Jerri leaned close. "Somebody in RiC let the bad guys know we were going to that clinic. Or someone in the director's office did."

"Okay, so we use the leak to set a trap," Gene said. "What do we use as bait? The papers?"

Jerri shook her head. "No. He wanted us not to have the papers. That cat's out of the bag." Gene nodded in agreement.

Jerri tried another. "Paul?"

"What about him?"

"He wanted Paul dead."

"That's true," Gene said. "But that cat's out of the bag, too."

Jerri frowned. "Damn. Well, what do we have that hasn't been spoiled?"

Gene triggered his COM. "Sam, have you sent the Lefkowitz report to A.D. Adams yet?"

"No," Sam said. "I've got a few more details to fill in. It'll get done. I can't fly to Atlanta and do your paperwork for you at the same time. I'll work on it on the plane. Sheesh." Even her harried complaints sounded cheerful.

"Great, Sam. Don't file that report. Lose it for now. Misfile it. Something."

"Right-o," she said. "Consider it lost."

Gene smiled at Jerri.

* * *

February 2nd, 3:29 AM EST; Summer home of Dr. Abraham Lefkowitz; Martha's Vineyard, Massachusetts.

Dr. Lefkowitz told his secretary that he was going to his summer cottage for a little winter solitude. Gene thought it was the perfect place to entrap a killer, an eighteenth-century cottage just west of the tiny town of Aquinnah on the southwestern tip of the island of Martha's Vineyard. A popular vote in 1997, just 39 to 36, changed the town's name to Aquinnah, a Wampanoag word for "land under the hill," from the original name "Gay Head." Marty had had a field day with that name, highlighting why the residents decided to change it in the first place.

The island was accessible only by aircraft and boat, and Aquinnah was more remote even than that. The only road leading to the town passed between Menemsha and Squibnocket Ponds, and it was washed out due to recent storms.

Fewer than four hundred people lived in the town, a full third of them Wampanoag. Everyone knew everyone, and everyone knew and liked the good doctor Abraham Lefkowitz. Gene introduced his team to the townspeople and asked them to report the presence of any strangers immediately. If asked, they were to say that the doctor was at his cottage, then call a toll-free number that patched through to Sam Greene.

The Gay Head Cliffs were on the west side of town near the lighthouse visible from Lefkowitz' cottage. The cottage sat at the top of the cliffs, a three-story edifice designed for the large families of yesteryear. It had a widow's walk on top from which Jerri and Doug took turns keeping watch over the water, and it also had a finished basement with an access door leading down a winding trail to the beach below. Motion-sensing cameras covered the trail. A location so remote was easy for a small team of agents to watch and presented itself as the perfect place to make a discreet kill.

Beautiful during the summer, at three in the morning on Groundhog's Day, Martha's Vineyard was a miserable place to be. It was twenty-four degrees, blustery, and frosty ice from the ocean spray crusted everything. Snow covered the ground, and a stinging salt wind blew in from the east. This was the second night of the stakeout, and the team couldn't wait for either something or nothing to happen so they could all go home.

Gene shivered in his parka. He'd been sitting in the lighthouse for four hours, alternately playing solitaire and looking around with high-powered, night-vision binoculars. Paul Renner sat next to him, reading an ancient issue of *Field and Stream*. Carl Brent slept on a cot in the next room.

Gene idly scanned the beach through his binoculars when his ear bead crackled to life. Jerri's voice was low and tense. "I have contact on the water. Three small lights, inbound from the southwest. ETA six minutes."

Sam replied over the COM, "Sighting confirmed. Performing image enhancement." The teams' binoculars were rigged with a video feed that relayed right into Sam's information-filled cocoon five hundred miles away. Paul stood, but came up short when Gene snapped out, "Wait!" He swung the binoculars out into the ocean and scanned the water. Three white-green pinpricks in the darkness of the ocean approached at a steady rate of speed.

"I see them. Be advised, Renner and I are en route to the house. Carl will maintain watch here. Everyone, get ready for contact. Assume suspects are armed and dangerous. Use your judgment here, people; we weren't expecting three boatloads of perps." He headed for the exit.

Carl stood at the door, yawning. As soon as Gene noticed him, Carl headed over to the .50 caliber sniper rifle swivel-mounted to the wall. He kneeled down, grabbed the stock with his better arm, and swiveled the scope back and forth, looking for the incoming boats. Gene ran down the stairs, a step behind Paul.

Gene got into the Hummer H2 that served as his command vehicle and gunned the engine while Paul clambered into the passenger's side. The roar was nearly inaudible over the surf, and he left the lights off. The run to the cottage crossed flat ground, and the area had been cleared of hazards the previous day. It would take two minutes to get there, which left them another two to prepare for the incoming hostiles.

Paul grinned at Gene. "I hope those boats don't hold a lot of people, or we're going to get slaughtered." He chuckled as Gene gunned the gas.

"Not funny, Paul. We were expecting two or three killers, not a football team."

"So what are the rules of engagement?" Paul asked.

Gene sighed, frustrated. The plan had always been to capture the killers and interrogate them. Eight or more well-armed mercenaries coming at them complicated matters. The last thing they needed was a running gun battle. As if reading his mind, a drowsy-sounding Marty spoke into the COM, his voice an awful impersonation of an old-West cowboy, "We lookin' at a shootout at the Gay Head Corral, pardners?"

Gene scowled. "Maintain radio discipline." He then followed up with a question. "Sam?"

"Hard to pick out anything," she said. "It looks like you've got three boats, the Navy SEAL-style fast inflatable ones, three or four hostiles per boat. I don't see any large guns or anything, and resolution isn't good enough to pick out sidearms, but there are at least two assault rifles in the group. I think they're wearing night-vision goggles."

This was his worst nightmare. Gene stopped the Hummer behind the house. He grabbed the megaphone from the dash and jumped out, then headed inside with Paul on his heels. "You stay right there on that couch and don't even twitch." Gene feared that Marty might try a friendly fire incident with Renner and was equally afraid that Marty might not survive the experience if he tried it. He found the solution to his dilemma next to the couch in the form of an ornate wrought iron end table.

He pulled out a pair of the over-sized zip ties that many law enforcement agencies use for handcuffs and looked at Paul. "Grab the leg of that table." With two tight loops he secured Paul to the bulky, fifty-pound weight. Paul lay face-down on the couch and began whistling a tuneless melody. *It's not perfect, but it should keep him from sneaking around.* That done, he turned toward the door.

"Everyone check in. Watch your targets," Gene said. They all knew the drill, so no one spoke over anyone else.

"Brent, lighthouse."

"Goldman, cliff path."

"Bates, third floor."

"Palomini, first floor."

"Renner, couch." The irony in Paul's voice carried over the COM. Gene ignored him and moved to the porch.

Sam spoke. "ETA one minute forty."

Gene surveyed the beach. "We're in it deep, people. Verify that they're hostiles, then neutralize them. Keep them alive if at all possible. Carl and Marty, on my mark you take out their boats, then Carl, you hit the beach with the spotlight. Jerri, you keep on them so Sam can feed us information. Doug, fall back to the top of the path and get a field of fire on the beach. We'll force surrender as they stumble to shore. Go!" Simple, tactical, and hopefully hard to screw up. It might keep anyone from getting killed. He could see the lights approaching the beach.

Off to his right, Marty lay in the snow, using the edge of the cliff as a defilade. He had a sniper rifle trained at the beach and an H&K MP5 lying next to him. Gene ran forward several steps, then dropped to his belly. "If they fire, return for effect, but we don't want a bloodbath here. If we can show them they're trapped, they'll give up."

"Twenty seconds," Sam said.

Gene replied back, "Carl, Marty, do it."

Over the COM, Sam reported agents under fire on Martha's Vineyard, requesting immediate support.

The muzzle flash from Marty's shot left afterimages in Gene's vision, and the report was the loudest sound outside of a jet engine that he had ever heard. Carl's shot popped one raft. Gene saw dark forms dumped into the icy water as the deflated rubber tangled their legs. Marty's shot demolished the motor of the second raft. More dim shapes dove for cover into the water. One man wailed; a wet, gurgling cry of desperation. Marty rolled to the right, denying the men below an easy target and lining up for his next shot.

The third boat sped for shore, the men aboard opening fire as they made landfall. Gene rolled hard to his left, flinching as bullets thumped into the ground near his position. He heard the staccato beat of Doug's H&K from the cliff path and the throatier return chatter of AKs from the beach.

Marty's second shot burst the last raft, even as the beach lit up like a midsummer day. Carl had redirected the lighthouse beacon onto the shore. The men below covered their eyes as their night vision goggles were overloaded by the harsh glare. Gene crept forward for a better look.

Four men had made the sand, one face-down, the other three firing blindly toward the cliff face and the lighthouse. Another seven were still in the water, taking cover amidst the craggy rocks and tearing off their goggles. One, tangled in the rubber of his boat, screamed and clutched his face.

Gene yelled through the megaphone, straining to be heard over the pounding waves and weapons-fire. "FBI! Drop your weapons! You're surrounded and caught in a crossfire!" If the men below heard, they made no indication of it. He screamed again. "FBI! DROP YOUR WEAPONS!"

A burst of automatic fire replied. A stream of bullets sliced into the upper cliff face and whizzed over his head. A window shattered in the house behind them as Gene scrambled backward. Doug responded with several tight bursts from his automatic. A man sprawled into the surf as Doug sprayed the rocks in the water with suppressing fire.

One man dropped screaming into the water as another shot from Marty's .50 caliber shattered his leg. Marty rolled to his left and reloaded in a single fluid movement, then scrambled to find another firing position. Another burst of automatic fire, and the beach went dark. Carl swore over the COM as bullets sparked off the top of the lighthouse.

Trying to adjust his eyes to the darkness, Gene looked out over the cliff face. Another dark figure knelt in the water, barely visible in the moonlight. The silhouette took shelter behind a rock and leveled what looked like a huge straw onto his shoulder. Doug's voice cried out over the COM. "RPG! RPG!" Machine gun chatter opened up from Doug's position, and sparks rang off the rock. The man ducked into cover until Doug had to reload.

The figure on the beach re-positioned the tube. His head burst like a melon hit with a sledgehammer. Carl's whoop of excitement came over the COM a split second before the rifle report hit Gene's ears. As the headless man crumpled, the RPG fired into the air, leaving a trail of smoke in its wake. It crashed back down into the water a few seconds later. The explosion ignited the gasoline from the ruptured motor.

As fire rippled across the water, men panicked. Most dove under the water to escape the spreading flame. The man clutching his face didn't. He flailed as the flames reached him. The grenades on his bandolier detonated. Shrapnel killed two men who had survived the gasoline fire and shredded the legs and back of a man on the beach. The others threw down their weapons and put their hands in the air. Gene tried again.

"FBI! STAND DOWN AND PUT YOUR HANDS ON YOUR HEADS!" The men on land dropped to their knees and folded their hands on their heads. In the water, men struggled to avoid the double danger of sharp rocks and burning gasoline. Marty lay in the snow and stared down the rifle scope. He swept it back and forth across the beach, searching for active hostiles.

Gasping for breath, his heart racing, Gene took stock. "Status," he said over the COM. The replies were immediate, breathless.

"Brent. I'm okay."

"Goldman, five by five."

"Bates, okay."

"Palomini, okey-dokey."

"Renner, still on the couch."

"All right," Gene said, "let's go get them. Marty, Doug, secure the suspects and check the injured. Carl and I will cover you. Jerri, you've got Renner duty. Be careful, everybody."

Nobody said anything as the team got moving. After a few seconds, Marty spoke.

"Fuckin' A, Gene."

"Yeah," Gene replied.

Chapter 20

February 2nd, 3:54 AM EST; Summer home of Dr. Abraham Lefkowitz; Martha's Vineyard, Massachusetts.

Twenty minutes later the scene flickered with red and blue lights, the product of one police car, one fire truck, and two ambulances, the entire emergency response force of the town of Aquinnah. A coroner had been called for the four dead and would arrive shortly from Boston.

Both of the injured men were in critical condition, one with a thigh that had been obliterated by Marty's .50 cal, and the other with shrapnel embedded in his back and legs. Four had extreme hypothermia, despite their wet-suits. Soon they would all be evacuated to Boston via ambulance boats due to arrive at any time at the main dock in Aquinnah.

The men wore government-issue, SWAT-style personal body armor, ski masks, gloves, and night-vision goggles. Gene's team recovered nine AK-47s, six pistols of Eastern European make, two bandoliers of grenades, and one tube RPG launcher. The weapons charges alone were enough to put these men away forever. None had identification, so the living and deceased alike had their fingertips scanned into Gene's PDA and uploaded to Sam.

They had laid the bodies out on the beach above the tide line. The ruined rafts were still tangled in the rocks. The survivors sat at the top of the cliff, wrapped in blankets taken from the house to protect them from the frigid wind. Carl stood watch over the prisoners. Gene, Marty, and Doug stood off to the side, their voices low but hostile.

Paul sat on the couch with his eyes closed, Jerri standing behind him on guard duty. The COM ear-bead he had been issued by Sam Greene was silent. It was also in his pocket. The one he had found near Gene Palomini's unconscious body almost a month before was in his ear. The encryption needed to break the lock on the COM had been pretty complex, but no encryption is unbreakable for someone with the right connections.

Marty's voice was pissed-off, as usual. "We can just fucking grab him, Gene. He's got nothing more to offer us. Nothing. Put him in a fucking box and deal with him later."

"Now's the time, boss," Doug said. "We won't get a better chance. He's got to know he's about out of usefulness."

"I gave him my word, Doug," Gene said.

"Yeah, but you never intended to keep it," Marty said.

"Right," said Gene, "but as long as he doesn't know that, as long as he thinks we can lead him to whoever sent an assassin after him, he'll stick close by. It'll be a lot safer to grab him once we're back at HQ."

"Goddamn it, boss, you're a fucking idiot sometimes," Marty said. "What's the difference between now and then, besides a little time?"

Gene looked his brother in the eyes. "I'd rather take him down in a secure facility, with no civilians around, surrounded by half the Bureau."

"Gene—" Marty said.

Gene held up his hand. "Just wait a minute, Marty." Marty rolled his eyes as Gene pulled Doug off to the side and muted his COM.

Gene leaned in close and kept his voice low. "Look, we're waiting to take him down because I'm protecting Marty, not Paul. He doesn't understand just how dangerous Paul Renner is." Doug raised an eyebrow. "He doesn't. He thinks he can just strong-arm him into submission like a common perp, and it's going to get him hurt. Just side with me on this, will you? It's just a few more hours."

Doug looked over at Marty, clenching and unclenching his gloved fists and swearing under his breath. "All right. I got it."

"Good," Gene said. They walked back over to Marty.

Marty took one look at Doug and snarled. "You're not siding with Gene, are you?"

Doug put his hand on Marty's shoulder. "Yes, I am."

Marty rolled his eyes. "You know what? Fine. But as soon as we're back at Hoover—"

"Yes," Gene said. "As soon as we're back at Hoover, Marty."

"Agent Palomini!" Gene turned around at the voice. The local Sheriff, Josephson, approached at a trot. "Hey! We need to get all these weapons secured. You can't just leave this stuff lying around my beach!"

Gene held up a hand to delay the sheriff and turned to his brother. "Look, we'll talk about this in a few minutes. Just keep your head." He turned back to Josephson, who glared daggers at Gene's upraised hand. "Forensics is en route via chopper. They're going to be here in fifteen minutes. Until they come, nobody touches anything."

Gene, Doug, and Sheriff Josephson walked away toward the beach, leaving Marty glaring at his brother's back.

Marty stepped into the empty living room. He saw no sign of Jerri or Renner. The bathroom door was closed, and he heard water running.

He drew his sidearm and tapped his COM. "Jerri, where are you?"

Marty stepped past the couch to the bathroom door. "Doug, can you get in here?"

"Let me finish this up. I'll be right there," Doug said.

Marty opened his mouth to reply. His breath left him as a knife punched straight through his Kevlar vest and into his back. It hurt, but not as much as it should have. *Oh fuck. I'm already in shock*. His knees buckled, and Renner held him upright against the door. Paul leaned close and plucked the COM bead from his ear, then spoke softly, intimately. "Didn't want to wait until Hoover, eh?" The knife came out with a gush of hot blood. "That was a lung." The knife went in again, lower, and twisted. Marty's legs turned to ice. "That was a kidney." Marty coughed, and blood flecked the white door. He tried to turn, but his body wouldn't respond.

"You think you're such hot shit, Marty? You think you're better than me? You fucking Feds are all alike. Holier than thou, sycophantic little fucks. You're just a bunch of killers. *Underpaid* killers." Marty gasped as the knife went in a third time. This one hurt like hell. "Liver, Marty. Time to quit drinking."

"Here." Paul's bloody hand came around Marty's side and grabbed the doorknob. "I left you a present." He turned the knob. The door opened and Marty fell through. He clumsily broke his fall and landed face-first on the floor. "You should have told her, Marty. Life is too short."

Jerri sat on the toilet, fully clothed, and stared at the ceiling with unblinking eyes. Her throat was an angry yellow bruise, already turning purple. Paul stepped over Marty's fallen body and wiped his hands on Jerri's shirt, then took her sidearm from her holster. Marty lay on the floor, trying to scream, trying to do anything, as the killer disappeared behind him.

Dressed in a heavy winter coat stolen out of the closet, Paul Renner climbed into the back of the ambulance. Two suspects, both critically injured, lay unconscious on their gurneys. A third, shivering despite a heavy blanket, was handcuffed to the door. The EMT changing an IV on the man with the shattered leg looked startled by Paul's sudden appearance.

"Okay, let's go," Paul said, flashing Jerri's badge in the darkness.

"You're coming with us, Agent?"

"Bates. Special Agent Bates. And yes, I'm coming with you. Let's get these three to the boats, pronto."

The driver nodded in the rear-view mirror and, triggering the lights but no siren, headed off toward Aquinnah and the docks that would take the wounded into Boston.

Sherriff Josephson droned on in his ear, and a flash of red lights caught Gene's eye as the first of the ambulances pulled out. *Good*, he thought. He spoke into the COM.

"Marty, which prisoners just left on those ambulances?" Josephson grunted in annoyance, and Gene realized he'd just interrupted him in mid-sentence. He held up a hand for patience.

"Marty, come in please?"

Nothing.

"Hey, Sam, can you check COM status, please?"

"Sure, Gene," Sam said. "Checking your signal." There was a brief pause. "Relays are still working fine, or they seem to be from this end. Carl, can you verify?"

"It'll take me a few minutes," Carl said. "Relay's back at the lighthouse."

"Where are you now, Carl?" Gene asked.

"I'm in the Hummer. I can do diagnostics on the way over."

"Hold on a second," Gene said. "Team, check in," he said.

"Brent here."

"Goldman."

Silence.

"Doug, meet Carl at the Hummer," he said. "Marty's supposed to be with the ambulance crew. Jerri's inside with Paul. Find them, now, and go together." He ran toward the house, leaving Josephson, mouth open, standing on the beach.

Marty took three pints of blood before the helicopter arrived and airlifted him to Massachusetts General Hospital in Boston. Jerri Bates's windpipe had been crushed. Forensics would tell them the murder weapon later, but Gene already knew. Paul Renner had killed her with his bare hands.

They found the ambulance at the Aquinnah docks. The critically injured men were still inside, unconscious. The EMT and driver were both dead, shot at close range with Jerri's sidearm, which Renner had left at the scene. They found no sign of Paul

Renner or the uninjured mercenary. Gene put out an APB on the missing speedboat, and Massachusetts State Police found it forty minutes later at a small private dock in Boston Sound.

Chapter 21

February 2nd, 8:27 AM EST; J. Edgar Hoover Building, Gene Palomini's Office; Washington D.C.

Doug and Carl made the trip back to Washington in silence. Sam let them. Marty was in ICU, and Gene had stayed with him, almost unresponsive. That left only the two of them and Sam in their heads when they needed her. Missing Jerri's talents already, Sam had brought in an outside team to conduct the interrogation, leaving Doug and Carl with little to do but wait for results.

Sam, unflappable despite her grief, continued to trace down leads on Renner's whereabouts. Acting on the assumption that Renner still hunted the man who had hired Lefkowitz, she focused on the killers from Martha's Vineyard and brought the full might of the Patriot Act to bear.

Airport security cameras had captured the commandos coming off a commercial jet. They picked up another two on Amtrak camera tapes. The plane tickets were purchased by an offshore dummy corporation, the train tickets from a numbered account in the Caymans. Sam started in on the grueling process of following the money trail in the hope of finding Paul Renner's next target.

* * *

February 2nd, 3:13 PM PST; Home of Geoffrey MacUther; San

Francisco, California.

Geoffrey MacUther was a large, grizzled man with a gray beard and a shaved head. Fifty-six years old, he was in better shape than most twenty-five-year-old athletes. Former Secret Air Service for Her Majesty the Queen, he was highly trained in stealth, surveillance, martial arts, modern weapons, and linguistics. A veteran of the first Gulf War and peacekeeping operations in Serbia, he was intelligent, charismatic, and had retired a highly decorated officer. He was also somewhat paranoid, but not without reason.

Geoffrey MacUther was proud to be known in the right circles for providing the best private security forces that money could buy. Private security forces weren't bodyguards or sentries. They were mercenaries, private armies hired out to the highest bidder.

He lived just north of Daly City, an affluent suburb south of San Francisco, where property values kept most of the riff-raff away. San Francisco wasn't far from Silicon Valley, and he managed much of his small empire from an office he had there. He bought goods coming up from L.A. and across the Pacific Ocean into the Port of San Francisco. He trained his men in the rugged Rockies, in the deserts of Nevada and Utah, and in boarding actions out at sea, all no more than a helicopter ride away.

For the past two years, he'd managed his business and laundered his money through a local startup called SoFiaK, named for his daughter, Sophia Karen MacUther, now Sophia Karen Brown and a proud mother of one. The brilliant thing about startups is that nobody really knew what they did, and everyone assumed that you couldn't talk about it for fear of competitors stealing your ideas. SoFiaK vans came and went from his home and his work at all times of the day or night, and people never got suspicious.

Running such an outfit required a great deal of equipment that the United States Government frowned upon, and so by necessity he had acquired a wide variety of black-market contacts. Most were basically good people who weren't interested in law and order, but some were complete scumbags, common criminals with no sense of honor or integrity. Sometimes, these common criminals would try to blackmail or rob him. Sometimes they would rat him out, and the police would come sniffing around. Once in a while, they even tried to kill him.

This made Geoffrey MacUther suspicious of last-minute meetings, even when set up by reliable contacts in the United States military. It was with this in mind that he stared out his front window. The Lexus pulling into the driveway had a single passenger, as per the arrangement made early that morning. House security frisked the man when he exited the newly rented car, just as the car had been searched when it reached the main gate. The man approached the front stoop, flanked by a pair of guards.

He was average height, average build, with black hair and blue eyes. MacUther opened the door. "You're Paul Renner?" The man nodded and stepped inside.

MacUther poured himself a cup of coffee. "Want some?"

"No, thanks," Paul said, admiring the decor. *Classic California asshole.* "I don't plan on being here that long."

"All right, Mr. Renner," MacUther said as he flipped a switch on the wall. Paul raised his eyebrows in question.

"Broad-band electromagnetic noise generator. No unshielded recording device, listening device, and so forth will work until I turn it off. No TV or radio, either. I've got random tumblers in the walls to fool laser microphones, too." He sat on the couch in the living room, and motioned for Paul to take the love seat. Two guards lurked in the doorway behind MacUther, hands inside their jackets with no pretense at subtlety. The tall guard stood behind the short one, so that they both had good fields of fire.

Suckers, Paul thought.

"I'm a very busy man, but you have some dreadfully important friends. So what do you want?"

"Well," Paul said, "it's sort of about the team you sent to Martha's Vineyard to assassinate Doctor Lefkowitz." In his peripheral vision, Paul watched as the short guard's eyes fluttered closed, then snapped back to the conversation. He suppressed a grin.

MacUther raised an eyebrow. "How exactly does this concern you?"

"Well, the concern is two-fold. First off, the whole thing was a setup to get to you, which worked. Second off, I'm pretty sure you sent a goon to kill me some time ago, and I want to know who hired you to do it."

MacUther cleared his throat, then took a sip of his coffee. "Did any of my team escape?"

Paul shrugged. "I don't think so."

"That's a shame. I feared that was the case when no one checked in. They were good men, Mr. Renner." Behind MacUther, the tall guard yawned. The short one closed his eyes.

"Good men?" Paul scoffed. "They were ambushed and slaughtered before they even knew they were in trouble. Who paid them to kill Lefkowitz?"

"I did," MacUther said.

"And why would you want the doctor killed, Mr. MacUther?"

"I wouldn't. That is to say, I don't care one way or another, aside from a contract. They were just men doing a job."

"I see. Operating under the assumption that the same person paid you to kill me, who paid you for the Lefkowitz job?"

The big Scot shook his head. "You know I can't tell you that."

Paul sighed. "I might have to kill you if you don't." Without looking, MacUther gestured to the guards behind him. They were fast asleep on their feet. "So be it," MacUther said. "I'm not one for breaking contracts. Nobody'd trust me after that, and then where would I be?"

Paul chuckled. "Living in a foreign country on the giant piles of money you've already made?"

"But I like my work. So no, I'm not going to tell you that. Is there anything else before I have my men throw you out?"

Paul smiled. "I don't think your men are able to do any such thing."

MacUther looked back at the men behind him. One tottered, his head lolling, as the other slowly slid down the wall. He turned back to Paul, who aimed a tiny pistol at his chest. MacUther remained cool and collected. "What did you do to my men, Mr. Renner?"

"Just a little contact poison when they frisked me. Nothing they won't sleep off."

"So you're here to kill me, Mr. Renner?"

Paul rolled his eyes. "No, you weren't listening. I'm here to find out who hired *you* to kill *me*. Whether or not you die is entirely up to you. Personally, I'd rather avoid it."

MacUther sat back and folded his arms. "I'm sorry, but I'm still not going to tell you. You have nothing to hold over me but my life, and if I talk to you about contracts, someone else will kill me. We're at an impasse, Mr. Renner."

Paul smiled. "No, we're not."

MacUther raised an eyebrow. "No?"

"No, sir. I know that there's something you value, and I know where she is. Your granddaughter's a cutie, just like her mom."

"Mr. Renner, you're treading on dangerous ground. Even so, I think we can be reasonable."

"Excellent," Paul said, even as MacUther's knife cleared its sheath. MacUther was fast for his size, but Paul pulled the trigger before the knife left his hand. The .38 round hit MacUther in the stomach. Paul knew it wouldn't hurt more than a hard punch, not at first anyway, but it threw off the big man's aim. He charged off the couch, and Paul shot him four more times, center of mass.

The impact barreled Paul right off the loveseat, and the two men crashed to the floor. Paul's chest compressed, forcing the air out his lungs, and they both lay still for a moment. Paul's ribs burned.

Paul punched MacUther in the stomach, twice. He grunted, but didn't otherwise respond. Paul rolled the large man off him and struggled to draw breath. He coughed and gagged his way to his feet, then examined the body on the floor.

MacUther was breathing, but wouldn't be for long. All five shots had hit him in the abdomen and chest. It looked like two had scattered off his ribs, but the other three had punched through. A .38 won't kill much of anything right away, but he'd hit something important, and MacUther was in shock. His breath came in a mess of gurgling wheezes, and he had blood on his lips. *Shit*, Paul thought.

Paul knelt and patted the dying man's pockets. He found a variety of objects that he pulled out to inspect. One was a remote alarm, the red LED blinking. *Who wants to bet that it works through the electric jammer?* Paul dropped MacUther's keys on the floor and turned his attention to the cellular phone. Paul turned off the jammer, then flipped open the phone and scanned through the caller ID.

Two calls stood out. One was from Gabrielle's Fine Jewelry, in the San Francisco area code, at 2:28 PM on January 30th. Another was to the same place, at 1:17 AM on February 2nd. *A few hours after the bait was set, and less than an hour after they sprang the trap. I don't know what kind of jewelry store takes calls at one in the morning.* He cleared the memory on the phone and put it back in MacUther's pocket. He picked up the house phone from its cradle, dialed 911, and dropped it on the floor.

Bending down, he flipped MacUther onto his stomach. He spoke in a low voice as he picked up the pistol. "That should help your lungs drain until help arrives. Sorry." *Speaking of help....* Paul heard gravel crunch in the driveway.

A peek out the front window revealed a white panel van next to his rented Lexus, *SoFiaK* emblazoned in bold red letters on the side. *Great*, thought Paul. He backed away from the door and stumbled up the stairs. Every step jarred his injured ribs. At the top he took a quick look outside, then popped open the window.

He swung out and grabbed the balcony railing. He tried to lower himself, but a chest spasm betrayed him. He dropped twelve feet to the ground, knees bent to absorb as much of the impact as possible. He stumbled to the wall and leaned against it, gasping.

He crept over to the dividing wall and clambered over the fence into the neighbor's yard. Within two minutes he was driving away, home-free.

* * *

February 2nd, 6:21 PM EST; Home of Emile Frank; Springfield, Virginia.

Doctor Emile Frank, his wife Nancy, and their four-year-old son Scott sat inside a 7,800-square-foot gated mansion, eating a delicious dinner of apple-glazed pork chops, Caesar salad, and fresh apple chutney. They chewed in silence while their son prattled on about preschool.

Emile's phone buzzed in his pocket, and his face flushed. This particular phone blocked all incoming calls except for a select few, and it had never rung before. He set down his silverware and wiped his hands on the napkin in his lap, then pulled out the phone. The caller ID said *Dino's BBQ Ribs*.

He stood, and placed his napkin beside his plate. "What is it, honey?" Nancy asked. She frowned at the phone. He knew she'd never quite come to fully trust him after his affair three years prior.

"Nothing," he replied. "Just work. Excuse me, I have to take this."

She pouted. "Honey, I thought we agreed no phone calls during dinner. This is *family* time."

He waved her off, flipped open the phone, and walked out of the room. Being in the dog house was the least of his worries. Behind him his son copied his mother's tone perfectly. "It's family time, Daddy!" Emile smiled at Scott's impersonation and put the phone to his ear. He kept walking and spoke quietly.

"This is Shelley."

The voice on the other end tried and failed to sound like a stereotypical Jersey goombah. "Hey, ah, this is Dino's calling. You got an order of steaks with us?"

"Yeah." He walked into the study and shut the door, then turned on the radio. He'd swept the room for bugs yesterday, but one couldn't be too careful.

"Um, well, they ain't coming in. Looks like trouble at the slaughterhouse. Union issues of some kind, you know?"

His heart raced. "What kind of trouble?"

"Can't say specifically. You'll have to call the foreman."

"I'll do that."

Emile Frank hung up the cell phone and put it in his pocket. He picked up the desk-phone receiver and dialed a string of numbers, activating the day's cipher. He heard a series of clicks as the encryption algorithm kicked in, then a dial tone. He dialed another number.

"How bad is it?" he asked.

"Geoff's down, shot several times, unknown assailant. We're en route to the hospital."

"Can he talk?"

"A little. Looks like a collapsed lung, but we're getting him stabilized, and he'll probably pull through."

"Great." *I don't give a fuck about his health, you moron.* "Who shot him?"

"Caucasian male, thirties, gave the name Paul Renner. Was asking about the Martha's Vineyard job."

"Did he learn anything?"

The ensuing pause was far too long for comfort. "He's not sure. He knows the guy got a look at his cell phone. Called 911 after he shot him."

"Anything in the cell?"

"We're not sure. The caller ID was wiped, but Geoff isn't sure if he'd done it himself or if the guy did it."

"Can you find the assailant?" Frank asked.

"Not sure. We got a picture from the security feed out front of MacUther's place."

"Send it to me, and stand by."

"You got it."

"Watch his hospital room. Let me know if anyone comes to see him."

He hung up the phone, picked it back up, and called yet another number, this one local.

A feminine voice answered, smothered in Southern twang. "Department of Homeland Security, Bioterrorism. How may I direct your call?"

He didn't bother to give his name. "Jeannie, put me through to my office, now."

"Yes, sir!"

Chapter 22

February 2nd, 4:23 PM PST; Highway 280, northbound; San Bruno, California.

Three thousand miles away, Gene, Doug, and Carl screamed north up Interstate 280, lights flashing and siren blaring as they blew past the traffic.

The GPS was leading them to the Daly City home of Geoffrey MacUther, just south of San Francisco. The money trail was circumstantial, but the forensic accounting team had led them to a California-based startup called SoFiaK. They'd all slept on the plane, and they looked it. The car reeked of body odor.

Sam's voice erupted from both the speakerphone and his COM ear-bead with an odd reverberation effect. "I have a Geoffrey MacUther, admitted a half hour ago under John Doe to the emergency room at Kaiser Permanente, 395 Hickey Boulevard, Daly City, with multiple gunshot wounds. They ran his prints on DigiLink, and the database flagged it for me." Doug slammed on the brakes. Onlookers gaped as the unmarked SUV skidded to a stop in the middle of the fast lane.

"How do we get there, Sam?" Carl looked down at the GPS and started punching in *Hospital*. He didn't have a clue how to spell "Kaiser Permanente."

"Hold on, I'm routing it to your GPS now."

Directions for MacUther's house disappeared. Directions for the hospital appeared. Doug hit the gas.

Ten minutes later Gene stalked through the Emergency Department entrance and up to the triage desk, flanked by Doug and Carl. It looked like the Boston hospital where Marty was recovering, only five times smaller and ten times cleaner.

Gene flashed his badge at the receptionist. Doug and Carl wore theirs. Other than the official identification, they looked and smelled like homeless men in wrinkled suits. "Gene Palomini, FBI. What room is the gunshot John Doe in?" Doug and Carl barged past her and started looking in windows.

"You gentlemen got here fast." The woman looked at the badge with mild suspicion and pecked at her keyboard. "One moment." She typed a little more. "4A, down on the right."

Carl hollered, "Got it!"

As they walked down the hall the nurse called to them, "He's scheduled for surgery in ten minutes!"

They ignored her and walked in together.

Uniformed policemen stood on either side of the bed. Their eyes widened as they saw the FBI badges. "Both of you, out." Gene was in no mood to argue.

"Sorry, Agent...." The younger-looking cop leaned forward to read the name off his badge. "Palomini, but we've got orders to watch this man. Standard procedure for a gunshot victim."

Carl looked at the man's badge. "Bullshit, Officer Mulroney. If this were a black man from the projects, he'd be in here by himself while you were out eating doughnuts and flirting with the receptionist. What you meant to say was that this is standard procedure for a rich white gunshot victim."

Officer Mulroney stuttered, "Well, I, uh—"

Gene repeated himself. "Out. Give us five minutes."

The men stood at attention. "We're sorry, but we have our orders."

Gene looked at Doug and Carl. "Arrest these men and place them in federal custody."

The officers looked at one another and reluctantly shuffled

out of the room.

Doug chuckled as he closed the door, but it held no joy. "That was diplomatic."

"Don't care," Gene said.

He leaned over the patient. MacUther's face was gray, his eyes sunken. Heavy bandages covered his chest. *He looks like I feel*, Gene thought without humor.

Gene pulled a printed photograph of Paul Renner from his pocket and unfolded it. He held it up in front of MacUther's face and patted his cheek to wake him. "Hey. Geoffrey MacUther." The man's eyes flickered open. He pushed the picture forward. "Is this the man who shot you?"

"Yes," MacUther said. "Said he'd...hurt Jordan. Couldn't...."

Gene interrupted. "Where did he go, Mr. MacUther?"

"Son of a bitch. Looking for someone...who hired me. Didn't get it, but I think he...." A spasm wracked his body, then settled. "He got a lead. I tell you...you get the bastard? Threatened my daughter...granddaughter...."

"We'll get him, Mr. MacUther. Just tell us what we need to know."

"Don't have much. Calls himself Shelley. All I have is a...phone number. The same one...." He leaned forward in a coughing fit, splattering the sheets with a faint spray of blood. Doug looked at his vitals and gave Gene a thumbs-up.

"The same one what?" Gene prompted.

"The same one...calls a front. Gabrielle's.... A jewelry shop...downtown San Francisco...to contract jobs."

Meanwhile, outside the room, "Officer Mulroney" made a telephone call.

"We've got a problem. Some FBI guys are talking to him now. An Agent Palomini and two other guys." He braced for the anticipated explosion.

Shelley's voice was shockingly calm. "Did they make you?"

"No," he replied. "If they check our badge numbers they'll hold up. They threatened to take us into custody, though."

"Do you have their names?" Shelley asked.

"Just the one."

"What was it again?"

"Palomini. Papa Alpha Lima Oscar Mike India November India."

"I'll take care of it. Inform me immediately if anyone else visits MacUther." Shelley hung up.

* * *

February 2nd, 5:08 PM PST; Gabrielle's Fine Jewelry; San Francisco, California.

Less than an hour later, the floor lights turned off at Gabrielle's Fine Jewelry. Paul Renner came out the front door while jotting a phone number into a notepad that he had purchased from the Walgreen's down the block. He verified that the sign on the door was flipped to *Closed*, fiddled with the keys until he found the right one, and locked the door.

That done, he pointed the automatic unlock at the row of cars across the street and pushed the button. A 2006 BMW sedan blipped and unlocked its doors. *Perfect*, Paul thought. *It always pays to kill people with good taste.*

He got in the car and admired the leather and wood interior. *Exquisite taste.* He put the key into the ignition and turned it. The car started with a throaty, masculine rumble. He eased it out of the tight parking spot and turned left toward Embarcadero Drive. He was only a few short minutes from San Francisco International Airport. He looked at his watch. *Or eight years in rush hour traffic.*

He stopped at a pier to get a snack and relax during rush hour. It was nice to be able to eat local food, and nothing beat a Pacific crab cake fresh off the pier. Paul took out his phone to book a flight to Dulles International Airport. *Nah, too predictable.* He booked a flight to Newark. He'd rent a car and drive to D.C.

Once there, he'd arrange an unfriendly in-home meeting with a Doctor Emile Frank of the Department of Homeland Security, where they'd have a little chat. Paul smiled. For the first time in days, things were looking up.

Chapter 23

February 2nd, 6:20 PM PST; Highway 280, northbound; San Francisco, California.

By twenty after six, Gene wanted to kill whoever was responsible for rush-hour traffic in the Bay Area. It had taken them almost an hour to travel at most a half mile up Highway 280. At this rate it would take another six hours to get to Gabrielle's Fine Jewelry. Their flight left in four hours, and they weren't going to make it.

"Hey, Sam?" Gene asked the air.

"I'm not done yet, Gene. This is going to take a while." An hour earlier Sam had started crunching the data on Shelley, trying to crack his identity.

"Not that, Sam. I know you'll send it when you're done."

"Sure will. What can I do for you, sweetie?" Her voice was saccharine, with an undertone of annoyance. She loved hacking and was obsessive once on a project. Like a pit bull on a leg, she had a hard time letting it go.

"Can you book us a later flight? There's no way we're going to make it to Gabrielle's and back to the airport."

"Sure," she said as if booking plane tickets was the best job in the entire world. "One new set of tickets, coming right up!"

Carl stared out the window at the never-ending trail of cars.

"We could walk faster than this, couldn't we?"

They'd made it another two car lengths when she came back with a reply. Carl was right. They *could* walk faster than this.

"Um, Gene, Homeland Security's grounded all flights out of the Greater Bay Area." Gene's head felt like it was going to explode. *As if catching Paul Renner wasn't enough to worry about.*

Carl piped up from the back seat, "Must be something big going on."

Doug was a little more useful. "Any idea what, Sam?" He turned on the radio and got an Emergency Broadcast System test. He changed the channel and got the same tone. Third channel, same thing. Gene slapped his hand away from the radio.

"Just leave it, Doug. They'll explain in a minute."

Sam replied, "Nothing's trickled through to the FBI yet."

After ten or so seconds the tone stopped.

"This is the Federal Emergency Broadcast System. This is not a test. This is not a test. The Homeland Threat Level is now Very High. A Homeland Security Emergency has been declared for the cities of San Francisco, Daly City, Pacifica, Millbrae, Colma, Burlingame, and San Mateo. If you are in your home or your place of work, do not leave. If you are within five miles of work or home, go there. If traveling by auto and not within five miles of work or home, pull to the side of the road and await further instructions. All military, hospital, and emergency personnel are to report to their stations immediately.

"This is the Federal Emergency Broadcast System. This is not a test. This is not a test." The message repeated. Numb, they listened to it a second time.

Carl leaned back in his seat. "Holy shit. They can't just lock down the entire peninsula."

Doug's face had turned a pale white. "Yeah, well, they just did."

Gene shook his head. "Well, forget that. We're the FBI, and we've got a killer to catch."

"Badges got to be good for something," Carl said.

Gene looked in the rear-view mirror. Ashen faces listened to radios in other cars. People yelled out their windows to other drivers, telling them to turn on their radios.

"Hey, Gene?" Sam's voice came from nowhere and everywhere at once.

"Yeah, Sam, go ahead."

"The FBI just got a national bulletin. You're not going to believe this shit. It says a radical group called the Aryan Ascendancy—never heard of them, but I'll bet they're a bunch of assholes—just smuggled a nuclear warhead into the country through San Francisco. They've put up a picture with the name Harold Trubb, and you're not going to believe who the prime suspect is."

Gene waited a moment and got no response.

"Goddamn it, Sam," Doug said. "Who the hell is it?"

"Renner."

Gene had to have misheard that. "Did you just say Paul Renner is threatening a nuclear attack on the Bay Area?"

"It's his picture, Gene, sure as I'm a fat broad. I'll download it to your PDA. Funny thing, though. Nothing we know about Renner ties him to neo-Nazis."

Carl muttered in the back seat, "Wouldn't surprise me." Gene's PDA blipped and a picture of Paul Renner appeared. It was fuzzy, as if taken from a security camera, but unmistakable.

Traffic had come to a standstill. Some cars pulled off the road. Most just sat there. Some people got out of their cars, earning honks, curses, and middle fingers from other drivers. The volume rose as shouts added to the horns.

Sam's whisper carried over the COM as clear as day. "*What the fuck?*"

"Yeah, go ahead, Sam, we heard that."

"Gene, something's desperately wrong here. I've got another picture here, an accomplice. Name's listed as Jim Palenti. I'm sending it to your PDA now." It blipped, and all three of them looked at it.

"Jesus, Gene, is that *you?*" Carl sounded as incredulous as Gene felt. The picture was from an FTA, field training exercise, almost eight years ago. Gene held a machine gun and wore forest-camo fatigues. With his shaved head, he really did look like a neo-

Nazi.

Gene stared at the picture, speechless. Doug replied instead, "Is this for real?"

Sam's tone was serious. "I wouldn't joke about something like this, guys. Not after Jerri and Marty." She cleared her throat. "Gene, what the hell is going on?"

Carl answered for him. "Renner was right. This goes pretty far up the chain of power. Shelley's worried we're going to find out who he is, and he's pulled out the big guns to stop us."

Doug chuckled darkly. "If I were him, I'd be a bit more worried about Renner."

Gene's grin held no humor at all. "Get out of the car. We've got to get out of the crowds before Homeland Security releases this picture to the public. Sam, keep working on Shelley, and get Adams to clear me. We'll make our way to Gabrielle's as best we can."

"Will do!" The order was like giving a kid candy. "Be careful, guys."

Carl replied for them, "We will."

They stepped out of the car into utter pandemonium.

Chapter 24

With two TVs and three computer monitors devoted to the situation in San Francisco and a message left on Adams' cell, Sam got back to work on Shelley's identity. All she had to go on was a cellular phone number, a fake name, and the fact that he worked for the federal government in Washington, D.C.

The average person would be terrified if he knew just what the government could find out about him, and writing code on the fly to mine data was Sam's bread and butter. She'd fueled up on jelly doughnuts and Mountain Dew from the mini-mart down the street, and was ready to work. She cracked her knuckles and set in for a marathon of data-crunching. *Here comes Big Brother, Shelley. Come out, come out, wherever you are!* For several hours Sam forgot about her teammates, San Francisco, nuclear warheads, and even food.

Using the Homeland Security database of cellular phone patterns, she traced the daily route of Shelley over the past eighteen months. Almost every weekday he started in Springfield, Virginia, moved to Washington, D.C. along the 395 artery, and went back home. That narrowed the suspect list down to eighty-or-so thousand people. His weekend patterns were all over the place, but nothing stuck out. The phone never left the greater Washington area.

She restricted the list to government employees and cut the original number by almost a third. She eliminated over twenty thousand more when she compared vacation records and sick time with the cellular tracking data, and even more than that when she added a cross-reference of the time clock databases of all government agencies. There were a lot of people who didn't actually punch a clock, so when she finished that, she still had more than eight thousand possible names.

She cut out the people on scheduled trips and conferences outside of Washington when the phone was on and in the D.C. area. That shortened the list by a few hundred people. Ninety percent in a few hours wasn't bad, but it wasn't good enough. She stared at the screen, unmoving. Her mind raced.

Sam chuckled at herself and eliminated the women. MacUther had told them Shelley was male and didn't use a voice scrambler. *That could have saved a lot of time.* Thirty-eight hundred people left. She sighed and looked at the clock. She'd been at it for five hours. *What else, what else?* She tapped her finger against her bottom lip. MacUther didn't mention anything about an accent, so she took a guess. She eliminated non-native citizens and late immigrants. Twenty-nine hundred people.

Who are you, Shelley? Come to Mama so she can spank your naughty little butt. She had a thought and smiled. *You can afford to hire mercenaries to kill people for you.* Her fingers flew across the keyboard, cutting everyone with a net worth of less than two hundred and fifty thousand dollars, barring primary residences. That was probably too low, but she needed to be somewhat conservative. He could be using government funds. Six hundred and twenty three people.

What else do I know that can narrow this down? In the next hour she wrote a program to track as close as possible the exact position of the cellular phone on an hour-by-hour basis. The granularity of the data was terrible. She only had what cell tower covered the phone at any given time, which gave her almost nothing at all. The one thing it did give her was the exact time the phone crossed from one cell area to the next.

She tapped her bottom lip. *Doesn't I-395 have HOT lanes?* High-Occupancy Toll lanes were special highway lanes for carpoolers, but also for people willing to spend extra money to drive faster from point A to point B. A wealthy government-type would almost definitely use them.

She looked up the locations of the HOT toll booths and overlapped them with cellular coverage maps. One HOT lane on 395 was within a quarter mile of a transition from one cell to the next. She cross-referenced the cellular travel patterns of the phone with government-owned EZ-Pass (HOT) toll card records, fed the new information into her program, and looked at the screen. A picture of a man in his late fifties or early sixties stared back at her.

There was only one wealthy, male, American-born or early immigrant government employee whose travel and work patterns exactly matched that of Shelley's cellular phone. Sam recognized Emile Frank. It was awfully hard to believe. She had to be sure. She double-checked the timing of calls made to or from the phone with calls made to and from Shelley's home.

Around the time Renner shot MacUther, someone made a call from the San Francisco area to Shelley's phone, somewhere in Springfield, Virginia. Seconds after that call ended, Doctor Frank made multiple calls out from his encrypted house phone. He received another call while Gene and the team were interrogating MacUther in the hospital, then called out on his house phone.

Sam indulged in a self-satisfied smile. She'd just proved exactly how much shit Gene and the guys were in.

She pulled up Frank's employee records and let out a low whistle. *Impressive guy.* She scanned his online resume and didn't find anything useful. She accessed his security clearance background check and a name jumped out at her. He worked as Chief Research Associate for Bailey Pharmaceuticals in the seventies but didn't include it on his resume. Her grin was fierce. "Gotcha, you bastard. You'd better hope Renner finds you before we do."

She looked at the clock. It was three AM. *Midnight in*

California.

She tried Gene on the COM. He didn't respond, but that wasn't a surprise this late. She tried him on his phone. Four rings, then a pleasant female voice relayed a message. "The cellular customer you are trying to reach is currently out of the service area. Please try again later."

Sam frowned and hung up the phone. Gene's team all had the same issue phone, and when they couldn't get cellular service, it switched to satellite coverage. *You could get a call in the middle of Siberia with these things.* She uploaded the data onto a secure personal server that she used as an FTP drop for Gene's team, but realized she had no way to tell Gene to go get it. Her mind raced; she knew where she had to go. She grabbed her purse and headed for the bus. A quick ride home to get her car, and she'd be off.

Chapter 25

Twenty minutes later Sam got off the bus a block from her apartment building. The short walk was quiet. She always preferred the night. It was so much more peaceful than the daytime, especially in the city. She trudged up the stairs, let herself in the front door, walked over to the elevator, and hit the up button, all without seeing another soul.

She fiddled with her keys outside her apartment door, found the right one, and put it into the lock. She turned and the deadbolt slid back. Acting on years of ingrained habit, she removed the key halfway and twisted it back the other way a quarter turn. Nothing happened.

She frowned down at the key in her hand, her heart thumping in her chest. The intrusion detection tumbler she'd installed when she moved in hadn't tripped, and that meant only one thing. Somebody who didn't know about it had unlocked, then relocked her door. *A little healthy paranoia goes a long way, Sammy-girl.* Her mind raced. *Too late to run—they already know I'm here. Well, best to play ignorant, then.*

She reached into her purse and grabbed the handle of the Ruger SP101 5-shot revolver she'd been carrying since college. The metal was cold and slick in her sweaty hands but tremendously reassuring, and the Trausch grip fit her hand perfectly. She buried her hand deep into the purse and tilted it, hiding the weapon. She opened the door as casually as possible.

Sam stepped inside and closed the door, rooting around in her purse as if searching for her ChapStick. In truth, she kept her hand on the grip and her finger off the trigger, just like at the range. She left the door ajar and did her best to pretend that nothing was amiss as she walked into the kitchen. She placed her purse on the counter, still rummaging, listening for any sounds of movement or breathing. She jumped out of her skin as a man spoke from the darkness of the apartment behind her.

"Don't move, and don't turn around." Even expecting the intruder to still be in her apartment, it terrified her to have an uninvited stranger in her living room.

She froze in place. Her body shook. Her fingers trembled on the pistol grip as her index finger found the trigger. *This is a lot different than target shooting at the range.* Her usual targets weren't breathing. She'd never even hunted before. Her mother had always told her to never carry a gun unless she was willing to use it. *Could be do or die time.* The SP101 .357 was known for stopping power and could do tremendous damage at short range. Sam didn't want to know how much.

"Who did you tell about the information you were searching for this evening?" The voice was warm, almost friendly.

When in doubt, play dumb. "What information? I don't know what you're talking about."

The man tsked. "Don't waste my time. Who did you tell?"

She looked at the ground. "No one. I didn't tell anybody."

"Turn around." She turned around, clutching the purse to her chest. It wasn't hard to act terrified. It wasn't an act.

The man wore blue jeans, a black turtleneck, black sneakers, and a black ski mask. She couldn't see anything that would help her identify him later. *Well, at least he won't kill me now that I've seen his face.* She cringed at the thought.

"Look me in the eyes and answer the question. Who did you send the information to?"

She licked her lips and looked him in the eyes. "Nobody. I tried to send it to my boss, but I didn't get the chance."

The man tensed. "I believe you."

The silenced gun snapped in the tiny apartment. Sam expected the shot and had half-turned when the man brought up the gun to fire. Her anticipation gave her an edge, but she wasn't fast enough to capitalize on it.

One bullet winged her in the left shoulder. It punched through muscle before exiting the other side. The other two punched into the wall behind her. She gasped in pain and fired her revolver. The clean double-tap blasted through the leather bag with a deafening roar. Both bullets hit their mark, the second higher than the first. Bloody chunks of the man's stomach and right kidney blew out of his back and all over the living room, and he dropped face-first onto the carpet. Ears ringing, she heard footsteps from the hall and a scream from the neighbor's apartment.

Her right hand numb from the tremendous recoil, Sam turned in place and pointed the gun toward the hallway with both hands, her feet spread wide for stability. Her shoulder hurt like hell, but she was pretty sure there was no serious damage. The apartment was dark, but the hall was well lit. It gave her a perfect view as the figure rounded the corner and jerked open the door. She saw the ski mask and machine pistol and fired another pair of shots. Blood splattered the wall as the man's body slammed into the doorframe and dropped to the floor.

Sobbing, Sam forced herself to silence and squeezed her eyes shut. She heard the neighbors, already on the phone with 911. She heard the people upstairs crashing around. She also heard the headset underneath her first assailant's ski mask.

She stumbled to the living room, dropped to her knees, and ripped off the mask. He was a young man, in his mid-twenties at most. He would have been handsome. The metallic tang of blood and fetid stench of shit filled her nostrils, mixed with some kind of cologne. With a sob she yanked off his headset and put it on. A voice flooded into her ear.

"—the target? Three? Two? Check in." She took a moment to

load four more rounds into the revolver, and for good measure picked up the machine pistol and shoved it muzzle-first into her purse. The man had a pair of tear gas grenades on his belt. She took those, too. A quick frisk revealed no ID of any kind. "I say again. Three, two, do we have the target?"

Her legs shook so hard that she could barely stand, but she pushed herself up on the couch and looked around. She held her breath to listen for other intruders. *Nothing so far.* She breathed in. The voice in her ear continued on as she looked around for something to use as a bandage.

"Team Bravo, we do not have a confirmed kill." She grabbed a roll of duct tape and a washcloth from the tiny pantry. "Cover the rear entry. We'll take the front." She thought about turning on the gas, but the voices of her neighbors made her change her mind. "On my mark. Three. Two." *Time to go!* She stumbled into the hall and held the cloth to her shoulder with her left hand, aiming the pistol with her right. She'd tape it in place once she got away. *If I get away.* She heard boots tromping up the front stairwell.

The others didn't have gas masks. She fumbled with the grenades, dropping the washcloth as she struggled to pull the pins without letting go of the spoons. She'd never done this before, only seen it in movies. She pushed open the crash-bar and let the little oblong canisters tumble out of her hands. They clacked and clattered down the stairs as she cowered behind the metal fire door. Both from the stairwell and the headset she heard a man scream, "Grenade!"

The world erupted in twin explosions, impossibly loud. The door jumped on its hinges. She felt shrapnel ping off the metal, then all she could hear was the ringing in her ears. A man screamed in the stairwell. It took her a moment to realize that they must not have been tear gas. She ran down the stairs at what was, for her, breakneck speed.

The remains of two masked men lay on the stairway. One stopped his incoherent screaming and started panting as she passed by. Each breath was a watery hitch, fainter than the last. The other lay face down, smoke curling from his body. She ran past them to the parking level.

As her feet touched the ground floor, a cool, collected voice erupted in her ear. "Alpha, we do not have visual on the suspect." She busted through the emergency exit door and into the parking garage, gasping for breath. She hadn't run down three flights of stairs since high school, if ever. She'd never done it that fast.

"Alpha, respond." *I think Alpha just had a close encounter of the fragmentary kind, asshole.* She reached for the machine pistol in her purse and grasped nothing. It must have fallen off her shoulder. She tried to get enough air through choking sobs and made a frantic scan of the area. A black H2 sat idling twenty feet away, parked sideways. The man inside the massive vehicle looked out the opposite window, his machine gun aimed at the far door. He wore a headset identical to the one she had on. She saw him speak, and she heard his voice in her ear. Her sobs vanished.

"Bravo, Alpha isn't responding. Move in and prosecute." Sam stumbled toward the car and pointed the revolver at the back of the man's head.

"Get out of the car, asshole," she said. The man whipped his head in her direction and tried to bring the assault rifle to bear. The bulky weapon hit the roof of the cab, and it gave Sam all the time she needed. She fired.

One bullet flew off into the garage. The ricochet pinged off a concrete pillar in the distance. The other bullet penetrated the base of the man's neck. Eyes wide, he dropped the rifle. He tried to stem the flow of blood that erupted from the wound, but the sticky red liquid gushed out between his fingers. *Jugular.* Sam gritted her teeth in fury and approached the car.

She opened the door with her left arm, the adrenaline overwhelming the pain in her shoulder, the pistol still aimed at the dying man's face. "I said get out." The man's eyes lolled as he struggled to maintain consciousness. She hauled herself up and into the massive cab.

Sam reached across the dying man and pulled the handle on the driver's side door. It popped open, and he leaned out drunkenly. She shifted toward the driver's seat and forced him to the left with the bulk of her body. He fell out of the car, flailing his arms in a vain attempt to catch himself. His head hit the pavement with a wet crack. Sam pulled the rifle the rest of the way into the cab and slammed the door.

Blood dripped down on her as she put the Humvee in drive and gunned the gas. She drove out of the garage and hurtled down the street at eighty miles an hour.

Can't go to the hospital. Can't go to the cops. Got to get a hold of Gene. She looked down at the GPS navigation system and snarled. There was no way to tell if "off" was off enough. *Got to ditch this deathtrap.*

Now that she had calmed down a little, her shoulder hurt like hell, but it wasn't bleeding much. She had no idea where the duct tape or the washcloth went, probably in the hallway outside her apartment, with her purse.

She pulled into an alley and killed the engine. Tears burst from her eyes as sobs wracked her body. *Get going, Sammy-girl. Get going.*

Chapter 26

February 3rd, 4:24 AM PST; Skyline College; San Bruno, California.

Skyline College dominated a hill that overlooked the south end of Daly City. Paul Renner sat on the back of a stolen Yamaha FZ6 motorcycle and surveyed the modern campus with a pair of stolen binoculars. Military personnel swarmed everywhere, even at this hour. They walked in and out of every building on campus, using every available inch of space as a bivouac.

From this staging ground, they maintained roadblocks all along the southern edge of the greater San Francisco metropolitan area. Standing orders were to shoot anyone attempting to break the roadblocks as well as anyone out after curfew. Helicopters patrolled the mountains, their searchlights flashing up and down gullies and over ridges.

A large truck blocked both lanes of the main access road, flares ringing it on both sides. He counted six men on patrol, all with radios. They looked tired, but there were six of them and nowhere to hide. A group of white, heavily windowed buildings sat off a quarter of a mile on the right. San Bruno Mountain towered in the distance, while behind him the little town of Pacifica sparkled beside the ocean for which it was named. Patrols ran every few minutes, spread out like a spider web from Skyline

College.

He swore under his breath. He couldn't get to Emile Frank if he couldn't get to D.C. He couldn't get to D.C. if he couldn't get off the peninsula, and he couldn't get off the peninsula without a military uniform. There was no way in hell he could steal one from the campus. It looked like someone had kicked an anthill full of men in gray camouflage. Even as he watched, a helicopter came in, landed, and disgorged eight soldiers.

He was stuck. If they saw him, he'd be dead. *Nobody outruns a radio.* He weighed his options and took the moment of reprieve to chew on a granola bar stolen from the nearby Hess station. He made a decision, then backpedaled the bike with his feet.

Paul coasted down the hill without putting any throttle to the motor, took a slow left onto Sharp Park Road, and killed the engine. He dismounted and let the bike fall in the middle of the intersection. He grabbed his duffel bag and walked into the small copse of trees in the park across the street. It was too dark to completely make out the sign, but oddly enough it wasn't Sharp Park. In the darkness he sat and felt through the bag, grabbing and sorting the components he needed. The cool metal under his fingers comforted him while he fitted together pieces of the sniper rifle. In less than a minute, he finished assembling the weapon, complete with a suppressor. Silencers were no good on a .50-cal because the bullets travel faster than the speed of sound, but Paul used a special subsonic load with hollow-point bullets. From thirty feet away they'd make big, big holes in people, and there'd be almost no report.

Paul went prone, popped up the legs on the rifle, closed his eyes, and listened. After a few minutes he was rewarded by the sound of an engine. He left his eyes closed until the headlights swept down the hill and past his position. He snapped them open. As he had hoped, a jeep carrying two men screeched to a halt in the middle of the intersection, narrowly missing the motorcycle.

Paul eyed them through the green glare of the night vision scope. The man riding shotgun got out, unslung his assault rifle and eyed the low wall that separated the college campus from the surrounding land. Behind him, the driver got out and circled the other side of the jeep. His head evaporated in a puff of red mist, and he dropped behind the car.

Paul chambered the next round as the second soldier turned. The man squinted to block out the glare of the headlights and called out to his squad-mate. *You don't even know you're dead.* Paul exhaled, then pulled the trigger again. He was up and running before the body hit the ground.

Paul dragged the bodies across the road and dumped them in the same spot he had used for the ambush. The motorcycle went with them. He couldn't do anything about the blood in the road, but the sun wouldn't rise for another few hours, and the darkness might give him the time he needed. Five minutes after he'd fired his first shot he pulled away in the jeep, dressed in the US Army uniform of Nigel Barrett, PFC.

Paul pulled up to the roadblock on Highway One. A massive convoy truck blocked the road and the entire shoulder on the left-hand side. The right-hand side had no shoulder, just a guardrail and a cliff leading hundreds of feet down to the ocean. Soldiers looked down at him from the truck. He reached up and handed them Barrett's papers. As one of the soldiers spoke into the radio, Paul drummed his fingers on the steering wheel. Nobody seemed eager to strike up a conversation.

Ten seconds went by, then twenty. *Maybe this wasn't such a great disguise.* After almost a full minute, Paul wondered if it might not be a better idea to jump out of the jeep, dive a hundred or so feet into the ocean, and take his chances with the sharks.

He covered a sigh of relief when the trooper handed back the manila envelope. He muttered a "Thank you" and tossed the papers on the passenger seat. The truck's engine started with the annoying, repeated beep of heavy vehicles everywhere. Moments later the road in front of him was clear, and he was on his way south. He cut north in Santa Clara.

Two hours later Paul Renner was most of the way to Sacramento in a stolen Chevy Corsica. He couldn't fly with the manhunt for Harold Trubb in full swing, and he'd have to watch his back, but that was an inconvenience he could live with.

He looked at the map from the glove box. If he took Route 80 across the country to New York State, he could cut through Pennsylvania on Route 15 and be in D.C in less than five days if he obeyed the speed limit. Sometimes, it paid to follow the law.

Chapter 27

February 3rd, 5:00 AM PST; Sunny Valley Super-9 Motel; San Francisco, California.

The alarm clock sprang to life with a newsman's deep, somber voice, shocking Gene into abrupt and unwelcome wakefulness. KSJO radio, though a modern rock station, was given over entirely to coverage of the impending nuclear threat.

"—at least seventeen dead by current estimates, all as a result of last night's rioting. Car-by-car searches on the bridges have brought traffic to a standstill, and even minor roads are backed up for miles with anxious residents trying to leave town.

"Angry protesters are questioning the administration's decision to search every evacuating vehicle, but FEMA spokesperson Nora Faulkner insists that containing the threat and apprehending the terrorists is the administration's highest priority. We turn to Elliott Marshall of NBC News for more. Elliott?"

Gene stretched and every muscle complained. He yawned as Elliott Marshall took over.

"Thank you, John. Rioting and civil unrest are now minimal. Many police and civilians were injured overnight, and two policemen have been confirmed killed as authorities struggled to restore order. FEMA has assured NBC News that military convoys will keep essential supplies such as food and medicine flowing into the peninsula and that there is no need to stockpile food or other supplies. Drop sites include hospitals, police stations, the old military base at the Presidio, and National Guard depots.

"If you run out of food or medical supplies, go to w-w-w dot FEMA dot gov, slash, San Francisco, all one word, dot h-t-m-l to find the closest supply depot, or call 911. Residents of the affected cities are advised not to go to grocery stores, as some store owners have taken to shooting at those who approach, fearing —"

The men droned on for a few minutes about the lockdown and the ensuing civil unrest. "The manhunt for Aryan Ascendancy ringleaders Harold Trubb and Jim Palenti continues. The Department of Homeland Security is offering a one million dollar reward for information leading to the arrest of either of these men, and a ten million dollar reward for the recovery of the nuclear warhead. If you have any information regarding the whereabouts of these men, or any members of the Aryan Ascendancy, call 911, or on the web, go to w-w-w dot DHS dot gov and click on the link in the upper-right corner."

Gene turned off the radio and looked over at Carl.

Carl looked up from the floor and met his eyes. "I think we're screwed, Gene." They both looked over at Doug, who nodded in agreement.

"Even so," Gene said, "we need to get to Gabrielle's. We've lost too much time already." He picked up his COM from the nightstand, put it in his ear, and spoke. "Sam?"

For the first time since he started working with her, she didn't reply. He tried again. "Sam?"

A sonorous male voice answered. "Ms. Greene called in sick today, Agent Palomini. This is Agent Johnson. What can I do for you?"

Called in sick? Sam almost never left work, much less called in sick, and would have called him if she had. He looked at his phone. Nothing. "Um, nothing. I just wanted to ask her a question." He cut the connection and pulled the COM out of his ear.

He used his cell phone to call Sam's apartment. After twenty rings the machine hadn't picked up. He hung up and tried her cell, with the same result. He called the FBI's main number and spoke to the receptionist. The connection was terrible; there was a lot of noise on the line. "This is Special Agent Gene Palomini. Can you patch me through to A.D. Adams' home, please?"

"Hold, please," she said. The phone beeped in his ear.

Adams' voice was hard to recognize through the static. "Hello?"

"Bernard? This is Gene Palomini. What's going on?"

"Gene? Where are you? Sam said you'd flown to San Francisco. Are you still there? Are you in the lockdown zone?"

"You've spoken to her? I tried her at home and couldn't get through." Gene's voice was full of worry.

"I haven't. I'm just working on the report from yesterday. Are you in San Francisco?" Adams' voice was tight, his words clipped. It wasn't normal.

Gene's reply was guarded, "Not exactly, but in the area."

"Where precisely?" Gene raised an eyebrow at Doug.

"I'm not sure exactly. We're on the road somewhere at a little motel."

"What motel? What's the number there?" Visions of helicopter strike teams danced in his head.

"Um, Lucky Seven in Cupertino," Gene lied. "Um, I'd have to go get the number; it's not on the phone here in the room." Doug and Carl gave him odd looks.

"Are Goldman and Brent with you?"

"Yeah, they're right here. What—?"

"Put Agent Goldman on the phone, please." It was clearly an order.

"Um, okay, but I have a question first." Gene mouthed to Doug, *he wants you.*

"Just put him on, Agent Palomini," Adams said.

"Okay, but he's not feeling well." Gene stalled. Doug held out his hand.

Adams' tone of voice brooked no argument. "I'm ordering you to give Agent Goldman the phone, Agent Palomini. *Now.*" Gene handed the phone to Doug.

Doug took the phone. "This is Agent Goldman."

Gene could hear the voice on the other end, but not what he said.

Doug mumbled an okay, rose slowly from the couch, and stumbled his way into the bathroom. He closed the door.

Once inside the bathroom, Doug spoke into the phone. "Done." The tile chilled his bare feet, and he was in no mood for games.

"Is Palomini listening?" Something in Adams' voice didn't sound right.

Doug opened the door softly, stepped back into the living room, and looked at Gene with wide eyes. "Um, no. He's not listening."

He held the earpiece away from his head so that the sound would project into the room. "I need you to take Agent Palomini into custody."

"That's preposterous. You and I both know—"

"Doug, I don't care what you think you know. We have it on very good authority that Palomini and Palenti are the same man." Gene's jaw dropped as he looked at the phone in Doug's hand. "You will—"

Doug interrupted him. "Pardon my French, but that's the dumbest fucking thing I've heard in my entire life, sir. I've spent almost every waking moment with Gene in the past two weeks, and most days in his presence for several years before that. Even if he is a racist bastard, which he isn't, he wouldn't have time to run some skinhead group or plan a nuclear attack. Sam's been tracking our movements for years, ask her. It's simply not possible."

Adams didn't say anything for a few seconds. When he spoke, his voice was cold and authoritarian. "Agent Goldman, my hands are tied, and so are yours. I'm ordering you to place Gene Palomini into FBI custody and transport him to the San José International Airport, where you will turn him over to Department of Homeland Security for processing. Agent Brent will assist you." Carl shook his head.

Doug didn't even try to keep the sarcasm from his voice. "I don't think that sounds like a good idea, Director. He's probably armed and dangerous."

"Of course he's armed and dangerous!" Adams hollered.

Now Doug was sure of it. Adams was born in Texas and had moved to northern Ohio when he was young, but had never fully outgrown his Southern accent. The man on the phone had emphasized the "r" in armed, and hadn't drawled the "a" like Adams would have.

"I'm not negotiating with you, Agent Goldman. Go relieve Agent Palomini of his weapons and place him under arrest."

"I don't think so, Director," Doug said. He flipped the phone closed before the man on the other end could protest. Gene sat on the bed and put his head in his hands.

Carl smirked at Doug. "That could've gone better."

Doug sat next to his boss and clapped him on the back. "I think we're in deep shit, Gene. That wasn't Director Adams."

"I suspected it," Gene said, "but your behavior confirmed it."

"Going dark, are we?" Carl asked. Doug and Gene locked eyes, leaving the agreement unspoken. "Then we've got to keep our phones off. Sam always tracks us with them. If she can, they can. You can bet they already know what cell tower's covering us, and they've got men not too far away. If we move, we're just going to help them pinpoint us."

As if on cue Carl's phone rang. He looked at it, then at Gene. "It's Adams' office." He turned it off and pulled out the batteries.

"Good idea," Gene said. They followed suit. Doug stuffed their phones in the backpack they'd bought the night before. When he looked up from the bag, Gene was looking at him. "Look, guys, you don't have to do this."

Doug rolled his eyes. Carl grinned. "Skip the crap about cutting you loose, Gene. We've got your back. What's the plan?"

Gene smiled back. "You realize we're all getting arrested, if not killed, right?"

Carl spoke. "Get to the point. What's the plan?"

"Okay, here it is. All we need to do is beat Renner to Gabrielle's, find our way off the peninsula through legions of military personnel, get across the country while evading a massive manhunt and million-dollar bounty on my head, find

Sam, get her to figure out who this Shelley guy is, arrest him, and get him to confess to the whole thing, leading to the downfall of the bad guys."

Doug put his hands to his head. With eyes closed he asked, "Is that all?" A faint grin betrayed his amusement.

"Nope. We do it without using an ATM or our FBI expense accounts, and without being able to coordinate anything through Sam. And we do it before Renner, who has a head start, gets to Shelley and kills him."

Nobody said anything for a few minutes.

Finally, Carl stood, clapped his hands together, and rubbed them in anticipation. "Well, better get moving then. But first things first." He walked into the bathroom and closed the door.

Chapter 28

February 3rd, 7:00 AM PST; Paul Renner's cabin; Lake Tahoe, Nevada.

Paul pulled up to an authentic log cabin nestled deep in the woods below Lake Tahoe on the Nevada side. Towering pines cast the driveway in shadow, but the house basked in early morning sunshine. He got out, slammed the door, and walked up the porch steps. He didn't have a chance to knock.

His dad opened the door, a worried look on his face. "Hey, Steve. You look stressed."

Paul shrugged. "Not really. I've got a lot on my mind, but that's pretty normal." His dad let him in, and he walked straight to the couch and sat. He looked up at the hart mounted on the wall, admiring the structure of the giant antlers.

"You get that one yourself?" his dad asked.

"It came with the cabin," Paul said. "I think it's older than you are. They aren't even indigenous to the United States."

"Oh." His dad sat on the couch next to Paul, his hands in his lap. "You want some coffee?"

Paul shook his head again.

"Okay," his dad said. They sat in silence for a while. Finally, his dad spoke. "Been reading the paper lately?"

Paul nodded. "Yup."

"It's kind of quiet up here. I don't watch much TV. But I do run into town to get the paper now and then. So you've seen the headlines?"

Paul nodded again.

"The pictures?"

Another nod.

"Care to explain about Harold Trubb?"

Paul gave his father a sad smile. "Harold Trubb is a figment of an overactive imagination, created by the man behind all this." He gestured to the cabin, then to his father. "I'm getting close to the answer, and he doesn't like it."

"So you know who it is?"

"Yes."

"Who?"

"It's bigger than this, but the man who tried to kill you is a doctor. Lefkowitz. Ring any bells?"

His father blushed and looked at the floor. "No. Why would a doctor want to kill me?"

"Are you sure, Dad?" Paul asked. "He ran a methadone clinic back in the seventies."

"Why would I know a doctor who ran a methadone clinic, son?"

"Because," Paul said, "you were a junky. Just like Mom."

His face a thundercloud, Kevin Parsons stood and towered over his son. "You take that back." He grabbed Paul's hair and wrenched his head back. Eyes blazing, he repeated himself. "You. Take. That. Back." He let go and stared at his own hand in shock.

Paul leaned his head into his father's stomach and patted him on the leg. "I wish I could, Dad. I wish I could." Paul sat back and looked into his father's eyes. "Mom didn't die in a car accident."

His dad collapsed onto the couch. He put his head in his hands. His shoulders shook, and a keening noise more animal than human erupted from his throat.

Steve looked up, his mouth agape. His father fired out the window, the bark of the pistol louder than anything he'd ever heard. His mother stood over the coffee table, shoving bags full of white powder into a duffel bag. The bullet hit her in the neck. She fell onto the floor, and he leapt on her, pressing his tiny hands against the wound. The blood covered him, spraying through his fingers. She gasped and gurgled and tried to breathe through the blood. Steve pressed as hard as he could, but the bleeding just wouldn't stop. His hands were too small.

After a while he asked a question. "Dad, what really happened?"

His father's voice was tiny, barely audible. "Don't make me go back there. I don't live there anymore." He squeezed his eyes shut. "I can't go back."

Paul grabbed him, pulled him close, and held him. He leaned close to his father's ear. His lips barely moved, and no sound came out. *Dad, I never left.*

* * *

February 3rd, 7:46 AM PST; Gabrielle's Fine Jewelry; San Francisco, California.

Gene lay in the back seat as the sedan pulled up in front of Gabrielle's Fine Jewelry. He wore a leather jacket with an upturned collar, sunglasses, and a baseball cap. *Like a perp on the lam,* he thought. Doug parallel parked in front of the store.

"There's nobody home," Carl said. Turning to the back seat, he smiled at Gene. "Coast is clear."

Gene sat up, made a quick scan of the street, then looked inside the store. The lights were off and nothing moved. "Wouldn't you expect someone inside?" he asked. "Guarding the store from looters?"

"Yeah, I would," Doug said. "Renner beat us here."

"Let's hope not," Gene said. "We don't know if Renner found out about this place or not." He scanned the street. Nothing. "Let's go. And be careful. These guys have no reason to trust or cooperate with us."

They got out of the car and approached the door, huddled together against the damp, cold wind. Gene rapped on the glass with his knuckles. Doug and Carl covered him, hands in their pockets. There was no response. "It was worth a try," he muttered.

Shielding his eyes with his hands, he peered inside. Everything looked normal for a high-end jewelry store. A series of glass cases filled with sparkling gems, gold jewelry, watches, tie clips, and so forth dominated the main room, all arranged in a jigsaw maze designed to make shoppers slow down and take it in. A marble-topped mahogany cabinet with an old rotary-dial phone and an antique cash register stood in the back. Behind it stood a single door marked *Employees Only*.

Gene stepped back and took a better look at the storefront. The phone number for the store was printed in large letters on the door. He took out the TrakFone Carl had picked up from Wal-Mart an hour earlier and dialed the number. The phone rang ten times, with no answer. He hung up.

Gene sighed. "Doug, hit the store with the Maglite."

The beam of light flared across the inside of the store, scattering and refracting through thousands of gems and reflecting off countless pieces of gold, platinum, and silver. "What am I looking for?" Doug asked.

"Anything out of—there! Right side of the counter!" Gene pointed, and Doug turned the light toward the rug.

"I see it," Carl said. "It" was a red stain on the carpet near the checkout. The back wall was misted with brownish spots. "It looks bad, Gene."

"Yeah," Gene said, surveying the interior. He pointed to a small gray box next to the door, connected to a modern-looking phone. "We need to get in there. How do you feel about bypassing the alarm?"

Carl raised his eyebrows. "This isn't the movies, Gene. That kind of thing takes time and the right equipment. I can't see the box very well. I think it's a GoldShield. The bad news is that they're a pretty reliable retail alarm. The good news is that I've bypassed a bunch of them."

"Can you do it?" Gene asked.

"I can definitely shut it off, but maybe not before it calls the police. Let me get my kit." He walked back to the car.

Doug looked at Gene. "You sure this is a good idea, Gene? If the cops show up...."

"Yeah, I know," Gene said. "I think it's worth the risk. You stay in the car, and the two of you take off if Carl botches the alarm. Assuming I get away, meet me at the diner two blocks that way." Gene indicated the direction with his thumb.

"What, and just leave you to the police? I don't think so, Gene."

Gene smiled. "I appreciate the support, but I'm not asking. Better me than all three of us. If they catch me, it's up to you to find Renner. Do it."

Doug stomped over to the car, cursing under his breath. Carl walked up to the door and set down his bag. "What's his problem?"

"His problem is that he's the getaway driver. If you can't shut off the alarm, run to the car." Carl looked annoyed, so Gene held up a hand to cut off an interruption. "I'll go inside and find out what I can in the few minutes before the local PD gets here. Get to it."

Carl opened his bag and removed something similar to a hand-held multi-meter. He touched the door and the frame of the building with the leads, fiddled with a dial, and did it again. Gene watched up and down the street. A few minutes later Carl put the device away. "There's nothing super-fancy going on. Seems like a pretty standard commercial burglar alarm."

He removed an electric screwdriver, a police-issue flashlight, and two pairs of wire cutters from the bag, one large and one small. He handed the large cutters to Gene and set the other two tools on the ground. "After I break the glass, we've got maybe sixty seconds, tops. You need to cut a hole through that wire mesh, open the door, then get out of the way so I can get to that box. Then we pray that I cut the right wire. Okay?"

Gene nodded and opened the cutter. Carl picked up the screwdriver and small cutters in his left hand, the flashlight in his right. Shielding Gene with his body, he smashed the window with the light. A recurring beep sounded over the tinkle of falling glass.

Gene hacked at the wires, jammed his hand through the hole, and unlocked the door. Carl barreled past him and hustled to the security box. He had it open in eighteen seconds. "Shit! It's custom." Carl spent thirteen seconds studying the wire layout.

"Hurry up," Gene said. Carl cut a wire. The beeping continued. He cut another, with no effect. A third cut and the beeping stopped. Carl inspected the LED display on the front of the box and gave Gene a thumbs-down. "We're toast." Gene yanked the phone off the wall and dropped it into Carl's hands. He pointed toward the door.

"Take that, get in the car, and get out of here. Call the new prepaid in twenty-four hours. Meanwhile, work on pulling info out of that phone." Carl opened his mouth to protest, and Gene shoved him toward the door. "Go!"

Carl stumbled out of the store and ran to the car, shaking his head at Doug. Doug waited for Carl to close the door, then gunned the gas. In seconds they vanished out of sight. Gene turned his attention to the store. He vaulted the first case and stepped around the back counter into a charnel house.

Gene turned off his emotional connection to the former humans on the floor and took in the scene. Two bodies, male, one Caucasian and one Asian, lay hog-tied on their stomachs with their shirts stuffed in their mouths. Their eyes gaped open, vacant, and unseeing. Flesh had been torn in strips from their backs. The Asian man's legs looked broken. The floor was sticky with congealed blood. A pocketknife lay on the floor next to several severed fingers. Gene noted that the register drawer was open, the till empty.

Gene knelt down and put his hand on the larger man's neck. The body was almost cold. *We're at least half a day behind him.* He searched the men for wallets, and the desk for anything that might lead him to Shelley. There were no books, no business records, no receipts. They'd been cleaned out.

A quick survey of the back room revealed a tiny office with an open, empty desk, and a small filing cabinet. A door stood in the middle of the right-hand wall; a trail of blood droplets led straight to it. Gene opened the filing cabinet and found four files. He stuffed them into his duffel bag, then pulled the cabinet away from the wall. There was nothing behind it. A quick search revealed no hidden compartments in the desk.

He looked at his watch. Four minutes since the alarm triggered. He was just about out of time.

He turned his attention to the door. It led to a tiny bathroom with traces of bloody water in the sink. A business suit, splattered with blood, lay on the floor next to the toilet. Whatever Renner had found here, he'd taken with him. Snarling, Gene left the office and shut the door.

He looked up into the waiting barrel of an SFPD service pistol. The uniformed officer behind the weapon looked like he was just out of high school, and he shook visibly. *Oh, great. A nervous rookie.* Outside, another officer took cover behind the door of a black-and-white, his pistol pointed into the store.

The policeman's voice was calm. "Slowly put your hands on your head and turn around."

Gene raised his hands. "You've made a mistake. I'm—"

"I know who you are, Mr. Palenti." Gene folded his hands over his head. He could hear the officer outside calling for backup. "Now turn around."

Gene turned. "I'm not Jim Palenti. Chief of Police Logan Stukly of the LAPD can vouch for me. My name is—"

"Shut up," said the cop. He twisted Gene's hands behind his back and zip-tied them together. Spun back around, Gene suffered a pat-down that took his pistol, his Swiss Army knife, and his wallet. The policeman opened the wallet and tsked at the FBI badge. "Looks good, Palenti." He flipped the wallet closed and put it in his pocket.

As he was manhandled toward the door, a familiar blue SUV screeched up to the curb. The officer at the car turned his pistol toward the newcomers. *What the heck?* Carl jumped out of the passenger's seat, flashing his badge as Doug put the car in park and climbed out.

Carl ignored the gun in his face and read the officer's badge. "Officer Russo, I'm Special Agent Carl Brent of the FBI, and I'm taking this man into custody. You're ordered to stand down and surrender custody on authority of Director Adams, PRD."

"This guy here's got a badge, too," said the other officer.

"Ours are real," Doug said, flashing his own. "We've been

tracking Palenti for eight months. You guys did good."

Russo hesitated, then looked at his partner. "Joey, call it in."

Carl's jab took Russo in the throat, and a chop knocked the pistol from his hands. Gene head-butted Joey even as Doug closed the distance and connected with a wild haymaker to the side of the head. Joey dropped to the ground, writhing. Carl followed up his strike with three more, then stepped in and slammed Officer Russo's head into the hood of the car. The cop dropped to the ground next to his partner, gasping and groggy.

Doug pulled a knife from his belt and cut Gene loose. He kneeled between the cops and cut the cords on their police radios before rolling them over and handcuffing them with their own zip ties. Gene recovered his wallet, knife, and pistol, then stabbed both drivers-side tires for good measure. Meanwhile, Carl did something to the cops' dashboard.

"Radio?" Gene asked.

Carl smiled. "Not anymore."

Doug patted the cops on the heads. "Be good, kids." He stood and looked at Gene. "Let's get the hell out of here."

They headed west.

"We need to ditch this car, Gene," Carl said. "Black-and-whites have front-mounted cameras standard these days. It's a fair bet they have our license plate as well as pictures of Doug and me."

"Stupid," Gene said. "They're going to be all over us."

Doug smiled at him through the rear-view mirror. "Yeah, it was. Did you find anything good?"

Gene shook his head. "Besides that phone, Paul cleaned them out. I've got four files, but I'll bet they're worthless." He pulled them from the duffel bag and passed them up to Carl.

Carl scrutinized them for a few minutes as Doug found a convenient back alley to ditch the SUV. "They look like receipts and warranties. Might be a cipher of some kind. We can pass them up to Sam to get some forensic accountants on them. If we can reach her."

"Yeah," Gene said. "If we can reach her."

"So," Carl said, "where are we hiding?"

Chapter 29

February 3rd, 12:35 PM EST; Massachusetts General Hospital; Boston, Massachusetts.

Marty looked up from his hospital bed as Sam entered the room.

"You look like shit," Sam said. He really did.

Marty's grin was glazed with painkillers. "Hey, Sam, how'd you get in here?" His voice was groggy and thick.

She gave him a half-smile. "Bribed the head nurse fifty bucks."

He chuckled as his head listed to the side. "Cool...." His head lolled, and his eyes rolled back, then snapped into lucid focus. "So how's it going, Sam?"

"Not so good, sweetie."

Marty teared up. "Not Gene—"

She cut him off. "Last I heard, the boys were in California," Sam said. Marty sighed with relief. "Something weird's going on out there, Marty. I think they're stuck in San Francisco, and I need to find a way to get them out past the barricades."

Marty's reply sounded hopeful, but puzzled. "They can't just leave? Why not?"

She explained. "It's a setup, Marty. The terror threat is fake, a front to set up a manhunt for them."

"Um...." His voice slurred. "Can't you just publish the fucking evidence we have so far, exonerate them?"

"Marty, I can't go to work. Someone tried to kill me last night." She reached up with her right arm and tugged her jacket down, showing the large bandage made with supplies from a convenience store.

"Holy fuck, Sam. Why?"

She put her hand on his arm. "I know who hired those mercs from Martha's Vineyard, who tried to kill Lefkowitz and Renner." Marty's face darkened at the name. He motioned for her to continue. "He's a government official named Emile Frank." He didn't reply. "Doctor Emile Frank?" she asked.

"Fucking hell, Sam, I've been stabbed, cut open by doctors, given several fucking gallons of other peoples' blood, and shouldn't even be conscious. I can barely fucking think with all these fucking painkillers coursing through me." He grimaced and hammered the button taped into his right hand, which sent even more morphine into his IV. "And I don't need you playing fucking coy with me. Spit. It. Out."

Sam gave him a half-hearted smile and patted his cheek affectionately. "He's the Director of Antiterrorism, Bioweapons, at DHS."

Marty mouthed a silent *wow*, his eyes starting to glaze as the morphine kicked in. "That's not good, Sam. You need to lie low."

"I know, Marty. I also need to tell Gene."

His eyes widened as he fought to stay conscious. "You haven't told him yet? What the fuck, Sam?" His eyelids drooped as he finished.

She patted his cheek, just hard enough to wake him back up. It mostly worked.

"Marty. Hey. I need you to tell me how you'd contact Gene in an emergency."

He opened his eyes and smiled at her. "Hi, Sam."

"Hi, Marty. How do I get a hold of Gene?"

"Try the COM, babe. Fucker's always wearing it, unless he's

sleeping. He's the boss, after all." He scowled, then smiled again. "Hi, Sam."

She enunciated every word, hoping she'd get through the opium haze and into his thick skull. "No COM, no phone. How do I contact him if he's gone under the radar? How would you do it?"

He tried to lean forward. She bent down to listen, and he grabbed her jacket with his left hand. "Ummmm…. E-mail."

"Okay. What address, Marty?"

"A secret one. Never use it unless there's a big trouble thing, Gene says. I told him it's stupid. But who's stupid now?" He nodded, as if sharing brilliant wisdom. "Little bro's got the smarts, you know?"

She nodded back. He copied her with ten times the enthusiasm. "I know, Marty, I know." He was still nodding when his eyes closed.

"What's the address, Marty? To contact Gene?"

He told her and passed out.

Let's hope this works, kids! She walked out of emergency by way of the main desk and passed another fifty to the head nurse. "I wasn't here."

The woman took the fifty. "Who wasn't where?"

* * *

February 6th, 9:18 PM PST; Home of Margaret VanDeSande; San Francisco, California.

Gene shook his head at Doug, his face blank. They were playing Russian Pinochle, a card game they'd learned in the service that was neither Russian nor Pinochle. They'd tried to teach it to Carl two days earlier, but he'd found it incomprehensible. They'd been holed up for three long and frustrating days after two near-misses with the authorities, so Gene and Doug were stuck playing cards while Carl looked for a way to contact Sam.

Margaret VanDeSande smiled at the two FBI agents from the doorway to the den. "Are you sure you boys don't want more tea and cookies?" she asked.

"No, thank you," Gene said. He could have gone for more of both, but was too polite to say so. They'd taken too much from this woman already.

Mrs. VanDeSande was a ninety-year-old Dutch widow with curlers in her hair and a faded pink nightgown. She was the proud owner of a large farmhouse built in 1947 by her dearly departed husband, bless his soul, and cared for most weekends by three of her eighteen grandchildren. The city of San Francisco had enveloped it four decades back.

Carl, Doug, and Gene had rented two rooms from her. They'd paid her a hundred dollars for the next week, with a promise of more once the lockdown had lifted. She took their hundred dollars and their promise of payment, and in return gave them not only a place to stay, but all the tea and cookies they could possibly want.

Almost every business in the city had closed because of the terrorist threat. People not waiting on bridges to evacuate were afraid to go out. Hospitals and newsrooms were the only things doing brisk business. The latter reported that the former were full and that there were over forty dead and two hundred injured from lootings, robberies, and home invasions. Close to a dozen had died in traffic accidents during the first hours.

The rest of the casualties came from people rushing roadblocks, trying to beat past the naval blockade or taking to the air. At least two hang-gliders and four hot-air balloons had been shot out of the sky, as well as one single-engine plane. The media warned of dire consequences that would befall any who tried to leave except through the still-congested and heavily searched approved routes. That is, they did so when they weren't busy airing a bunch of made up "facts" about Trubb and Palenti, or clips from the president's speech about the dangers of terrorism and the resolve necessary to fight it.

"Suit yourself, boys," Mrs. VanDeSande said. "I'm going to bed." She set a small tray holding a cup of tea and a plate of six shortbread cookies between them. "Just in case your friend gets back and wants a bite to eat," she said with a smile. She wandered into her bedroom and closed the door.

Gene took a cookie and munched. *No point waiting for Carl on these.* He studied his hand. "Three clubs, no twos."

Doug rolled his eyes at Gene's bid and threw down a seven of hearts. "Remind me to never take you to Vegas."

Gene followed with a nine of spades. "Don't worry about that. I like to win," Gene said with a smile. Doug was saved from utter defeat when Carl strolled into the den.

"You look awfully proud of yourself," Gene said.

"I got an open WiFi node a block over, near the gray apartment building with the trees on top." Carl grinned ear-to-ear. "I boosted the signal with another wireless router, ran the cable over the roof top, so we should be lights-on in here."

"Really?" Gene was excited for the first time in days. Mrs. VanDeSande's computer was old in 1992 and had no Internet access. "Who'd you get to sell you a computer in this mess?"

Carl's grin turned downright evil. "Who said anything about selling?"

"Ah, shit, Carl," Doug said. "You stole it?"

"Ain't stealing," Carl said. "I appropriated the computer for emergency government use. If movie cops can do it with cars, I can do it with a laptop."

Doug favored him with a withering stare. "You know that's illegal."

Carl grinned. "Sure! But he didn't. I flashed my badge...." Gene looked at him in alarm, and he added, "real quick, too fast to read anything, and he handed it right over."

Gene threw up his hands. "Whatever. I don't care. Just give me the computer."

Carl produced the laptop and set it on the desk. He logged in and slid it over to Gene. Gene opened a web browser and went to Gmail.

To: Maggot Face
From: Zipper

Hey its S. Zip sez 'Mellow Cricket'. If ur stuck and 1 2 get back _Yellow Brick Road_ is how. Zips ok.

Gene slammed his hands on the table. "YES!"

He clicked on the link embedded in the phrase _Yellow Brick Road_. While he waited for the page to load, he explained. "It's Sam. Mellow Cricket's a code phrase. Don't ask, but it means this message is legit."

According to the web browser's navigator bar, the web page name was "How_ya_like_them_apples.com." The web page showed a bunch of gibberish. Cyrillic and Chinese symbols scrolled down the page before disappearing at the bottom and reappearing at the top. Gene furrowed his brow. "How ya like them apples?" he read aloud.

Carl responded. "Over easy."

Gene looked up at him, confused. "What?"

"It's a me-and-Sam thing. Just type *Over Easy* into the computer."

Doug gave him a puzzled half-grin. "Are you blushing, Carl?"

Carl shook his head with far too much enthusiasm. "I never blush," he lied. "Just type."

Gene did so.

The gibberish dissolved away into an empty chatroom. Words flowed across the screen.

SayItAintSo: Hey there! This is as secure as I can make it, which means the right computers can hack it in a couple of weeks or months, if they know where to find it.

GMan: Hi, Sam.

SayItAintSo: Don't use names. It gives the cryptoweenies a crib. Are you guys where I think you are?

GMan: Yes.

SayItAintSo: Stuck?

GMan: Very.

SayItAintSo: All three of you ok?

GMan: Yes. How's M?

SayItAintSo: Good. Bored. Confined to bed rest.

GMan: What's up with A.D. A? Called and got impostor.

SayItAintSo: Not surprised. Long story. Will send file. Decrypt with first thing I ever said to you.

GMan: I remember.

SayItAintSo: Of course you do, baby.

GMan: Ok. How are we getting out?

SayItAintSo: Now I know you're alive, gotta talk to a friend. Wait for e-mail.

GMan: Ok.

SayItAintSo: Log off now. Don't just close the browser, log yourself out then shut down.

GMan: Ok.

Gene logged out, then looked up at Carl and Doug. All three of them were grinning like maniacs. It was nice to hear from a friend.

A long moment went by before anyone said anything. Finally, Carl spoke. "What now, boss?"

"We wait, Carl. We wait for our knight in shining armor to come rescue us."

"Giddyup, Sam," Doug said. They all agreed.

Twenty minutes later they received an encrypted e-mail from Sam. Gene typed the phrase, *Why do I always get the cute ones?* into the computer. In moments they learned everything they never wanted to know about the man trying to kill them.

* * *

February 7th, 12:21 AM EST; The Java Jungle; Fredericksburg, Virginia.

Sam beamed as she logged out of the chatroom. *I love Internet kiosks. Can you get more anonymous?* Now that she couldn't go to work, the café near her hideout in Fredericksburg, Virginia had become her new favorite place. It had four computers with broadband access that coffee shop customers could use free of charge. In Sam's case, "free of charge" meant at the cost of a dozen biscotti and three double-shot lattes. Best of all, it was open 24-7. The staff had already gotten used to the husky girl who never moved.

It was the middle of the night and the coffee shop was deserted, so she placed a call through the Internet to an old friend, using Federal encryption protocols. The phone rang twice before it picked up.

She was glad to hear a familiar voice. "Govind Agrawal."

She kept her voice low, conscious of the barista at the other end of the shop.

"Hey Govey, it's Sam."

"Hi, Sam! That puzzle you gave me is quite the 'doozy,' as you put it. We are getting nowhere very quickly, but I think somewhere rather slowly." Despite the hour his voice was alert and cheerful.

"Well, quicker is better than slower. Lives depend on it."

"I got that impression before, Sam." He paused. "What is it I can do for you today?"

Sam took a deep breath. He wasn't going to like this.

"I need to ask a favor. A huge favor." She didn't have to try to sound desperate.

"If it is in my power, it is yours, my friend."

She smiled. "Wait until you hear what it is. I need to preface this by saying that someone tried to kill me a couple of days ago. Some bad shit is going down, and it involves Emile Frank. He's responsible for the nuclear threat in San Francisco, too." *Sort of.*

For a moment she heard nothing at all on the other line.

"You are sure of this?"

"As sure as I can be, yeah."

"I have met Doctor Frank on several occasions. He seems to be quite a pleasant man, all in all. I find it difficult to believe that a man in our own government is consorting with terrorists."

"The manhunt is phony," Sam said. "They're not Aryans, and there's no bomb. Trubb is a guy who was working with us, and

Palenti is my boss. They're not even named Trubb and Palenti. They found out that Emile Frank is into some serious shit, and next thing we know they're inside a DHS lockdown and the whole goddamn country is out for their blood. Frank also worked for Bailey Pharmaceuticals, the same company that developed the 'cure' you're working on. It's not a coincidence."

Another long pause. "Why do you not turn in Frank yourself? If he has killed a bunch of people with a fake nuclear emergency lockdown, the government will put him away for a million years."

"Remember I said someone tried to kill me? They were in my apartment, waiting for me when I got home. I was shot in the arm. Don't worry, it's not too bad. They've hacked the phone system and are intercepting calls going in to my boss. If I go to work, I'm dead. If I don't, I'm just an anonymous crackpot on the phone who nobody's going to believe."

Govind sighed. "All right. And what do you need me to do?"

Now it was Sam's turn to pause. If he said "no," she didn't have a plan B.

"I need you to help me smuggle three men in my team out of the lockdown area."

Govind didn't say anything for a long time.

"Will you tell me all about the adenovirus?"

Curiosity killed the cat, Govey. "Yes."

"Everything you know? Where it was developed? On whom it was tested? Everything?"

"Absolutely everything."

"Let me make some telephone calls. Call me back in two hours."

Relief flooded through her. *Thank God.* Worry replaced relief. "I will, but you have to be careful, Govind. These guys knew what I was doing on my FBI computer within minutes of my search."

Govind's reply was flippant. "This is the CDC. Careful is what we do." It didn't reassure her at all.

"Watch yourself, Govey. You've got a family to protect."

"Two hours, Sam." He hung up the phone.

Sam's chair groaned in protest as she leaned back in it. She found herself with two hours to kill and nothing to do. She hated having nothing to do. She looked around the vacant coffee shop. *When in Rome.* She ordered another latte and two more biscotti.

Chapter 30

February 7th, 3:47 AM PST; St. John's Lutheran Hospital; San Francisco, California.

Gene waited for the police car to pass before he signaled to Doug and Carl. *Go!* His teammates hustled across the street, heads ducked as if evading sniper fire. Gene trailed, hot on their heels. They crept into an alley that opened into a loading dock in the back of the hospital. Two trucks half-shielded a rusty metal door. One read *St. John's Mortuary* in stark white letters, the other *St. John's Hospital*. A quick inspection revealed no one inside.

They traded point positions in a classic leapfrog maneuver, covering one another as they approached the building. Gene moved up to the door while Carl and Doug took defensive positions behind the trucks.

He knocked twice and waited. He knocked again. Ten seconds later, the door opened a crack. A young, scruffy man in wrinkled hospital scrubs favored Gene with a wary look. He said nothing.

Gene spoke. "Don't you ever sleep?"

The man shook his head. "Only on Tuesdays."

Gene stuck out his hand. "Gene Palomini, nice to meet you."

"Ted Sanders. Same. Your crew with you?"

Gene turned around. He didn't see Doug or Carl. He smiled

and waved to the alleyway. The men emerged from the shadows, weapons stowed in the duffel bags, and approached the door.

"Get inside," Ted said. "We've got everything set up." He handed them white air filters and put one on himself.

Doug swallowed and put his on. He didn't step inside. "Is there some kind of contamination?"

Ted shook his head. "Nope, but they're doing some asbestos removal one floor down, and this will make you harder to recognize if someone sees you." He walked inside. Doug hesitated, then followed.

They hurried after him, scanning for potential hostiles. Blue industrial tile covered the floors and went halfway up the walls, where it was replaced with white tiles of the same size. Fluorescent lights hung from the exposed metal girders that made up the ceiling, illuminating everything with the same sterile, lifeless glow. Wooden doors, stained with age, punctuated the hallway at regular intervals.

Sanders led the trio through several twists and turns. The subbasement looked the same everywhere, as far as Gene could tell. They followed Sanders through aluminum double doors labeled *MORGUE*.

Carl crinkled his nose. The morgue smelled of formaldehyde, bleach, and an underlying lemony scent that just served to make the other two that much worse. Gene and Doug had both been through enough morgues not to react.

Four people stood inside, their white lab coats labeled *CDC* in large blue letters on the front breast and again on the back across the shoulder blades. Three Caucasians and one Indian-looking woman, none of them younger than fifty, turned to look at the FBI agents. The woman shook her head.

"The duffel bags won't do. You must get rid of them." Her accent was Bangladeshi. Her voice was almost sultry but all command. "We will take your gear while you get ready for transport." She stepped aside, leaving a clear view of the tables behind her.

Three black body bags were lined up on three tables, each open and empty. A fourth lay sealed and bulging beside them.

Stickers showing the international symbol for *Biohazard* covered them on every side. The team looked at one another, then at the bags, then at the Bangladeshi woman. Doug started to sweat.

The doctor clapped her hands. "We don't have time to waste, gentlemen. You may keep your underpants but your clothing must go."

They undressed. The lab-coated men came forward and helped them. They took each item of clothing, folded it, and placed it inside clear plastic bags, also labeled *Biohazard*. Doug trembled with every movement.

Carl grinned at him, misunderstanding. "Wait till you get your socks off. Floor's cold, man."

Doug's face turned ashen. Gene gave him a concerned look. Doug closed his eyes and shook his head. Almost to himself he said, "I'll be all right, Gene."

Gene patted him on the shoulder and finished taking off his clothes. "Excuse me, ma'am, but why are we doing this?"

One of the gentlemen stepped forward and explained. "You can't just leave town, sir. Homeland Security has everything locked up tighter than—" The Bangladeshi gave him a withering stare. "Well, awfully tight. Doctor Agrawal at CDC Atlanta has an order that he's to be shipped four bodies with a rare Southeast Asian infection, so the disease can be studied. Guess what, gentlemen? You're three of those bodies."

With a sidelong glance at the fourth body bag, Carl raised one eyebrow. "Three of them?"

"Yes," he replied. "The fourth is well sealed and will be transported with you. There had to be some truth to this farce."

Doug looked at Gene, his eyes bloodshot. Sweat dripped from his forehead in spite of the cold, and his face got grayer by the second. Carl dropped his pants and kicked them off to the side. As the black man hopped up onto the table and slid his legs into the bag, Doug stumbled to his knees and retched.

"You sick, Doug?" Carl asked. The doctors ignored the question and rushed to Doug's side. He waved them off.

"I'm okay, I'm okay." He spat and stepped away from the sticky pool on the floor. He looked at Carl and Gene with shame.

"Diseases make me nervous."

Carl smiled sympathetically. The Bangladeshi woman stepped forward and took a vial and syringe from her pocket. She grabbed Doug's wrist and pulled. "Stick out your hand." He did so.

She removed two cc's of medicine from the bottle, squirted a little of the liquid out of the syringe, and injected the medicine into his arm.

"What is it?" Doug asked.

"It will calm you. Get undressed and into the bag. We have no time left."

Ninety seconds later they lay in body bags with small, scuba-style oxygen tanks fed into their mouths. The Bangladeshi woman leaned over them and spoke.

"You must not betray your presence with the slightest noise until the plane has left the runway. To do so would jeopardize all of our lives, if Govind is to be believed." She hung a toe tag on each of them. "I don't know what he owed this friend of yours, but I'm certain at this point that they are even and that the three of you owe him much, much more. Be silent until we get you. You have forty minutes of air if you regulate your breathing. So do it." She zipped the bags closed and plunged the world into darkness.

Muffled voices continued another few minutes, then it fell silent.

Doug worked to control his breathing. In the darkness the red *Biohazard* logo clawed its way into his psyche with directed precision and headed straight for the panic, fight-or-flight center of his primitive subconscious. He'd never considered himself claustrophobic, but the fact that this was a *body bag* made the enclosure that much worse. The leathery, heavy plastic stank like the morgue. It blocked out even the tiniest traces of light.

He kept his eyes closed against the darkness and concentrated on the facts. *Nothing in here is infected. The CDC people are experts. The other body is well sealed. Totally safe.* The biohazard symbol flashed across his vision again, but the intensity of the panic dulled, as if filtered through cotton gauze. *We're going to be in the air soon. In body bags. With an infected corpse.*

He heard Gene's voice in his head. *You can do this, Doug. It's like being in a sleeping bag, that's all.*

A sleeping bag for dead people.

A sleeping bag. Just relax, everything's going to be fine. Just relax. He knew the voice wasn't real, but he took comfort in it nonetheless.

He took a deep breath, held it, and let it out. *Better.* His heart rate came down, his breathing slowed to an almost normal pace.

See, Doug? No problem. You'll be fine. Just fine.

He tried to shriek when hands grabbed him through the rough plastic of the body bag. He tried to panic. His body didn't move as strong arms lifted him and placed him on a gurney. His heart raced; his adrenaline level shot up. He tried to struggle, but couldn't move.

The world turned fuzzy. The gurney felt soft, like a giant pillow. It rocked like a cradle. It was warm, too. Comfy. Doug Goldman fell into a drugged sleep.

Gene heard voices as they wheeled him down the hallway, the closer one female, the farther one male. They didn't sound familiar.

"So where are these four going?" asked the female voice.

"Helicopter. Rooftop. I guess they're shipping them out somewhere."

"Why these four?"

He couldn't hear the reply over the clatter of the gurney wheels against the tiled floor.

"Yeah. There's some order from the CDC or something. Some sort of killer flu." Her voice was sad. The man asked a question Gene couldn't hear.

"I don't know," she said. "I've only been home twice since all this started. It's bad out there, you know?"

The clattering stopped with the movement. His stomach lurched. *Elevator.*

"What about you?" the woman asked.

The man grunted. "I live in Marin County. I haven't been

home in most of a week. My kid's almost three, got to be missing me big time, and my wife's convinced I'm going to die in a giant fireball."

"Wow." The reply was as automatic as it was stupid. "That sucks."

"Sure does. The sooner this is over, the better."

"Yeah. And the sooner the feds catch those racist assholes and hang them by their balls, the happier we'll all be."

The elevator dinged a final time and came to rest. Gene heard the doors open, then he was on the move again. In the distance he heard the muffled drone of a helicopter. It got louder by the second, until it filled his world with throbbing sound and utter blackness.

Voices he couldn't understand yelled over the noise. He felt the gurney being raised, then rolled. A sliding rush marked the closing of the helicopter door, then he lifted from the earth.

Unlike Doug, Gene had never minded flying. He'd always found it relaxing. What he liked most about it was the view. This experience was different. The only sensations were unpleasant.

The noise was incredible. His body shook with the pounding beat. His stomach lurched with every change in motion. His left knee itched, and he knew he couldn't scratch it. Even his thoughts were unpleasant. *Do we know these people don't work for Emile Frank?* It would be just wonderful if, instead of being rescued, they were just minutes from being weighted down and dropped into the ocean.

Gene wondered if it was possible to spontaneously develop a simultaneous fear of the dark, drowning, enclosed spaces, infectious diseases, and flying. *If any experience would do it, this would be it.* He added paranoia and profound pessimism to his list of encroaching mental conditions.

The helicopter touched down with another lurch to his stomach. *Even if they do drown us, this day can only get better.*

Rough hands lifted him from the gurney. The world dropped out from under him, and he almost wet himself. *This is it. We're dead.* He hit the ground and suppressed a groan of pain.

"Careful! We don't need postmortem trauma!" It was the

woman who'd injected Doug. "Just load them on the plane gently and be on your way."

"Sorry," said the female voice. "I thought he'd be stiffer."

"Rigor mortis is temporary. If you were good at your job, you'd know that. Now hurry up."

"Bitch," the girl muttered.

Two pairs of hands lifted him into the air and out of the helicopter. He felt himself hoisted, carried several dozen steps, then dumped onto something hard that sounded like metal when his head hit it. *I guess gentle means something different when you're handling a corpse.* He hoped that Doug and Carl were getting better treatment. Three more clangs marked the arrival of the other body bags.

Gene heard what sounded like a large van's sliding door. It closed and muffled the sound of the helicopter outside. He tried to quiet his breathing, but it was hard to do with an oxygen hose stuffed in his mouth.

Five minutes later the world lurched into motion. A minute more and he felt thrust. They had to be on the plane. *Here we go.* The moment the wheels left the tarmac, the Bangladeshi woman unzipped his bag. She stared down at him with cold brown eyes and tore the breathing apparatus from his mouth.

"I am Doctor Nazeem binte Saleh. Your nervous friend is fast asleep. The paralytic I gave him will dehydrate him. He'll wake with a bad headache and will be needing a lot of water. Welcome to life outside San Francisco, Agent Palomini. We'll be touching down in approximately six hours." She handed him a blanket.

He looked around the airplane. The cabin was empty except for Doctor Saleh and two of the doctors from the morgue, plus Carl, Doug, and the corpse. Doug slept in his body bag, the zipper down far enough that he could breathe easily. Carl stretched and let out an enormous yawn. It looked like he'd been napping. "Put your clothes on, Carl," Gene said, as he reached for his own. Gene's attention turned back to Doctor Saleh.

"Tell me, Agent Palomini, why was all this necessary?"

Gene buttoned his shirt. "I'm sorry, but I can't do that. Maybe someday, but certainly not today. Or tomorrow." He let the implication hang in the air.

Her frown deepened. With a flick of her wrist she produced a business card, severe black lettering on a creamy taupe background. "When someday comes, you will tell me."

He took the card out of her hand, put it in his shirt pocket, and smiled. "I'll do that."

She smiled brightly then. "Yes, you will."

Carl walked over and sat on the plane floor between them.

"Nice nap?" Gene asked.

He leaned back, spoke around a yawn, "Either I'm especially tired, or those bags are especially comfortable." He looked over at Doug. "He's still asleep, huh?"

Doctor Saleh gave Gene an inquisitive look, then turned to Carl. "He is well drugged. Make sure to get plenty of liquid in him when he wakes up."

Carl smiled enthusiastically. "Will do." He looked at Gene. "Hey, where are we going?"

With a smirk, Gene turned to Doctor Saleh.

"Atlanta. You'll be disembarked at CDC headquarters and taken to Govind's lab." She stretched her index finger toward the body bags. "In those."

Carl looked at Doctor Saleh. "What then?"

"Then you're no longer my problem, and Govind owes me a very large favor."

Chapter 31

Emile Frank's direct line rang. The caller ID read "White House." The FBI had been hounding him for days for his source on the nuclear-weapons tip, and he was tired of hiding behind "need to know." Suppressing a sigh, he picked up the phone and put it to his ear. "Doctor Frank."

"Hi, Emile," said the pleasant male voice on the other end. "This is Trubb. Or is it Palenti? I don't remember which one I am."

Emile went cold. He kept his voice neutral. "You're on a secure line?"

"Duh," Paul Renner replied.

"What can I do for you, Mister Renner?"

"What you can do is give me every piece of information you have involving your research on heroin addiction."

"And why would I do that, Mister Renner?"

"Because if you don't, I'm going to kill you. And call me Paul."

Emile paused. "You might find that more difficult than you think, Mister Renner."

"Oh, please," Renner said. "I know where you live, where you work, what you drive, and I have your travel itinerary for the next two months. Do you honestly believe that the extra security you have lurking around your house is going to stop me?"

Emile closed his eyes. "So my choice is life in prison or you kill me? I think I'll take my chances."

"I have no interest in ruining you," Renner said. "I don't care what happens to you one way or another."

"Then why would you want the research?"

"It doesn't matter." Renner's voice was tense.

"Yes," Emile said, "it does. It matters a lot. So either you're going to tell me, or this conversation is over."

Silence. Emile began to sweat.

"Mister Renner?"

Paul Renner's voice was flat. "My father was one of your patients."

Oh, shit. "I see," Emile said.

"I don't think you do," Renner said. "But I'm going to have to insist. Your research. All of it."

"And you'll leave me alone? You'll leave my family alone?" Emile hated the desperation in his voice.

"You give me everything you have, everything, and you can go on living your life as if nothing ever happened. After you do whatever you're going to do to Palomini's team."

"Where do I drop it?"

"Get out of your eight-thirty meeting and get your car. After you've retrieved the information from wherever you have it, go home. There's a scrubbed cell phone in the drawer of your nightstand, under the old newspapers where you kept that unlicensed pistol. I'll give you instructions from there."

I'm going to fire every one of those meat-headed sons of bitches. "All right," Emile said. "I'll have the files in fifteen minutes, but they're going to be heavily encrypted. I'll deliver them to you and will send you the password as soon as I'm safely away. Then you and I are done. Finished. Permanently."

"You'll call me with the password within twenty minutes of the exchange." The line went dead.

Emile disengaged the magnetic failsafe on his bottom drawer, opened it, and pulled out an external hard drive. *This should have made me rich.* He locked the drawer and headed out, an excuse on his lips.

Doug watched Dr. Frank though his binoculars. "He's heading to his car, alone," he said into the mini-COM that Sam had set up. "A blue Volvo, Virginia tags. Seven-Echo-Three-Zulu-Charlie-One."

"Roger," Gene replied.

Doug pulled down the binoculars and put his car in drive. "He's heading south. Stay behind me and out of sight." In his rear-view mirror, Gene's car pulled out from two-hundred yards behind him.

"Roger again. Just don't lose him, Doug. This might be our last chance at Renner."

Tell me something I don't know.

* * *

February 9th, 9:37 AM EST; Anacostia Park; Washington, D.C.

Paul watched from a park bench as Frank's cobalt-blue Volvo XC90 pulled into the restaurant parking lot. The air was bright and clean, and the sounds of morning traffic had faded from an insane cacophony into dull background noise. "Okay, I'm here," the doctor's voice said through his phone.

"I know. Get out of the car and walk into the park, toward the swings." A little girl shrieked with glee behind him as another child chased her across the grass. "Okay, now turn right down the jogging path."

He let Dr. Frank spot him as he got close. Paul stood and stepped forward. "The data, Emilio?" he said without preamble, his hand outstretched. Frank plucked a small paper bag from his breast pocket. He placed it in Paul's hand and jerked back. Paul chuckled.

"This is everything, but none of it points back to me. Even if you try to connect the dots."

Paul looked inside the bag, then put it in his pocket. "I told you I don't care. Get out of here. I'll call you in twenty minutes for the password."

"You'll have it as soon as I—" He was interrupted when a blue sedan jumped the curb, followed by a white SUV. Emergency lights flashed from the dashboards of both vehicles.

Paul turned blankly back to Dr. Frank. "You set me up."

Frank cowered. "No, wait!" The bullet hit him square in the forehead. A woman screamed as the body fell. From the two vehicles poured Gene Palomini, Carl Brent, and Doug Goldman.

As the car slid to a stop, Gene bailed out with his sidearm drawn, shouting orders and using the door for cover. "Drop the weapon and put your hands on your head or we *will* kill you!"

"Watch his left hand." Doug clicked in over the COM.

Renner slowly took his left hand from his pocket as he dropped the pistol with his right. "You can't shoot me, Gene. Me holding this detonator is the only thing stopping the hundred-odd people in the restaurant behind you from being blown to bits."

Gene hesitated.

"He's bluffing," Carl said over the COM. "Let me shoot him."

Gene stood his ground. "Put your hands on your head, turn around slowly, and get on your knees."

Paul held the object out toward Doug, to give a better view. "It's military," Doug said. "It appears to be activated."

"He's bluffing," Carl said again. "I'm going to shoot him."

"Hold," Gene said.

Renner smiled. "Goodbye, gents. I have a camera in the restaurant and a couple surprises waiting along my way out of here. If you try to follow me or evacuate anyone or I even smell a cop for the next fifteen minutes, they all die." He turned and jogged down the path as Gene stood helpless.

"He's bluffing, Gene. He's bluffing." Carl's pistol tracked Renner as he disappeared through the trees. "We've got to go get him."

Gene looked back at the restaurant. The patrons inside rubbernecked at the windows to see what the commotion was all about. "We can't risk it, Carl."

Thirty minutes later, Gene, Doug, Carl, and Sam were en

route to HQ in D.C. The restaurant had been evacuated and the bomb squad sent in. Gene sat in a holding room for two hours before he was told that there was no bomb in the first place.

* * *

February 11th, 11:02 AM EST; Fort George G. Meade; Anne Arundel County, Maryland.

Captain Sara Belonga looked at the caller ID on her desk phone. It read, *USAIC, Huachuca, AZ.* She picked up the phone on the fourth ring. "DYQ CNC." Anyone who called this number either knew what that meant or had called the wrong number. At the National Security Agency, you didn't give out information you didn't have to. Ever. Besides, only one person ever called her personal line from Fort Huachuca.

The voice on the other end was softly male, pleasant, and polite, with just a hint of Alabama to it. "Hello, Miss, this is Lieutenant-Colonel Jacob Rostan with the United States Army Intelligence Center. Is Captain Belonga in?" Sara smiled in spite of herself.

"Jake, you asshole, I mean Lieutenant-Colonel, sir, you know it's me. What's up?" She'd known Jake for two years, since she'd been assigned this post, but only over the phone. He always called her directly when he wanted something and was an insufferable flirt. They'd worked together several times on joint USAIC-NSA code-breaking problems.

"I've got an encrypted drive I need cracked, and I need it cracked as quickly as possible, then re-routed to me immediately."

"All right," she said. "Let me take a look at it." It took two minutes for their computers to shake hands, verifying access codes and identities, then another fourteen minutes to upload. They killed time talking about their families, then bad first dates. It never took Jake long to bring it to dating, even though he was, to all appearances, happily married. She was in mid-laugh when the computers finished.

She snapped back to business. "Okay, I've got it. Let me take a look."

She clicked on the icon, and a logo popped up–an exploding star surrounded by a halo of binary zeroes and ones.

"Ouch, Jake. SuPeRnOvA is a hard nut to crack. This could take months."

He replied, "Yeah, I know, but I need you to task a team with appropriate clearances to it immediately. I don't care what you have to pull people from. This could be huge. I'm sending another file with some possible cribs. It goes without saying that this information goes nowhere except back to me. But I'm saying it anyway."

"Yes, sir. I won't even read it myself, sir," she replied with no hint of irony. "We'll get right on it and send it to you as soon as it's done. Still, we're talking two to six weeks, absolute bare minimum."

"Very good," he said. "Do what you can."

"We'll get on it as soon as we get the official order through chain of command."

"Under five minutes. Assemble a team."

"Roger that. Catch you next time, Jake."

"Bye, darling," he said and hung up the phone.

A few minutes later Lieutenant-Colonel Rostan had the order dispatched through official military channels. That done, he picked up the phone and dialed another number.

"Hello?" said the voice on the other end.

"Done. I'll send everything as soon as it's cracked."

"I've wired the first hundred grand to your account. You'll get the rest when I have the data."

"Pleasure doing business with you, Paul."

"Sure thing, Jake. Keep me posted."

Jake Rostan hung up the phone.

Chapter 32

February 13th, 12:16 PM EST; St. Angelina's Cemetery; Gregory Falls, New York.

The gravestones were goosebumps of snow on the landscape, white and harsh in the midday sunlight. The priest droned on in the background while the mourners said their goodbyes. Jerri Bates's mother sat stoically in front; her father sobbed in the bitter cold.

Gene and his team stood in the back, separate from the civilians, the small-town crowd that had grown up with Jerri Bates. Her family, friends, and neighbors mourned the loss of one of their own.

"No Marty?" Carl asked.

Gene shook his head without looking up. "Doctor wouldn't clear him to leave. He tried to bust out, against medical advice, but he didn't make it past the nurse's station."

"He's always had more heart than brains, Gene," Doug said.

"Runs in the family," Gene said.

They stood in silence, listening to the priest pray for the living and the dead, and they muttered "Amen." They listened to Jessica Bates ask the Almighty for justice to be done, and they said "Amen." They heard her pray for forgiveness for the man who had taken her sister's life. They said nothing.

Doug turned and walked away, blazing a path through the snow toward the small parking lot. Sam followed in his wake. Carl looked at Gene, then at the retreating forms of Doug Goldman and Sam Greene. With an apologetic, sad smile, he turned and followed his friends, leaving Gene alone with his thoughts and the family of the girl he had killed.

* * *

April 10th, 6:00 PM EST; Gene Palomini's Apartment; Washington, D.C.

Two months after Jerri Bates' funeral, Gene unlocked his door with a sigh and stepped into the front hallway. His shoes splattered the wall and door with speckles of mud as he kicked them off. *April showers....* He hung his jacket on the doorknob, walked over to the fridge, pulled out a Heineken, and popped the tab. A quick swallow quenched his thirst as he unbuckled his pistol and put it on the counter. He set his cell phone and COM ear bead next to it.

He shuffled into the living room and collapsed on the couch, reached for the remote, and noticed an envelope on the coffee table. Instantly alert, he sat up. Beer spilled down the front of his shirt. He ignored it. "Don't move," Paul Renner said from the bedroom doorway. Gene froze, then settled back down onto the couch.

"We're going to catch you," Gene said.

Paul sighed. "If the time comes, and you get close, I'll have to kill you, and I'll regret it. In the meantime you haven't turned up shit, and you're not going to, so there's no reason to go there. I'm not toying with the FBI anymore."

Gene patted the envelope. "This from you?"

"Yeah. There's some information there about Emile Frank you might find interesting."

"Ah. Thank you." Gene didn't feel like thanking him. "Is that all?"

"Yes."

Gene reached forward and opened the envelope. Inside was a single, unlabeled USB memory stick.

"What is it?"

"The truth. Emile Frank helped engineer the gene-therapy technique. He knew it caused immediate psychosis in about one percent of the chimps. He buried the data and went to Bailey Pharmaceuticals with his 'miracle drug.' The rest you know. Sort of."

"Sort of?"

"Over three thousand subjects, Gene, in that clinic alone, between VanEpps and Lefkowitz. But Frank continued his research elsewhere. Boston, Chicago, Cleveland, D.C. One percent went nuts almost instantly, and he killed them with overdoses. The rest are time bombs, waiting to go off."

"That...." Gene hesitated. "Covering that up might be sufficient motive for killing a lot of innocent people."

"Yep. Lefkowitz was doing Frank's dirty work and didn't even know it."

Gene turned around for the first time. Paul Renner leaned against the doorframe, a compact pistol pointed at the floor. Gene knew he had no chance of taking him down from fifteen feet away. Another man, maybe, but Renner was way too fast. His blood pounded in his ears as he stared at the face of the man who had killed Jerri Bates. Somehow, he kept his voice calm.

"Does it include names of patients?" Gene asked.

"Of victims, yeah."

"How many, Paul?"

"Over ten thousand." Paul's voice held no emotion.

"My God. Are they on the disk?"

Paul shook his head. "Only the dead ones. I'm keeping the rest of the list myself."

"Why?" Gene asked.

Paul didn't respond.

"Why did you come here, Paul?"

"Can it be cured?" Paul asked back. Something in his voice sounded desperate.

"We're not sure. People are looking into it. Why?"

"Not your business, Gene."

"Why not turn the list over to the FBI?"

"FBI are scum, Gene. What do you think they'd do to those people?"

Taken aback, Gene didn't reply at first. "I'm not sure."

"I am," Paul said.

"Okay, then, what about the CDC?"

Renner gave him a sad smile. "I will at some point. There's something I need to take care of first." He frowned at the floor.

"Who's Kevin Parsons?"

Paul snarled. "I said it's none of your fucking business."

Gene cleared the couch in a single leap. Paul flinched and pulled the trigger. The bullet blasted a mound of fluff from the armrest. Gene slammed into him. His full-body check carried them both into the doorframe. Paul gasped for breath as Gene slammed his spine into the wooden molding. The pistol fell from his grip.

Gene backed up half a step and body-checked Paul into the doorframe again. Paul head-butted Gene in the nose. Gene felt cartilage crush under the force and stumbled back a step, tears in his eyes. *If he gets any distance, I'm a dead man.* Gene swung with a wild haymaker, forcing Paul to duck and splattering them both with blood from his broken nose. With the killer crouched before him, Gene kneed him in the side of the head. Paul fell backward into the living room, scrambling on all fours to regain his feet. Gene charged after him.

A swift kick to the knee knocked Gene crashing to the floor. Paul rolled out of the way, flipped to his feet and turned toward the door. Gene grabbed his left foot with both hands and twisted, hard. Paul tumbled to the floor and cracked his head on the coffee table. Gene dove on top of him, grabbed him by the throat, and hammered him in the face with his fist.

Gene hit him again, and again. Paul's eyes lolled sideways, his bloody mouth open. His eyes snapped into focus as Gene cocked back for another blow. Gene recoiled as knuckles slammed into his throat. He fell back, sucking in air.

Paul scrambled to his feet and bolted out the door.

Gene grabbed his gun off the counter, and shoved the COM bead into his ear while he ducked out the door.

"Sam!" he gasped. "I'm in pursuit of Paul Renner." He took the stairs two at a time. "Backup. Now!"

"On it," Sam said.

Bullets ricocheted through the entryway as he reached the bottom of the stairwell. He took cover behind the door, counted to three, and looked out. More shots peppered his position, and he ducked back.

Tires screeched. Gene rounded the corner, his pistol leading. A blue sedan peeled away. He unloaded his gun, shattering the back window and punching holes in the trunk. The car took a hard left and disappeared from view.

"Blue sedan headed north on Wisconsin Ave," he said into the COM. He gave the plate number.

They found the car ten minutes later. There was no sign of Renner.

* * *

April 18th, 1:22 PM PST; Motel 6; Reno, Nevada.

A week later, Paul sat on the edge of the bed, his eyes half closed. His right hand held the list of names from Emile Frank's computer, his left held a pen. Behind him a perky news anchor droned on about the Methadone Psychosis Syndrome scandal and the continued civic unrest it had been causing, a video-feed of a mob scene behind her. Half-listening, he stared at nothing in particular, lost in thought. He heard her say a name he recognized and looked up at the TV, surprised.

Gene Palomini stood in front of a blue curtain, an American flag on a stand over his left shoulder. He had haggard bags under one eye, a fading yellowish bruise around the other, his nose swollen, and his government-issue dark navy suit rumpled. It would have been hard to make a more striking difference with the perky, cute little anchorwoman. The FBI agent read from a script, staring into the camera. His face was a mask of rage, but his voice was as steady as Paul had ever heard it.

"This message is for the man who calls himself Paul Renner." He cleared his throat. "Paul, please listen. We need to get treatment for those afflicted with MPS. We aren't asking for you to surrender yourself. We aren't...we aren't even asking for you to give us your whereabouts. We just want to help those in need. The government is willing to pay handsomely for this information, both in money and...and the possibility of a presidential pardon. Please call before it's too late. We...I.... Please call." Gene looked down.

The screen switched back to the anchor, who wore her best "grave and serious" face. "Again, that was Special Agent Gene Palomini of the FBI, asking for alleged assassin Paul Renner, the same man who broke the story just a week ago, to surrender the list of those suffering from MPS. More on this story as it breaks." It was the sixth appeal that Paul had seen since he'd sent the information to CNN, but the first from Gene.

Paul turned off the TV and looked down at the list. Quite a few names had been crossed off: people who had died of causes natural or unnatural, from heart attacks to car accidents to simple old age. Many had died over the past couple decades trying to commit homicide of one form or another. For the hundredth time tears sprang to his eyes.

He wiped them away and stood. He put the list into an envelope, then stuffed it into his jacket pocket. He grabbed a semiautomatic pistol from the table and tucked it into the back of his pants.

He dropped the envelope into the mailbox outside the lobby. It was addressed to Special Agent Gene Palomini of the FBI. That done, he walked to the parking lot and got into the silver sedan he'd rented earlier that day.

An hour later, Paul Renner knocked on the door to his Lake Tahoe cabin. "Just a minute!" came the reply. He took a breath, held it, then let it out. His dad opened the door, ever-present cup of coffee in his hand and a worried smile on his face. He wore forest camouflage and a black WWE baseball cap.

"Hey, Steve," he said, and wrapped him in a hug. He pulled back and looked his son in the eyes. "You been watching the news?"

"Yes."

Kevin Parsons clapped Paul on the shoulder. "Well, come on in, the coffee's only about an hour old." He stepped into the house, still talking. "You in town for long? I could sure use the company about now."

"No, I'm not going to be here long. How about that coffee?" As Kevin turned toward the pot, Paul's hand went behind his back, up under his jacket.

Thirty seconds later, Paul Renner left the house, alone.

The End

CPSIA information can be obtained at www.ICGtesting.com
Printed in the USA
BVOW07s1348151013

333792BV00001B/14/P